Coming Home to *You*

Cheri Ritz

Other Bella Books By Cheri Ritz

Vacation People
Let the Beat Drop
Love's No Joke
Low Key Love
An Acquired Taste
Under New Management
It Had to Be Brew

Praise for the works of Cheri Ritz

Under New Management

There are some twists and reveals that added complexity to our main character's journey... Because the path to love never runs smoothly! Overall, this was a fun and feelgood story that also included some amazing sounding Italian dishes. Be prepared to feel hungry!

-Leane, *NetGalley*

I liked the neighborhood feel of the story, and even the side characters were vibrant. I thought I knew where the story was going, but I was still surprised by the twist. I definitely recommend if you want a lighthearted foody romance. And now I'm craving Italian food...

-Jasmine S., *NetGalley*

An Acquired Taste

An Acquired Taste is very cute! I appreciated how sweet the romance is and I enjoyed spending time with these characters and watching them fall in love.

-*The Lesbian Review*

This is the first time I've read a book by Cheri Ritz, and I wasn't disappointed. ...This book was cute, with some funny moments. I found once started, it was difficult to put down, 'Just one more chapter' comes to mind.

-Cathy W., *NetGalley*

...Ms. Ritz has brought together two women that you will find yourself rooting for. Great characters and great supporting cast has made this a very entertaining read. Very, very good.

-Bonnie S., *NetGalley*

...The cooking in the book made me itch to start prepping, creating, cooking and eating. The visuals you get in your mind's eyes while Elle brought Ashley on a culinary learning journey were such a plus that you can literally smell and taste the food and of them falling in love. I thoroughly enjoyed the read as the book has the same satisfying end akin to a good meal that leaves you feeling upbeat, wholesome and all around happy.

-Nutmeg, *NetGalley*

Vacation People

The character work is solid, the relationship is developed well, and the settings seemed vivid. If you like vacation romances, you should pick up *Vacation People*. I'm looking forward to seeing more stories from Cheri Ritz in the future, because this was a great debut.

-*The Lesbian Review*

About the Author

Cheri Ritz is a Pittsburgh native, wife, mom of three, and author of several books published with Bella Books. She loves reading romance novels, so writing happily-ever-afters is a dream come true for her. She enjoys binge-watching her favorite TV shows, crafting, and '80s and '90s pop culture. You can catch her around Pittsburgh trying new IPAs, hanging at home with her wife and two rambunctious cats, or working on her next novel.

PUBLISHER'S NOTE

Coming Home to *You*

Cheri Ritz

For My Sisters

Acknowledgments

Thank you to Jessica and Linda Hill, and all the fine folks at Bella Books. I appreciate all you do to put these stories out into the world. To my editor, Heather Flournoy, I can't tell you enough how grateful I am for your guidance on this book. Not only was working with you enjoyable, I also learned a lot along the way. From the bottom of my heart, thank you.

A big thanks to my writing pals who brainstormed with me and listened to me talk about this book while it made the years-long journey from idea to actual novel. Brooke and E.J., your beta read input was so very appreciated and a huge part of making this project happen. The sisters of Fisher's Creek have finally arrived!

Thank you to my sisters, Shelly, Stacey, and Jaymie. I'll always cherish the laughs we had hashing out this story, and I hope I've captured some of that magic in these pages. Jaymie, we miss you so much. This one is really for you gals—I love yinz.

Of course, I couldn't do any of this without the support of my wife. Jaime—thanks for always being my greatest supporter as I pursue my dreams. Love, love, love you!

FISHER'S CREEK HIGH SCHOOL

1993

Three final exams done and only two to go. It was the last week of high school for the Fisher's Creek senior class. Nic was almost there. Almost free.

Grabbing the books she would need to study at home, she paused to admire the Polaroid taped to the inside of her locker door. Her best friend smiling and squinting into the sun. She was especially cute in her cheerleading uniform. Her long, lush brown hair—that smelled like lavender—was especially shiny in the early evening light. The picture was taken before the first pep rally of the fall and had hung there in the locker all year, right next to the strip of pictures of the two of them in the photo booth at the Fisher's Creek Strawberry Festival.

It's been a hell of a year, but in one week we get that diploma.

Summer had always been Nic's favorite season, and she was excited to kick this one off. Their last summer before they both went off to college. She didn't know how she would bear it when they had to go their separate ways at the end of August. *No.* She quickly pushed that thought out of her mind. They had almost three whole months of nonstop fun ahead of them, and she wasn't about to waste a moment of it stuck in her sad feelings.

She touched her fingertips to the image, wishing she could apply that gentle caress to that gorgeous jawline in real life. But in their sleepy little hometown, that was not a risk she was willing to take.

Nic had figured out she was gay sometime during her seventh-grade year, but she didn't tell a soul. That was the same year that a young gay man had been beaten and left for dead just over the county line. She still remembered her mother's frightened whispers to her father when she thought the kids weren't listening. Even though she hadn't come out to her parents, Nic wondered if they somehow just knew, and if her mother's hushed tone was because she was scared for her. Right out of the gate for Nic it was clear Fisher's Creek hadn't exactly embraced the *Free To Be… You And Me* mindset. She continued wearing the mask of who everyone expected her to be. It was just easier that way.

Even if fear for her personal safety wasn't holding her back, Nic was much too afraid of losing her best friend altogether if she admitted her true feelings for her. A powerful yearning in her heart was all this would ever be. Yes, leaving Fisher's Creek would be so freeing for Nic—she could finally be her true self, but it would also be bittersweet because it meant leaving Roxy. The one bright spot in her Fisher's Creek life.

"Oh my God. Nicola Dickenson is so in love with Roxy Fitzpatrick!"

"She practically just kissed that picture of her!"

Nic slammed her locker shut and spun around just in time to catch a glimpse of the giggling eleventh-grade girls who went scurrying down the hallway. She didn't realize there was anyone else standing nearby—at least not anyone who was paying her any attention. Classes had ended nearly thirty minutes ago and most of the students had cleared out. Hell, she would've been long gone too if she hadn't stayed to help Mrs. Barnes clean up the classroom after a particularly rowdy game of Grammar Jeopardy in her eighth period Honors English class.

She'd been careless and let her guard down in public. A mistake. Her cheeks flushed with heat as she slung her backpack over her shoulder and put her head down to try to duck out of the school without seeing anyone else. But the second she turned the corner, that plan went up in smoke. She nearly ran a stunned-looking Roxy Fitzpatrick over on her way to the exit. Had she been standing right there the whole time?

"Was what those girls said true? Are you in love with me?"

Apparently, she had.

Nic would never forget that look of shock and confusion on Roxy's face. It only took a second to burn it into her memory before she pushed past her and ran for the door. She'd left Roxy there alone with her unanswered question.

Nic never looked back.

CHAPTER ONE

Nic Dickenson rolled into Fisher's Creek on Sunday afternoon in her sleek, solid black Tesla Model 3. The car was expensive, and sophisticated, and cool, and…she hated the ostentatious thing.

The Tesla was her wife's—nope, her *ex*-wife's—car. It was one of maybe three things Nic had actually gotten in the divorce thanks to an airtight prenup. A consolation prize. But screw that. Whatever. Dana had moved on, and Nic was doing that too. She smiled to herself thinking how pissed off Dana would be if she saw the amount of dust and dirt that had kicked up on the car while traveling on the old country roads en route to Fisher's Creek, Pennsylvania. This last stretch was particularly rough. The road had been paved, although how long ago that paving occurred was questionable. Years of Pennsylvania winter weather, topped with a hearty helping of neglect had left the surface warped and covered in fissures. Chunks of road were dislodged or altogether gone. Patches of dirt had been washed across the asphalt by heavy rains, filling in where pavement once belonged. It didn't make for the smoothest ride, nor the cleanest. Dana was always so damn obsessed about the car being clean. Whatever. Moving on. Nic had other things to worry about.

The actual reason she was returning to the town she grew up in, for one. She'd missed Great-Aunt Aggie's funeral two months earlier, which Nic didn't think was a big deal since she barely knew the old lady. But it turned out she'd been left something in Aunt Aggie's will. Something Nic's mother insisted she had to come back to Fisher's Creek to retrieve. It was probably just her mother's way of guilting her into coming back for a visit, but curiosity on top of a longing to see her sisters convinced her to make the trip. Thank God her sister Maggie had offered Nic the empty guesthouse on the back of her property for her three-night stay. She could visit with family but still retreat to her own space when she needed respite. If she was going to return to Fisher's Creek, this was the way to do it. Get in, get out. Three days and she would be good to go. Back to New York, where she belonged.

Back in New York writing her book, God willing. Was she the author of a *New York Times* best-selling novel that had been chosen for Reese's Book Club and acclaimed by reviewers and readers across the country? Yes. Would she be able to replicate that success with her sophomore release? Possibly not, since the first two-chapter deadline she'd already extended twice since she'd signed the contract for the book was rapidly approaching and she was totally stuck. No story. No chapters. She'd totally forgotten how to string words together. She hadn't had a dry spell like this one in over thirty years. The last was back in high school when she'd been asked to write a "What Senior Year Meant To Me" article to be published in the yearbook. She'd agreed to the assignment figuring it would be a breeze, before her breezy high school life had lost all the wind in its sails because…well, whatever. The thing was, her publisher was expecting chapters, and since she'd already spent a sizable amount of her advance on divorce lawyers and sorting out her personal life, she had to produce something—and fast.

Maybe the change of scenery from New York City to her hometown in the middle of nowhere would help jar something out of her brain.

Lost in her deep thoughts, Nic didn't see the pit in the road until it was too late, and the front right tire of the Tesla made a heart-dropping pop, quickly followed by a gut-clenching grind and rattle as the vehicle lurched from left to right following the impact. Nic struggled to get the jerking car under control then eased over to the side of the road to assess the damage. At least she would be out of the way of passing traffic. *Right.* Okay, there was no passing traffic. She was stranded on a lonely old country road. The nearly three-mile stretch of road that shot off Route 15 was the only vein into Fisher's Creek. It was lined on both sides with full-bodied greenery that smelled to Nic like summer camp. In the winter, through the bare trees, there was nothing but woods to the left and the right as far as the eye could see. All snow and sticks. Just as lonely, only colder. In either season, help wasn't likely to stumble upon her. Of all the dumb, fucking luck.

She climbed out of the car and slowly circled it to get a full assessment. The front tire on the passenger side was definitely flat. Beyond that, it was hard for her amateur eye to determine what else was wrong much less put a name to it. One thing was sure: She would need assistance—the Tesla didn't have a spare, so the tire would have to be addressed by a professional. Luckily, it was a mild May in this part of Pennsylvania. Cloudy but dry, and not too hot to stand outside and wait. She sighed and pulled her phone out of her back pocket to make the call.

Less than thirty minutes later, Peter "Peewee" Palone stood with his hands balled on his hips, squinting at the dusty Tesla while he chewed on a toothpick. The toothpick thing always made Nic nervous. Wasn't that a choking hazard? What if the pointy end jabbed you in the gums? Peewee wasn't concerned. "Yeah, I'm gonna have to tow it in and take a good look underneath. Might've bashed up the undercarriage good, you know? Gotta be real careful driving cars like this on back roads like these. Luxury vehicles can be real delicate."

He pronounced it like *dell-ee-cut.* And was *bashed up* a technical mechanic term? She knew the car was ridiculous. He didn't need to rub it in.

She and Peewee had graduated from Fisher's Creek High the same year. He played offensive guard for the Fisher's Creek Smiling Crawfish back then, and while he still had the same hulking size that had earned him his ironic nickname, his shape had shifted some in the thirty-ish years since then, now a little less buff shoulders and a lot more beer belly. Same thick neck, though. His dirty tan Fisher's Creek Garage uniform had a patch on the shirt with his name on it and the red cap he wore backward pressed a ridge into the meaty flesh above his sweaty brow.

"Thanks, Peewee. I appreciate the heads-up on that."

Nic blew out a sigh. It wasn't Peewee's fault she drove a stupid, *dell-ee-cut* car, and he'd been nothing but friendly since he pulled up in his rusty old tow truck. She could at least dial back the sarcasm.

God, it wouldn't be long before the constant reminders to keep her attitude in check would be flowing freely from her mother's lips: *Small towns don't work the same as your big city life in New York. You'll catch more flies with honey than with vinegar.* Momilies. They would be starting up in exactly two and a half hours, when Nic stepped into her parents' house for the Dickenson family's traditional Sunday supper: Welcome Home, Nic Edition.

"Nic?" Peewee waved a meaty hand in front of her face like he was trying to wake her from a trance. He'd said something to her. She'd missed it.

"Oh, yeah. Sorry."

"Do you mean, yeah, you'll call someone, or yeah, you need a lift?" He scratched at the back of his beefy neck.

She could call Maggie to pick her up, but that would mean her sister would have to leave work at the family practice where she was a nurse practitioner to drive all the way out to the edge of town. She'd texted earlier and informed Nic she'd been called into the office on an emergency. Calling her other sisters, Bella and Janie, would disrupt their weekend routines with their husbands and kids. And calling her parents to come rescue her? Absolutely not. It was too soon into reentry to face them. Plus, that would lead to extra hours at their house without her siblings. She wasn't quite ready for that. "I'll take that lift. You can just drop me at Zachroll's."

Zachroll's Watering Hole was a little dive bar near the edge of town, just far enough out not to be a nuisance to the main drag, but not so distant that you couldn't take a long, drunken stumble back home if necessary. The Dickenson sisters had spent plenty of nights over college breaks wasting time, shooting pool, and singing karaoke in that bar. Some of those times they'd needed to sneak an underage Janie in with them, but Zachroll's wasn't the kind of place that paid much attention. It was dark and smoky, and possibly the only place in Fisher's Creek where people kept their head down and minded their own business. If you kicked up too much of a ruckus, Old Man Zachroll would throw you out on your ass, no questions asked. Other than that, if you didn't give him a reason to look up from the newspaper as he sat on his barstool perch in the corner, he didn't. Old Man Zachroll. Hell, Nic hadn't thought about him in years. He'd seemed ancient as dirt back then, he had to be pushing one hundred by now. Was Zachroll's Watering Hole even still there?

"Zachroll's it is," Peewee grunted as he hooked the Tesla up to the chains of the tow. "Anything you want to get out of the car before I lift it?"

Although the Tesla had one of the more well-sized trunks among vehicles of its caliber, it still wasn't what she would call expansive. Somehow she'd still managed to squeeze in two suitcases, a duffel bag of linens, and two boxes filled mostly with books she intended to pass along to her sisters before the car was stuffed to the gills.

"Me and Maggie will swing by the garage later to get it."

The ride to the bar passed quickly with the two old school chums catching up. Peewee ended up marrying his high school sweetheart, Cathy Christopher, and they had two sons who were both now in college. Peewee boasted about the little boutique in town that Cathy owned, which tracked with what Nic remembered about her. Cathy was always into fashion and the latest trends, even back in school. Although, Nic always pictured her ending up in New York City, or LA, or somewhere much more fabulous than their hometown. That was what Fisher's Creek did to people—it held them tightly in its clutches. Some people just never escaped.

That wasn't Nic, though. This visit home was exactly that. A *visit*. She would check in with her parents, pick up her inheritance, spend a little time with her sisters, and recharge. Three days and she would blow that popsicle stand and head right back to New York. It was a solid plan.

Peewee slowly pulled the truck into the gravel parking lot of Zachroll's and slipped the gear shift into park, letting the engine idle while Nic gathered her purse and the zip hoodie she'd brought along in case the weather turned.

"You sure I can't drop you at your folks', Nic?" He squinted past her out the passenger side window at the nearly empty lot. Only two cars sat parked, one dirty as the other was rusty, and other than a flickering neon *Open* sign in the front window, the place looked abandoned.

Nic didn't care. Desperate times and all that. "I'll be fine. I'm just going to sit a moment and call my sister. She'll come get me. Thanks again, and tell Cathy I said hello."

She hopped out of the truck and gave Peewee one last wave before he pulled away. She gave the bar a once-over as she headed toward the entrance. Not much about the exterior of the place had changed in the seven years since she'd been back in town for a quick Christmas weekend, but the door had been painted a fresh coat of turquoise to match the lettering on the Zachroll's sign, which appeared to have been touched up as well. There was a four-foot-tall wooden bear carved from a tree trunk that she didn't recall, but other than that, it was almost like time there had been standing still. Par for the course in Fisher's Creek.

She pushed through the heavy door that still stuck against the jamb like she remembered, whether from a warped frame or the general coating of beer slop on everything in a dive bar she did not know, and blinked hard as her eyes adjusted from trading sunlight for the dim bar lighting. High-backed vinyl booths lined one wall—that was new—and the old, tattered beer ad posters on the walls had been replaced with actual framed prints of vintage advertisements and photographs of the town. Even the floor was new, although still sticky to the step, but improvements had been made for sure.

Old man Zachroll was no longer seated at the front corner, but the two locals in the joint hunched over the bar nursing whiskeys, eating complimentary peanuts from a bowl, and staring at the baseball game on the one television might have been sitting in those seats the last time Nic stopped in. Just two nondescript old white guys in well-worn jeans, flannel shirts, and trucker's caps.

"Be right with you," the woman behind bar taking inventory called over her shoulder.

Nic hummed along to the Hendrix song playing as she settled herself on a barstool and assessed the brunette bartender. She was a couple inches taller than Nic, which put her at five seven or eight, but it was hard to tell for sure with her hair all piled up in a poofy bun on top of her head. Plus, the way she stretched and reached as she checked the bottles of liquor kept her in constant motion. That same motion emphasized the cut of muscles in her long, shapely legs extending from the frayed edge of her denim cutoffs with the bar towel hanging out of the back pocket. Even from behind, Nic could tell this woman had curves in all the right places. She was an improvement to Zachroll's as well.

A warm flush rushed Nic's chest and she felt her lips slide up into a pleasant grin, ready to charm the barkeep. Old habit. *Easy, Nic. This is Fisher's Creek, not New York City. There's likely one lesbian in town, and you're it.*

The woman finally turned to take her order, and Nic immediately realized she needn't have admonished herself at all. There'd be no pickup lines spit today. Staring back at her from behind the bar, looking just as surprised as Nic felt, was the very reason she'd gotten the hell out of Fisher's Creek in the first place all those years ago.

CHAPTER TWO

"Well, well, well. Look what the cat dragged in: *New York Times* best-selling author Nicola Dickenson."

Nic didn't care for being compared to a decimated rodent's corpse, but she did enjoy learning that her name hadn't fallen too far off Roxy Fitzpatrick's radar over the years. She obviously knew about the book. It gave Nic a sense of power.

"I'm still just Nic."

"I'm sure you are," Roxy said, pulling the towel out of her back pocket and wiping the surface of the bar top between them before laying down a cocktail napkin. "What'll it be?"

Nic forced a smile. She could still be polite even if Roxy seemed to have lost her good graces. She asked for a draft and wondered what the hell was up with Roxy's cold shoulder. Sure, they hadn't talked since high school, and the last time they did cross paths had been the most humiliating day of Nic's life. But really, what the hell? If anything, Nic should be the one with the attitude. She could remember the horror in Roxy's eyes all those years ago when she learned Nic had more-than-friends feelings for her like it was yesterday.

Whatever. She'd drink her beer and hit the road. With Roxy Fitzpatrick behind the bar, Zachroll's was no longer the oasis on the long voyage back Nic had originally hoped it would be. All she wanted to do was drink a cold beer and enjoy a little quiet time before total transition into Fisher's Creek. Instead, it appeared she had been tossed into the deep end of the swimming hole before she was ready to start doggy-paddling.

Foam spilled over the edge of the frosty mug Roxy set on the napkin before leaning on her elbows and regarding Nic with wide eyes. "So what brings you home? You're not back for good, are you?"

Nic nearly choked on her beer. The panic in Roxy's eyes settled it—she was definitely less than thrilled to see Nic again. "Oh, God no." The response was out of her mouth before she could filter it. But seriously, *home*? She was in town, sure, but Fisher's Creek hadn't been home to Nic since she was a kid. And even then, well, Roxy knew as well as anyone how that went. "I'm just visiting. Staying at Maggie's." Why had she said that? She didn't owe this woman an explanation much less an apology for her reaction.

Roxy blinked her big, emerald eyes at her as if waiting for her to say more, but Nic took a long drink of beer and let the silence stretch, refusing to flinch under that sexy, long-lashed gaze. "How long you sticking around?"

"A few days." Nic hoped that answer was enough. She didn't want to discuss her return—or anything really—with Roxy. They didn't need to make conversation any longer. Clearly neither was exactly thrilled to see the other. She blew out an exasperated breath and took another drink, hoping Roxy would take the hint and leave her to finish her beer in peace.

"You know, for a woman known for her words, you're sure being stingy with them." Roxy frowned as she pushed off the bar. "I'll leave you and your bug alone."

"What bug?"

"The bug up your butt." She gave Nic one last scowl, slung her towel over her shoulder, and sauntered down the bar.

"Ha ha. Were you this funny in high school?" Nic called after her.

Roxy didn't look back, she just went about her work emptying a rack of clean glasses. Nic forced herself to look away from Roxy's shapely ass bending over to line the glasses up on the shelf by the beer taps. Was it possible that she was even more attractive now at forty-something than Nic had found her when they were teenagers?

Nope. Don't even start thinking that way.

Nic pulled out her phone and texted her sister: *Pick me up at Zachroll's?* She needed to get out of there, and the sooner the better.

She took another drink and stared at the phone, willing it to light up with a response. A watched phone screen was no better than a watched pot. Her gaze slid back down the bar. Roxy had finished putting away the glasses and moved on to wedging a lemon. It was really something how she could shake her hips in time with the Bad Company song on the jukebox while slicing fruit and look so damn sexy doing it. *Stop it.* They were never anything more than friends in high school, and they weren't even friends now.

What did she expect anyway? Some kind of warm welcome from the town that had beaten her down all those years ago? She was being ridiculous.

Luckily, Nic's phone chirped with an alert, giving her a reason to look away. Maggie's response.

Still working. Can't leave the office for about twenty minutes.

Twenty minutes and then the drive time out to the bar? No way could Nic hang around in Roxy's presence that long. Screw that.

I'll just walk there, she typed out before draining her glass.

She threw a few bucks onto the bar and left. Hopefully that would be the last she'd see of Roxy Fitzpatrick.

Five minutes down the road, Nic began to regret her choice of footwear. She hadn't planned on taking a hike in from the edge of town. Flip-flops were not made for distance, and little chunks of broken pavement poked at her rubber soles. Hadn't the trek felt a hell of a lot shorter when they were kids? Maybe another sister could give her a ride. Bella was probably still at church or something. And what would she say when she heard Nic had been day-drinking at a dive bar on a Sunday? That was like sacrilege. Too much like breaking the rules. Very un-Bella. She pulled up Janie on her phone instead and tapped out a text: *What are you doing, baby sis? Can you give me a ride?*

By the time she kicked some rogue gravel out of her flip-flop, her phone was chirping with a response. Good ol' Janie—she was never far from her phone, and usually not far from her laptop either. She was a stay-at-home mom these days, but she still put her IT background to use. She'd organized her whole household schedule using apps on her computer and was always trying to push her latest and greatest find onto her sisters. Nic was amused by Janie's organized online persona these days, since when they were growing up she was always the wildest and most free-spirited of them all.

At a T-ball game. Can't leave now. The twins are tearing it up on the diamond.

Crap. Maybe Bella was worth a shot. She was pulling up her older sister's contact info when her foot connected with uneven pavement. Before she knew what was happening, she was tumbling toward the ground. She'd tripped and landed on her hands and knees. Then she felt the sharp slash of pain in her cheek.

Fucking hell! Her eyes stung with tears as she sat down, ass on asphalt, and assessed the damage. The tears were partly from the pain, but she couldn't deny they were rooted in the humiliation she'd been feeling since she started the walk. Her knees were throbbing, and the denim of her capris had dirty patches where they'd made contact with the road. The palms of both of her hands were an angry red, both with gravel embedded in the flesh. But worst of all was the burning in her cheek, and when she brushed her fingertips across it, her fear was confirmed—she was bleeding. When she fell, a stick had popped up and scraped her face.

Welcome back to fucking Fisher's Creek.

She pushed herself up to standing and tried to dust herself off. It was a losing battle—she was a mess. She'd have to change her clothes before Sunday supper at her parents' house, which meant she'd need to get her belongings out of her car. She needed to get to Peewee's garage. She took a tentative step and pain shot through her right ankle. She'd twisted it when she tripped. With a grimace of determination, she resumed her path down the road, limping as she went. She would not be beaten down by this town again. Especially not on her first day back. A tickle on her cheek drew her hand, and she realized that the cut was still actively bleeding. Maybe a stop at Maggie's office first before collecting her belongings would be prudent. Maybe Maggie would even take pity on her and give her a lift to Peewee's.

An approaching car behind her caused her to limp closer to the edge of the road, this time making sure to watch where she stepped. The car slowed down beside her. Just what she needed—some redneck asshole hassling her while she was limping along in tattered jeans with a bloody face to top it off. She lifted her head to tell the driver to get lost when it registered that the vehicle was a Fisher's Creek police cruiser.

She stopped walking when the window rolled down. "Hey, big sis, need a ride?"

"Junior? Oh my God. Talk about good timing."

Her little brother to the rescue. As the youngest of the Dickenson clan, Junior had grown up with four older sisters who tortured and tormented him—in the most loving ways, of course. The girls would dress him up like their very own living doll and dared him to do more than a few things their mother would still be mad about if she had known. Junior was a "late in life" baby for Marie Dickenson, or as she referred to him, their "little miracle." He'd survived his sisters' treatment and grown up to follow in their father's footsteps, going into law enforcement and becoming a member of Fisher's Creek's finest. Junior's unexpected arrival on that back road was the first good thing to happen since Nic's return.

"Maggie called me." He shrugged. "C'mon. Get in."

"You really got into it this time, huh?" Maggie adjusted the light above them and peered at Nic's cheek. She wasn't judging, simply stating a fact. Her saintly patience, along with her ability to roll with the punches, were qualities that served her well as a medical professional. "Just like when we were kids, always rough and tumble. Always tough as nails."

Maggie's ash-brown hair was cut in a neat bob, much shorter than the last time Nic had seen her, the front of it clipped back off her face by a silver barrette. She studied Nic's face from under the bright red frames of her eyeglasses.

"This wasn't rough and tumble, this was me literally taking a tumble. I tripped—ouch!" Nic flinched as the suture needle pierced her cheek.

"Don't move," Maggie gently scolded. "I'm trying to spare you a scar. You're lucky this is right by your hairline. It will hardly show."

"No worries. Chicks dig scars, right?"

"And always still about the ladies." Maggie smirked and tugged on the Vicryl as she carefully stitched up the wound. "Hold on, I'm almost done."

"God, Maggie, I was not always about the ladies. I held that back until I went off to college."

"If you say so."

"And after everything with Dana—" Nic blew out a breath. Nope. No need to go there. She didn't want to dig into that pathetic story. "I think me and the ladies are on a break. Why don't we talk about your love life for a change?"

"Oh, sure. If you're in the mood for a horror story." Maggie laughed as she snapped her gloves off and deposited them in the bin. "Let's not and say we did."

Anytime Nic was with her sisters this happened—it was like they were kids again, falling into their old ways, talking in comfortable phrases that telegraphed their special sister bond. Mercilessly teasing each other. Fiercely protecting each other. Their own code. She missed it while she'd been away, and falling right back into it was a balm to her raw nerves and gloomy soul.

"So, truce, then," Nic offered.

"Enjoy it while it lasts." Maggie winked. "You know Mom's not going to give us any peace tonight. *Let's shame my single daughter* is one of her favorite games. I'm just glad you're back in town to absorb some of the heat."

"It's dinner—two hours—how bad can it be?"

Two hours later, Nic had her answer.

The whole ride down from New York, Nic had been dreading Sunday supper with the entire Dickenson clan, but a few bites into the meal at her parents' table with her siblings, their spouses, and her niece and nephews, Nic was transported back in time. Some of the best times of her childhood happened while gathered in that very dining room. Jolly holidays, dinner parties with friends and neighbors, Friday night pizza and game nights when they were all young. Memories wrapped around her like a cozy throw blanket, warmed her heart, and brought that feeling of family alive for her again. Maybe it had been too long since she'd been back.

Nic's son, Asher, was the oldest of the cousins, and spending time with her sisters' kids made her really miss him. He was off at college and teetering on the edge of being a full-fledged adult. He would be flexing his freedom once classes were over for the semester by working at the shore with friends. It was just as well, since Nic's habitational situation was currently in flux. Nic would've loved to have him there with the rest of them, though. Intelligent and independent, the kiddo made her heart burst with pride and ache from missing him. She pushed the thoughts of her absent son to the corner of her mind and focused on the family members who were gathered at the table.

Bella's boys were both in high school, and while they minded their manners for the most part, Nic caught them elbowing each other good-naturedly and stifling eye rolls at the conversation more than once. They reminded her of her own siblings at that age. Collin, Maggie's twelve-year-old, was sweet and stayed engaged in the conversation at the table, whether it was his grandfather speaking or one of the younger kids. Then, of course, there were Janie's twins, Mia and Mason. At seven, they were cute and giggly and made Nic think of their mother at that age. Janie had always been like sunshine breaking through the clouds. Bright and bubbly, contagiously enthusiastic.

Despite her prior misgivings, dinner turned out to be quite enjoyable. But by the time her mom started passing the dessert at the end of the meal, Nic's curiosity was starting to get the best of her. Her mother had made such a big freaking deal about how she had to come back to Fisher's Creek to get her inheritance from Aunt Aggie, but she'd made it through the entire dinner without word one about what this mysterious item was. The suspense was thicker than the cheesecake her mom was serving up.

While everyone else dug into their dessert, Nic sank down in her chair. Her plan to take care of business and get out of town felt like it had gone slightly off track, and that made her antsy. That was the only reason why she let a heavy sigh slip out while still seated at the dinner table.

"Is something wrong, Nicola?" her mother asked as she finally sat down to her own slice of cheesecake. "Eat some sweets. You'll feel better. Everyone feels better when they're eating cheesecake."

"Not the lactose intolerant." Junior laughed through a mouth of cake. His wife, Kellie, fixed him with a warning glance and he quickly covered his guffawing mouth with his napkin.

"Ma, I don't need any dessert. I'm stuffed," Nic protested. "I can't remember the last time I ate like this."

"It's probably been seven years," Bella offered. "You know, the last time you graced us with your presence."

Junior snorted. This time Nic shot him a look.

"She's here now, that's the important thing. Right, Pop?" Maggie. Always the champion of her siblings. The rolling river of the bunch who tried to keep things moving along nice and easy like.

"We're glad to have you home, sweetie." Her dad's gruff voice was somehow a comfort to Nic. A constant. A reminder of her childhood and sweeter times.

"Thanks, Pop. And dinner was delicious, Ma." Nic fixed her face into a more pleasant expression. There was no reason to be impolite. "I just can't believe nobody's mentioned the Aunt Aggie thing."

"We're not going to talk about an inheritance matter at the dinner table. That's tacky, even if Aunt Agatha was an old crab pot," her mother said as she poured herself a cup of decaf from the ancient carafe on the table. "Besides, I'm not in charge of Aunt Agatha's affairs. I was just the messenger. You'll have to talk to her attorney about it."

"Her attorney?" Nic's gaze ran down the row of faces at the long table to her older sister. "Bella, aren't you Aunt Aggie's attorney?"

The entire table burst out in laughter. Nic took a deep, *stay cool* breath.

Finally, Bella held up a hand to calm them all down. She had a way of doing that. She was like the wind blowing in and whipping everything in her path into shape. Strong and persuasive. Sometimes a little bit scary. "Okay. Let me finish my cheesecake and we'll talk shop."

Nic stood in the middle of her parents' living room, a space that was so familiar to her, and felt like the world was tilting on its side. According to her sister, and the piece of paper she held in her hands, she had inherited a house. A big, old stately house in Fisher's Creek. "Aunt Aggie left me her house? Grumpy old Aunt Aggie, who barely ever spoke to me except to bark 'Merry Christmas' once a year, left me, her lesbian great-niece from New York, her house."

"Yes." Bella nodded solemnly, officially in serious attorney mode. "I think you really captured the essence of what occurred in that statement. Well done."

Nic blew out a sigh. "I'm serious, Bella. Is this some kind of joke? Because I came all the way down here for this, and if you—"

"It's not a joke." Bella stuffed the papers she was holding back into the manila envelope and placed the package on the side table. "The house is yours. And beside the fact that we all wanted to see you, it was just easiest for you to come here and handle all the paperwork. Plus, this way you can go over there and see the house for yourself before you decide what you want to do with it."

"What I want to do with it? It's salable, right? I mean, I can just sell it, right?"

"Well, sure. But—"

"I'll hire you to handle the real estate transactions, and that will be that."

Bella chewed her bottom lip as if she was carefully considering her response. "I'm not a real estate attorney, but I can handle it for you if that's what you want. I just think you should at least go over and have a look around before we sign anything."

Why was Nic's stance on selling the house not computing with Bella? She didn't need to see Aunt Aggie's house. She'd seen it a handful of times when they were young and the sisters tagged along with their mother when she went over to the big house to drop things off for her aunt after running errands. At no time did Agatha even seem to acknowledge their presence. It was like children were invisible to her, which made sense since Nic had heard her say on more than one occasion that "children should be seen and not heard." Why the old woman had left the house to her was a complete mystery.

"Just think about it, Nic," Bella said in her important, big-sister voice. "In the meantime, I've hired someone to do a few necessary repairs around the old place, so you need to be at the house tomorrow to let them in."

"What?" She had to have misheard that. "Why me?"

"Because someone needs to be there and I have to work and—" Bella threw her hands in the air, clearly frustrated. "It's *your house*. These things need doing to get the house up to code if you're going to sell it." Bella turned to head out of the room, but before she left she said over her shoulder, "Plus, there are some of Aunt Aggie's personal things that still need clearing out of there."

Clearing out Great-Aunt Agatha's personal belongings. Great. It wasn't how Nic thought she would be spending her Monday, but she didn't exactly have a full schedule while she was in Fisher's Creek anyway. And with her car at Peewee's awaiting repair, she had some unexpected time on her hands. She folded the paper she was holding, carefully running the crease between her fingertips. This trip was supposed to be a grab-and-go operation, but now here she was, a homeowner. A homeowner in Fisher's Creek, Pennsylvania.

Her mom was washing the dishes and Janie dutifully drying when Nic marched back into the kitchen. How could they carry on like normal, like this wasn't extremely weird?

"The house, Ma? Aunt Aggie left me her house? Why would she do that?"

"Well, I don't know." Her mom's voice was a little too songlike for the words to be entirely true. "Agatha was a woman who did whatever she wanted. Besides, I don't know why you're acting like leaving you a home is a bad thing. Seems like you could use a house right about now."

Nic's shoulders went tight at the base of her neck. "Ma, don't start, okay?"

"I'm just saying, you leaving Dana there in the apartment is practically handing it over to her. It's like you're giving up your right to it."

There it was.

"Mom, it's not like that at all." Nic rubbed at her temples. They'd had this conversation before, over the phone. The in-person version wasn't any more pleasant. "As I've told you, I have no right to it. She lived there before we were together. It was hers, and that prenup I signed guaranteed it remained that way. That's how I ended up with her stupid car. It was the best my attorney could do for me."

"But you love that apartment." Her mother fanned her hand on her chest. Was she tearing up? *Come on.* "How can you just give it up?"

Nic did love that place in Manhattan with the built-in bookshelves and hand-scraped hardwood floors. She loved it so much. Until she didn't. After that day when she came home early from a meeting with her publisher and found Dana in bed with her yoga instructor, she had no interest in staying in the home they'd built together. The image of the yoga instructor's bony butt in downward dog pleasuring her wife was not one Nic was likely to forget anytime soon. She'd just as soon leave it behind with the apartment and most of the other material items she and

Dana had acquired over the years. She'd been too devastated to even fight. Hell, she barely had any money in her bank account. Nothing to fall back on in case her muse had left the building for good and she was never able to write another novel and she had to take a job flipping burgers at the Burger Barn. *Motherfucking Dana.* Throwing away a twenty-two-year relationship, nine of those years actually married, to plank with some skinny-assed, Lycra-clad thirty-year-old.

"Loved," she sighed. When her mother gave her a questioning look, she clarified, "Past tense. I *loved* that apartment. Things change, Ma."

"But still." Apparently, her mother wasn't done drilling her point home yet. "What about poor Asher? That's his home too. Where will he live?"

"For a few more weeks he'll live on campus at Penn like he's done all year long, then he's off to the shore with friends for the summer. He's got a job lifeguarding." Nic shrugged. "In between the job and school, he can land wherever I am or with Dana. She's his mom too."

Nic become pregnant with Asher in 2003 when she and Dana had been together for just over two years. It would be another eleven years before it would be legal for them to get married, but they knew they wanted to start a family and have a life together. They found a donor and decided Nic would carry the baby. Dana officially adopted Asher after he was born, making everything neat and tidy.

Her mom stopped cleaning long enough to pose with her hand balled on her hip and shoot Nic a pointed look. "I know she's his mother too. All I'm saying is, if something ever happened between me and your father, I hope you kids would pick me. And I hope Asher picks you."

"There's no picking!" She scrubbed a hand over her face. Dana had turned out to be a shitty wife, but that didn't mean she wasn't a wonderful mother to their son. "We're his moms. He loves both of us no matter what happened between us. And he's practically grown—he's starting his own life." Her mother's snort of judgment made Nic's ears burn with anger. "You know what,

Ma? He can come here and live with you. Is that what you want? You think you can raise my son better than I have?"

"I didn't say that." Her clipped tone betrayed her feelings.

"You didn't have to. I got your message loud and clear."

Her mother sighed. "Asher's a wonderful boy. He could come visit a little more often, but he's learned that from you. You raised him in that big city life—much too important to come home even for a visit. I'm used to it. This is the first time you've shown your face in Fisher's Creek in nearly ten years."

A silent beat stretched between them as Nic bit back a snarky retort. So damn dramatic. It had definitely been less than ten years, but still, the nasty cocktail of truth, pride, and guilt that only family could cause swirled in her stomach.

Janie cleared her throat, reminding them she was in the kitchen too. The sun breaking through on a cloudy day. "Speaking of kids, Aunt Nic, two are waiting as patiently as seven-year-olds can for you to set up the sprinkler out back so they can run through it."

Janie to the rescue. Even if Nic didn't come home to visit often enough, she could still count on her sisters to be her saving grace. Her mother turned her full attention back to her dirty dishes, finally having said her piece. Nic took the opportunity to escape and followed her youngest sister out to the backyard.

"And that's exactly why I've put off returning home for *nearly ten* years." Her Marie Dickenson impression was spot-on. Nic yanked the garden hose through the grass. "It was only seven years, by the way—right after you had the twins, remember? All that time, and the mom guilt can still punch me right in the gut."

"Come on, give her a break, Nic." Janie handed her the garden sprinkler. It was the same one they had used to cool off in the yard when they were kids. Still stored in the shed in her parents' backyard after all this time. "She misses you and she's worried about you. That's called love."

"Funny thing, love."

"No, Nic. Don't start with that."

"Don't you start," Nic countered. She felt stupid kneeling in the freshly cut grass struggling to connect the sprinkler onto the hose. She couldn't get the threads to line up. Was this even how it was supposed to go on? "First it will be about how I'm mean to Mom, then you'll hit me with the whole 'Fisher's Creek loves you and you left' thing. It's a tired old story."

"Right. I know the story too." Janie nodded and took the sprinkler back from her, clearly out of patience for Nic's inability to complete the task. "You get mad thinking Mom's picking on you, when in reality she treats all of us in that same mother-smother way of hers, only the rest of us all live here so we get it constantly with no break in the action. It's just her nature. It's her way of loving us, so we all accept that. All of us but you. Then you'll move on to how horrible Fisher's Creek is with absolutely no regard to the fact that all of us still choose to call this place home. We make that choice, you know. And you should really get over all that too, because Fisher's Creek is actually a great place to live, you just need to open your eyes and give it a chance."

Nic picked grass clippings from the skin on her knee as her baby sister screwed together the sprinkler and the hose with an ease that declared she'd been at her parents' house and done it a million times. Despite the message delivered in her little speech, there was a twinkle in Janie's eyes that was like the spoonful of sugar that helped the truth go down. It was hard to be or stay angry at her, always had been. "Since when did you become such a straight-talking, wise woman?"

"Without you here to do it, someone had to take on the role." Janie dusted her hands on her shorts as she stood. "Seriously, can you just hold that attitude in or at least tone it down while you're here? We're all so happy you're home. Can you please just let us have that?"

The sunny smile on her sister's face softened Nic's heart, the same effect it had always had on her even when they were kids. Truthfully, she wasn't asking for much. Nic only planned on being in town for a few days. She could try a little harder to enjoy them and let the little crap roll off her back. Don't sweat the small stuff, right? God knew she'd had enough big stuff on her plate to worry about lately with her divorce and the book. She grabbed Janie's hand and gave it a squeeze. "Okay, sister. I'll try just for you."

"Thank you," Janie said and kissed her cheek. "And you can start by convincing Maggie to host Dickenson Sister Tequila Night after we get out of here tonight."

"Dickenson Sister Tequila Night? Finally, a Fisher's Creek tradition I can get behind!"

CHAPTER THREE

Later that evening, the sisters reassembled at Maggie's house for a more relaxed catch-up.

"I've got the limes!" Janie burst into the kitchen through the back door, holding two of the bright-green fruits up in one hand. It reminded Nic of the way she used to hold billiard balls while racking them up at Zachroll's on a Friday night.

"It's about time." Bella's curls danced around her face as she grabbed the limes and traded her sister a shot glass. She had the same shade of strawberry-blond hair as Nic—they got it from their mother. "We had to do our first round with salt only."

Bella and Nic got their hair color from their mother, but all four girls got her name. Isabella Marie, Nicola Marie, Margaret Marie, and Jane Marie. Her mom always joked she named them that way to keep them easy to remember. Nic suspected her mother actually wanted to give the girls one more thing to connect them to her Italian father's side of the family. As if Marie's cooking wasn't enough to keep that family history at the forefront of their stomachs, minds, and hearts.

"Not Mags." Nic grabbed the bottle of tequila and started pouring. "She shot a chaser from the squeezy lime thing in her fridge."

"It's the same damn thing," Maggie argued as she grabbed a freshly cut slice. She bit into the flesh and shook her head, quickly amending her statement. "Nope. This is definitely better."

"I would've been here sooner, but the kids asked for one more story, and you know I can't resist their cute, sleepy little faces."

"I told you, you could've brought them over," Maggie said. "They could've had a sleepover with Collin."

"And I told you." Janie shook some salt onto her hand. "I needed uninterrupted sister time."

Nic held her shot glass up in a toast. "To sister time. My very favorite part of Fisher's Creek."

"Sister time!" the others echoed before partaking in the tequila shot routine.

"Mmm." Janie licked her lips. "Except do you think Junior feels bad that we leave him out?" Even after all this time, she continued to stick up for their little brother. As one of the youngest two of the pack, she'd always been his protector. Totally loyal, that was Janie.

"Oh, please." Bella rolled her eyes. "I heard him talking to Dad at dinner about how we had one of our 'hen parties' planned for the night. He's perfectly content to be passing on the occasion."

Nic slid onto one of the reclaimed wood stools at the breakfast bar. Maggie's house had a country inn charm to it. The kitchen had distressed cabinets in a creamy white color, and pots hanging from the dark wood beams on the ceiling. It was homey and comfy, the kind of room that encouraged people to gather. "Go easy on Junior. He saved my life today."

"God, Nic, dramatic much?" Janie pushed her chin-length, ash-brown hair out of her eyes. She was the same shade as Maggie and Junior. "He told me you were staggering down the road away from Zachroll's. Very classy. What happened? Did you get a little rowdy and make Roxy have to throw you out?"

"First of all, I was not staggering. I tripped and fell. My knee was sore." Nic rubbed her right knee. Why did talking about aches and pains always make them worse? "Secondly, do not ever speak that name in my presence. I've been in Fisher's Creek less than eight hours and I've already had my fill of Roxy Fitzpatrick."

"You can speak Roxy's name, but we can't? That doesn't seem fair," Maggie teased over her shoulder as she ambled toward the fridge. "Who needs a beer?"

"Me," the others said in unison.

Nic reached for one of the brown bottles her sister was passing out. She'd been trying unsuccessfully all evening to get the image of Roxy's green eyes out of her mind. Eyes that once used to look at her with brightness and mirth but today held nothing but disdain for Nic. And now, here Roxy was the topic of conversation in what should be a safe space. She took a long pull on her beer bottle. She would be wise to put that woman out of her mind. Roxy clearly had no intention of picking up their friendship where they left off back in the early nineties. "Since when does Roxy work at Zachroll's anyway? And why didn't any of you tell me? A little heads-up would've been nice."

"You haven't been home in like, *ten years*." Bella hit her with some major side-eye, indicating she'd been brought up to speed on Nic's conversation earlier with their mom. "We should've told you Jimmy Ehrman was valedictorian at the high school last spring and Mr. Terrance won two hundred bucks on a scratch-off lottery ticket down at the Gas-N-Go five years ago too."

Maggie gave Nic's shoulder a sympathetic squeeze, smoothing over Bella's teasing before settling onto the stool next to her. "Roxy doesn't just work at Zachroll's, she owns it. Bought it from the old man almost three years ago. Fixed it up herself and everything."

"And we didn't tell you because Roxy Fitzpatrick is like your least favorite subject." Janie shrugged. "How the hell were we supposed to know a dive bar would be your first stop in town?"

"Seriously, Nic, after all these years you're still mad at Roxy?" Maggie swiveled on her stool and fixed Nic with an exasperated look. "Aren't we supposed to grow out of high school angst? You two used to be inseparable. Can't you just get along?"

The words made perfect sense. Nic was well aware the past was best left in the past, but Roxy Fitzpatrick was like a scar—a reminder of days gone by that would always be with her. One that sometimes still hurt in the late quiet hours of the night. It was the kind of pain that came with being betrayed by a friend. Or maybe something worse. And Roxy didn't exactly give her a warm welcome earlier at the bar. No, it sure didn't feel like she'd be letting go anytime soon. "You know what? I don't really feel like talking about Roxy anymore."

Bella arched a perfectly sculpted eyebrow in her direction. "Then should we talk about Dana?"

"Absolutely not."

Janie slammed her beer bottle down on the counter, causing foam to bubble over the neck. "But if we don't rag on your love life, then what are we going to do for entertainment?"

"Oh!" Nic exclaimed, struck by inspiration and the beauty of dodging a bullet. "We could rag on Maggie's love life."

"As I told you earlier, there's nothing to get excited about there." Maggie shook her head. "Certainly won't be entertaining. So…next subject, please."

"Nothing? Are you sure about that?" Janie left her beer on the counter and helped herself to Maggie's laptop. "We might get a little excited to hear about your Perfect Pair profile. What do you think, sisters?"

"Get out!" Bella slid off her stool to peer over Janie's shoulder at the screen, like she needed to see it with her own eyes to confirm. "You're on a dating site?"

"How do you know that?" Maggie threw her hands in the air, clearly at a loss. "I haven't told anyone. Can't a girl have any secrets around here?"

"I Googled you. I Google all of you every once in a while for the hell of it. Sorry, I love you." Janie didn't look up, and her expression definitely didn't look apologetic. She kept pecking away at the keys to pull up the site. "You're my sisters and I like to keep an eye on you."

Nic knew she shouldn't take delight in the invasion of her sister's privacy, but as long as the spotlight was on Maggie, it was off her. She was…relieved. Besides, she'd taken the brunt of the heat at their parents' house. It was someone else's turn.

"That's a great picture of you. Good choice." Bella nodded approvingly as Maggie's profile filled the laptop screen. "You've got message alerts. Have you met anyone on here?"

Maggie chewed her bottom lip for a beat as if trying to decide whether to go down that path, but then her lips relaxed into a grin that held a glint of pride. She grabbed her phone from the countertop and pulled up her text messages. "Yep. I've been texting with three of them. One says he's a 'born-again virgin,' one has a great sense of humor but lives in Ohio, and the last one, well, he's really hot but I think he's just looking for a sex hookup. He doesn't say much, just sends a lot of…dick pics."

"Ew!"

"Oh my God!"

"Let's see them!"

"Ew," Nic repeated. "No, Janie. She's not going to show us. Besides, I'm more interested in this *born-again virgin* thing. Exactly how does that work?"

"He's holding out for Miss Right before he has sex again. Don't look at me like it's weird. I think it's really sweet." Maggie pouted and held out her phone. "And he's handsome too."

Janie squinted at the picture of the born-again virgin, then started typing again. "Email me that picture. We'll see how sweet your virgin is."

While Janie worked her computer magic, Bella swiped through the other pictures on Maggie's phone. "Yowzer! I found the dick pics."

Janie finally looked up from the laptop. "What did you say the virgin's name was?"

"I didn't." Maggie shook her head. "But it's Greg. I'm thinking about asking him to meet me IRL."

"You're not meeting your sweet virgin Greg *in real life*," Janie said, crossing her arms. She had a know-it-all grin like the one she used to get when they were kids and she would beat them all at Monopoly. Such a smart-ass.

"You can't tell me what to do, little sister." Maggie balked.

Janie angled the laptop to show the others what she'd found. "I mean, you can't meet a virgin named Greg because he's actually

Allan Garrison, and he's definitely not a virgin. He's a stay-at-home father of three."

"Aw, his kids are cute." Nic kept her focus on the computer screen and tried her best to avoid catching an eyeful of the naked man that Bella was still gawking at on Maggie's phone. "Does he talk about them a lot?"

"No. Never mentioned them." Maggie's brow furrowed. "Allan? Are you sure?"

"Yep." Janie nodded. "I'm guessing he never mentioned his wife either. Here's a picture of them all on a family vacation to the Grand Canyon last month."

"That sonofabitch."

Nic put a sympathetic hand on Maggie's arm. "Looks like you were catfished, Mags. You caught yourself a cheating, lonely househusband."

"I can't believe it. I actually liked Greg. I mean Allan. I mean… Ugh." Maggie scrubbed both her hands over her face. "How did you figure that out?"

"I did a reverse search on the picture you sent me. It matched up with another on the Internet." Janie shrugged. "A couple of clicks led me to his social media presence. Sorry, Maggie."

"No, thank you. You saved me from making a big mistake." She crossed the kitchen. "Who else needs another beer?"

Bella raised her hand along with the others before turning back to Janie. "Can you do it with Mr. Dick Pic?"

"I think that *you* want to do it with Mr. Dick Pic." Janie smirked. "Sure. Forward that picture to me."

While Maggie handed out beers, Janie did her thing. Within seconds she had her results.

"That one was easy." Janie pressed a button and the screen was filled with an array of images of the same man in various stages of undress, a couple in which he was totally au naturel and fully frontal. "He's a porn star. Smith Hardcock."

"Maggie's been texting a porn star?" Bella's eyes were practically popping out of her head. She'd been married to a man for twenty-two years and had two sons, but she was acting like she'd never seen a naked male before. "You met a porn star on a dating site?"

"Bella." Nic stared at her sister in disbelief. Her older sister was the most book-smart person she knew, but sometimes basic common sense seemed to elude her. "She met a guy pretending a porn star's parts were his."

"You're like a dick-pic detective." Maggie stared with amazement at her younger sister. "A dic-tective."

"You should start a business," Bella chimed in. "You could call yourself The Dic-tective."

Nic nearly choked on her beer. "Dic-tective? That's appalling."

"Don't be anti-dick," Bella scolded. "There are straight women out there who need Janie's help lest they fall prey to the fake dicks out there. Just like Maggie did."

"I can't believe this. Are there no honest men left out there?" Maggie whined and dropped back onto her barstool.

Nic's heart went out to her. Maggie was only eighteen months younger than her. It was hard to meet new people at their age. Well, it hadn't been hard for Dana and the yoga instructor. But for normal, noncheating types…

She put an arm around Maggie and pulled her close in a side hug. "Aw, sweetie. There are nice guys out there. You just have to be more careful when you're looking for them online."

"Yeah," Janie chimed in. "From now on you send any new guys you're thinking about meeting to me. I'll check them out and report back. No sweat. Nic, you should send me any of your prospects as well. Women can be creeps in cyberspace too."

"I'm not on Perfect Pair."

"You are now." Janie finished tapping at the keyboard and sat back to let the others admire her handiwork. "I just made you a profile."

"Your hair looks gorgeous! Awesome pic." Bella nodded approvingly.

"That's because it's my author headshot. If my publisher sees that they'll have a fit." The last thing Nic needed was to draw their ire about something like image copyright infringement when she was trying to lay low in the first place. "Take that down."

"Don't you dare!" Maggie pushed between Janie and the computer. "If I have to have my online dating life scrutinized by the sisters, so do you."

"I don't have an online dating life," Nic protested.

"Do you have any dating life?" Maggie shot back.

"Ouch." Nic winced at the ugly truth. Despite the mounting number of lonely nights that had passed since she'd left Dana, she had a book to write, and until that happened, romance would have to remain on the back burner. In the meantime, it wouldn't hurt to show a little sister solidarity if it helped Maggie to feel better. "Fine. But switch out that photo. I don't have the bandwidth to deal with fallout from the good people at Mountain Pass Press."

Janie swooshed Maggie out of her way and went back to work the profile. "There you go. And now let's take a look at who these potential prospects might be. I set your filters to reflect your location here in Fisher's Creek, so you don't have to wait until you get back to New York to start making connections."

The filters didn't matter to Nic. She wasn't really going to use the dating app. Plus, how many queer connections could there possibly be in the Fisher's Creek area? "How very thoughtful of you."

"Yeah, yeah. Very thoughtful," Maggie parroted as she and Bella peered at the screen over Janie's shoulder. "Let's see Nic's matches."

"By all means, let's." Nic surrendered and focused on the computer as her sister clicked through the profiles of the women the site claimed were the other part of her Perfect Pair. One after the next were pleasant looking enough, but none really stood out until—"Oh my God."

Janie let out a whoop. "Looks like you matched with the most eligible bachelorette in town."

Bella leaned forward, squinting at the photo. "Wait. Is that—"

"Oh, yeah." Maggie nodded, confirming what everyone was thinking. "That's Roxy Fitzpatrick."

A shiver worked up Nic's spine as she stared at the photo of those shining emerald eyes. *Well, I'll be damned.* "Roxy Fitzpatrick is looking to meet women on a dating site."

"Yeah." Janie grimaced as she gazed up at Nic. "Did we not mention that Roxy came out as a lesbian a few years back?"

So maybe one thing in Fisher's Creek had changed.

CHAPTER FOUR

Heading north on Main Street in the heart of Fisher's Creek and turning left on the street that lined the side of the park led to a row of five Victorian houses, two of which had those wooden tree-stump bears in front of them. So very Fisher's Creek. There was originally a sixth house in the row, but one burned down in the seventies and the owners never rebuilt, just moved away and left the lot vacant. The third one in had belonged to Great-Aunt Agatha for as long as Nic could remember. It was the Hill family home, the home Agatha had grown up in. According to family history, her parents passed when she was just nineteen and she took over the house from there forward. As far as Nic knew, it was just Aunt Aggie rattling around in the big house all alone. Which was especially amazing to Nic once Bella handed over the keys Monday morning and she actually stepped into the vast interior of the house for the first time since she was a kid.

She took a quick walk-through to get the lay of the land. Six freaking bedrooms, although two of them were up on the third floor. The rooms on the first floor had high ceilings and wood paneling on the walls, and between the parlor and dining room were pocket doors that could slide shut for privacy. The kitchen was terribly out of date, but it had plenty of counter space, a huge pantry for storage, and a back staircase to the upper floors of the house. Despite needing some work and updates, it was a really great house. Too bad it was smack in the middle of Fisher's Creek—the last place Nic would want to settle down.

Most of the flooring in the house was hardwood, but the kitchen had been tiled at some point. In addition to having several chips across the surface, the once white tiles had taken on a dingy yellow hue like the teeth of a heavy smoker. A problem for the next owner, along with the gold and burnt orange floral wallpaper. Straight out of the seventies. How had she forgotten about that decor?

The cabinets could have a vintage-style appeal, or maybe someone would just want to rip them all out and start fresh. Nic could see that going either way. But that was also someone else's problem. She swung open the wooden doors on the cabinet in front of her and gasped—it was still full of dishes and ceramic mugs. Neatly—but definitely—full. Yanking open the next one to it, and the next, she found similar contents. Didn't anyone clean anything out? She opened the pantry and found it fully stocked with both canned and dry goods. She'd inherited much more than a house. She'd inherited contents too, and it needed to be cleared out before she could put the house on the market. It was one thing to ask Bella to handle the sale, but it wasn't fair to dump this on her too.

But if the kitchen was still full of her great-aunt's stuff, did that mean…

She raced up the steps to the bedroom and pulled open the wardrobe. Packed from wall to wall with garments. And the bottom was rows of shoeboxes stacked three layers high. More stuff to sort and pitch. The dresser drawers were stuffed too. So was the closet. Apparently, what Bella had conservatively described as *some* of Aunt Aggie's personal belongings was actually *all* of Aunt Aggie's personal belongings. There was a houseful of possessions—a whole former life—to deal with. Where the hell would she even start with this?

"Hello?"

Nic nearly jumped out of her skin at the sound of another person in the old house with her, but then she remembered the whole reason she'd come to the house in the first place: the handyman—or woman, more likely, based on that voice.

"Be right there," she called as she headed for the stairs. She'd figure out the mess later. Right now she needed to get the handyperson handying. The sooner the projects bringing the house to code were completed, the sooner she could sell the house, and the sooner she could just get on with her—

"Roxy?"

Roxy was the handyperson? *What the fuck?*

"Of course." Roxy looked even less thrilled to see her than Nic felt. She also looked very sexy in cargo pants that hugged her hips and a threadbare Rolling Stones T-shirt with a notch cut into the neck providing just a peek of cleavage. But it was the work belt currently slung casually over her shoulder that made Nic's heart skip a beat. "This is why you're back in town—to help your family with the house."

"My house," Nic corrected her. "Agatha left it to me for some reason."

Roxy had the gall to roll her eyes. "Bella failed to mention that when she hired me."

"I know the feeling. She failed to tell me you were the handyperson she hired."

"Handyperson?"

"I'm sorry. Do you prefer something catchier like... handyma'am?"

"I'm a full-ass contractor, thank you very much."

"How would I know that? I haven't seen you in almost thirty years. I thought you were a bartender." The look that flashed in Roxy's eyes made it clear Nic had said something wrong again. "Ugh. I'm sorry. Bar *owner*. What's with the side hustle fixing up old houses anyway?"

Roxy opened and shut her mouth as if she had thought better of answering the question. Instead, she scowled and raised her toolbox. "Can I get started here, or what?"

Nic stepped aside and gestured in the direction of the powder room that needed attention. She couldn't deny she was more than a little curious about the answer Roxy had appeared to bite back, but it really wasn't her business. As Roxy silently pushed past her and on to the task she'd been hired to do, it was very clear they were no longer friends—that relationship had come to a screeching halt many years ago. Besides, she had a houseful of contents to address. And a sister who had hired Roxy to work on her house to bitch out.

The minute she was back upstairs and safely out of earshot, she dialed up her older sister.

"You hired Roxy Fitzpatrick to do the work at the house?"

"How nice to hear from you, little sis."

"Bella."

"Nicola, I'm at work. I don't have time to talk about this. The work needed done, and it's getting done."

"But Roxy?"

"She was available now, her price was right, and she knows what she's doing."

"Does she, though?"

"Nic, don't be ridiculous. That's the field she went into. She's a licensed, bonded professional."

"I thought she owned Zachroll's."

"She does, and she did all the renovations herself. But before she was a bar owner, before she came home to take care of her mother, she was a contractor. She still picks up jobs here and there around town. I'm sure the money helps to pay for her mother's care. The way I see it, Roxy's your best bet to get it done quickly and for a reasonable price." Bella blew out a lengthy sigh surely meant to convey her annoyance at the conversation. "Are you satisfied? Can I get back to work now?"

Nic wasn't satisfied. Her former high school best friend-turned-first crush, who now seemed to totally hate her guts, was downstairs bringing the house that Nic had unexpectedly inherited from a great-aunt she barely even knew up to code. Plus, the house was unexpectedly full of every last earthly possession of said great-aunt. That was yet another thing Nic had to figure out how to deal with. "Did you know all of Aunt Aggie's stuff is still in the house? And I mean *all* of it."

"Listen, Nic, can we talk about this at lunch? I've got to go. Bye."

Damn it, Bella.

She slipped her phone into her back pocket and surveyed the hallway. Where should she even begin with this mess? And what should she do about Roxy? Bella had mentioned availability and price, which were both valid points. Roxy had already started working downstairs, and who knew how long it would take to find someone else and get on their schedule to do the job. She needed the house up to code ASAP so she could sell it, and she'd only have to deal with Roxy for a couple more days until she went back to New York, so what the hell?

Her gaze landed on the door that hid the stairway that led to the third floor of the house. She hadn't even looked up there yet. There was probably plenty of space for storing old shit up there too.

She braced herself for what she would find as she climbed the narrow staircase, but when she reached the top, her heart sank. Even before she found the pull chain to click on the bare overhead bulb, she could tell. Generations' worth of discarded furniture and stacks of boxes no doubt holding family members' old belongings were covered with dust and waiting for someone to clear them out.

"Fuck me," she groaned as she bent over to read the label on the closest boxes.

Polly's Accessories, and below that, *Childrens' Belongings 1940*. The children of the house at that time would have been Agatha and Virginia, Nic's grandmother. Might be an interesting glimpse into the past anyway.

"Oh, man! You've got a lot to clean up."

The voice startled her, and Nic let out a scream as she jumped to her feet. She caught a glimpse of Roxy's amused face just before hitting her head on the bare bulb, breaking it and casting the large room into darkness.

"Crap." Nic's head stung where it hit. She'd probably been cut. "Don't move, there's shattered glass."

Roxy's footsteps cracked on it as she ignored the warning and approached. "Don't worry about me. Steel-toed work boots are pretty tough. But you might want to watch yourself in those flip-flops. Hold on."

Before Nic could even ask what she was doing, Roxy picked her up and carried her across the attic to the glass-free section of floor. Upper body strength was surely a benefit of that contracting gig. That explained the shapely biceps Nic had admired on Roxy when she was tending bar.

Being wrapped tight in Roxy's arms—even for this brief moment of rescue—sent a rush of endorphins whizzing through Nic's system. Maybe Roxy hated her guts, but Nic's guts were having a completely different reaction to the situation, and it definitely was not unpleasant.

Even after her feet were back on the ground, Nic's heart was still fluttering wildly in her chest. She willed her body to chill out, but her expression must've betrayed her because Roxy looked at her with serious concern.

"Are you feeling woozy? Hold on to me—let me help you down the stairs."

Agreeing to that seemed like a better idea than admitting what she was actually feeling—*that I kind of want to kiss you.* That was… surprising. She opted for a submissive hum and grabbed Roxy's arm as instructed.

Back in the second-floor hallway, Roxy directed her to the sunny window at the front of the house. "I think we better check your head."

"I was thinking the exact same thing," Nic said before she could stop herself. She couldn't help it. This was the same woman who broke her heart all those years ago, rejecting Nic when she learned of her true feelings. Perhaps her thinking was a little fuzzy.

"Does it hurt?" Roxy asked, peering at her scalp. "There's a little blood and…yep, there's a sliver of glass. Hold still." She pulled a pair of needle-nose pliers from her tool belt and raised it to Nic's head.

"Wait. What are you doing?"

"Hush. Don't move," Roxy commanded. "Got it."

Nic glanced up in time to catch the tender look in Roxy's eyes as she stood holding the tiny piece of bulb she'd extracted. "Thanks. I owe you one."

Roxy's lips parted and she leaned forward, her voice holding a tiny note of mirth as she whispered, "I'll keep that in mind."

In that moment, it seemed like they were on even footing again. Like maybe they still held a piece of that magical best friends connection from their teenage years.

But just then Roxy's phone chirped, bringing them both back to the present, and the spell was broken.

Roxy's expression shifted back to all business mixed with a hint of disdain. "Anyway, I'm about to drive into town to hit the hardware store for supplies. That's what I was coming to tell you when…well, before. Do you want me drop you at the med center so Maggie can take a look at you?"

The velocity with which the vibe between them had changed was enough to give a gal whiplash. At least it had cured Nic's urge to be wrapped in Roxy's arms again. "Why are you even doing this?"

"Doing what?"

"Why are you still doing the work on my house if you can't stand being around me?"

For the briefest moment Roxy looked like she'd been caught off balance, but she recovered quickly. "I've had my eye on the Victorians off Main Street since I moved back here. Working on one of them is a dream come true for me."

Nic nodded slowly. That sounded like it could be true. But Bella had hired Roxy to do a couple upgrades to a powder room and install a railing. Not exactly any projects that required fine craftmanship. It seemed like maybe that wasn't the whole story.

Roxy sighed. "And I need the money."

"You own a bar."

"You may have a skewed idea of what the nightlife in Fisher's Creek is like." Roxy smirked. "The bar makes enough money to keep chugging along, to pay my staff and keep me clothed and fed, but it's not necessarily enough to…I have some other expenses to cover."

"Your mom's care," Nic blurted out and knew right away she shouldn't have. "I mean—"

"Yeah, no, you're right." Roxy's uncomfortable grimace was apparently meant to signal the end of that subject, but at least it wasn't the look of contempt she'd been giving Nic only moments before. It was almost like something between them had softened. "Anyway, I'm going to run to the store and get some supplies, then I'll probably grab some lunch. But I'll be back this afternoon."

Now it was Nic's turn to smirk. "I'll still be here trying to dig this house out from under every last one of the material things Aunt Aggie amassed in her lifetime."

"A little more to this house than you bargained for?"

"It's a lot of stuff that nobody in the family wants, and I need to clear it all out fast so I can get the house on the market," Nic confessed. "I guess I'll have to haul it to Goodwill or have the Vets pick it up or something. Maybe I could call one of those places that advertise they'll haul away your junk?"

"Junk?" Roxy's voice was incredulous. "I only got a quick look at the contents of the attic, but based on the other stuff I've seen in the house, you've got some nice things here. They have value."

"I don't mean to sound ungrateful." Nic tried to walk it back a bit. "It's just that I didn't expect this. The house, the stuff, any of it. And I need to get it all sorted, and fairly quickly."

"I see." Understanding washed over Roxy's face. "Well, I could probably help you with that if you want."

"Do you want it? The stuff? You can totally have it."

"Oh no." Roxy shook her head vehemently. "I couldn't take it. That wouldn't feel right. But maybe we can make a deal."

Making a deal with Roxy seemed like trying to use the slippery felled trees to cross the wide part of the creek; it was possible with an abundance of caution and delicate footsteps. But if she had a possible solution to Nic's stuff problem, she at least needed to hear her out. "What kind of deal?"

"I know about selling stuff at flea markets and selling stuff online, and I know about refurbishing items that have been neglected and need a little TLC. I'll help you sort through what you've got here and determine what we can sell. And then I'll help you sell it."

"As part of your handyperson services?"

Roxy let out a genuine laugh this time. "Sort of. How about we split what we make?"

Clearing the stuff out of the house and making a little extra cash along the way? It sounded like a reasonable solution. Especially if Roxy truly knew what she was doing. Definitely worth a shot.

"I'd say you have a deal." Nic stuck out her hand to shake on it and barely flinched at the jolt of excitement that shot through her as they connected.

Janie pulled up with her minivan full of cardboard boxes ready to help clean out the pantry twenty minutes later. A total lifesaver. It was only a small piece of the mess compared to the rest of the house, but she had to start somewhere, and the two of them working together was better than Nic going it alone.

While Nic sorted through old repurposed plastic containers, Janie started on the canned goods.

"Some of this stuff is expired, but we can take the rest of it down to the food bank," Janie reported over her shoulder. "They'll put it to good use."

"I can't get over how much stuff she held on to. Look at these margarine tubs. There's a couple of dozen of them that she must've reused for food storage." Nic tossed a stack into the recycling bin. She actually knew the answer—people who lived through war rationing usually knew how to renew, reuse, and recycle. Aunt Aggie was just being a responsible citizen of planet Earth. "And the sheer quantity of canned beans and tomatoes I saw earlier. What did she need all that food for? She was the only one who lived here, and I'm guessing she ate most of her meals alone."

"She wasn't always the only one who lived here," Bella said by way of announcing her arrival as she breezed into the house. The bags of takeout in her hands were a welcome sight, even if she did release a deep sigh as she deposited them on the table. "Why did you ask me to bring lunch when you have so much food here already anyway?"

Janie dropped what she was doing in the pantry and rummaged through one of the takeaway bags, extracting containers of food and setting out their lunch. "Unless you're into condensed soup right out of the can, I'm not sure there's an actual meal in that pantry."

Nic joined her sisters at the table and pulled one of the grilled chicken salads toward her. "Forget the pantry. Bella, what do you mean Aunt Aggie didn't always live here alone? Like way back in the day when she lived here with her parents?"

"No. Haven't you ever heard Mom mention Miss Polly?" Bella asked as she pulled open various drawers on the hunt for eating utensils.

"Who the hell is Miss Polly?" Janie passed around the thin brown paper napkins that came with the food.

Bella shrugged. "Some other old spinster friend of Aunt Aggie. I don't know if Polly rented a room from her or what, but they both lived here for a while, and they used to have guests from out of town stay with them, and they would throw huge, fancy dinner parties. I remember hearing Grandma say something about it one time. When I asked Mom about what I overheard, she said Grandma and her sister never got along and she didn't want me upsetting her by bringing it up and sticking my nose where it didn't belong."

Nic had follow-up questions, but before she could think them through, Janie reached across the table.

"Cool story, sis," she said, poking at Bella's lunch. "But I want to know what's going on here. Your salad has chicken on it. I thought you and Chad were giving up meat."

She was right. Bella breaking a rule? Especially one she set? That did not compute.

Bella drizzled ranch dressing from a little plastic cup across her salad, chicken and all. "Red meat, yes. We're still eating chicken, turkey, fish."

"What about pork?" Nic asked, intrigued by this new topic as well. Her sister's meatless agenda was news to her.

"No pork," Bella confirmed around a mouthful of lettuce.

"You're denying Chad bacon and ribs?" Janie shook her head. "No wonder he was so grumpy at Mom and Dad's last time he was there. He barely said two words all night. Is that why he missed dinner yesterday?"

"Yeah, he's not loving the change," Bella admitted. "But that's not why. He had a meeting at the Lodge he had to show up for. I think they're just playing poker, but whatever."

"I wondered why he missed my welcome home meal." Nic had always liked her sister's husband. Chad was a quiet guy, but very sweet. And he treated Bella like a queen. "For goodness' sake, let the man have his meat. Life's too short."

"Life *is* too short." Bella poked her fork in the air, punctuating each word. "That's why I'm trying to extend ours by cutting out unhealthy habits like eating red meat."

"Okay, okay." Nic put her hands up in surrender. Once Bella had her mind set on something, it was usually a done deal. Poor Chad. "Speaking of time running out, I'm still planning on heading back to New York on Wednesday, so thank God Roxy has agreed to help me clear this place out."

"You think the two of you are going to get it done in the next two days?" Janie pulled a doubtful face. "I think you better rework your timeline. We've barely even made a dent in that pantry."

"I'm just glad to hear you and Roxy are getting along." Bella smiled knowingly.

"I don't know if I'd go that far," Nic responded with a scowl. "Neither of us has killed the other yet, so that's something. Thanks for that surprise, by the way."

"Stop making such a big deal out of it." Bella waved a hand like she was swatting away an annoying gnat. "You need the help anyway. It's not like I can drop everything at the firm and come over here every day."

Nic turned a pleading gaze to Janie. She needed all the help she could get. And maybe someone to act as a buffer while she and Roxy sorted through Aunt Aggie's belongings. Or possibly a referee.

"Don't look at me like that." Janie cringed. "You know I have two little kids, right? Besides, this job is too big even for three of us to finish in two days. What do you have to rush back to New York for anyway? You're a writer, you can work from anywhere."

"Where exactly have you been living up there since the divorce anyway?" Bella asked.

Nic took a long drink of water. Stalling. She'd been doing what she had to, but she wasn't necessarily proud of it. Living in New York City wasn't cheap, and she'd just gone through a divorce that had been rough on her financially as well as emotionally. "I've been staying in an extra bedroom in my friend Maryann's apartment."

"You're staying in an extra bedroom in your friend's home?" Bella frowned. "You're a full, grown-ass woman and you're basically couch surfing."

"Hey, give me a break. I just spent a fortune on my divorce, and I've been trying to hold out on making a commitment to real estate until I turned my book in to my publisher."

"But you admit you have nothing to rush back for," Janie pushed. "Just stay here a little longer. So what?"

So what? Her sisters didn't get it, and that was no surprise to Nic. She had left behind her life in Fisher's Creek for a reason, and even if she was currently a homeowner in that town, she fully intended her stay to remain on the brief side. Yet she couldn't deny she would need more than two days to sort out this house thing. Even if she had help. Plus, she still had to wait for Peewee to finish the repairs on her car. "My life is in New York, even if there's nothing demanding I rush back in the moment."

Nic caught the eye roll glance her sisters exchanged, followed by something that looked a lot like disappointment on both of their faces. Truthfully, she'd had a really good time with them at Maggie's house the night before. She wouldn't mind having a little more time like that before she left again. Staying a few more days wouldn't be the end of the world. She blew out a sigh of surrender. "I guess I can stick around through the end of the week. Friday, that's it. As long as you two—and Maggie—promise to help me with this place when you can."

"Deal," Bella said without hesitation. She tossed her napkin into her empty salad container, signaling her lunch hour was ending.

"Not so fast." Janie held up a hand to halt Bella's exit. "I'll help too…we all will help, but I want something from you. This is the first time you've been back for an extended visit in forever, and who knows how long it will be before you come back again. I want a sisters' night out before you leave. We can do it Thursday night at Zachroll's."

"You got it." Bella stood and grabbed her bag. "I've got to get back to work."

"I was talking to Nic."

"Oh, please. She'll go." Bella shot Nic a pointed look. Daring her to defy her. "Don't even start acting like we're putting you out by asking you to go out for a couple of beers. I mean, it's not like you're going to have anything better to do in Fisher's Creek on Thursday night."

"Come on, say you're in." Janie pulled a puppy dog eyes, another one of those little sister faces that had always been impossible to resist.

What the fuck? By Thursday night, after nearly a week in that town working with Roxy on the house, she'd either want a cold one to celebrate her forthcoming exodus, or possibly need a beer to cry out her frustration into. "Fine. I'm in."

It wasn't until Bella had left and Nic was back to packing dishes and glassware that it hit her exactly just what she'd agreed to. A night at Zachroll's would mean spending even more time in Roxy's orbit. Roxy, who earlier had fixed her with a stare that contained genuine tenderness. Kind of like the way they used to look at each other when they were kids. Only now she had a lesbian online dating profile.

It was still unbelievable. After what had happened at the end of their senior year—the way Roxy had regarded her when she learned of Nic's feelings—Roxy was now an out lesbian? Thinking about it made her head want to explode. And made her even more nervous about spending all this time together. At least she'd be blowing town at the end of the week, but still…

Damn, her sisters were going to owe her big time for this one.

CHAPTER FIVE

Nic met Roxy at the house bright and early Tuesday morning. Even with agreeing to stay in town for the full week, cleaning out the house seemed like a daunting task. She'd more or less resigned herself to the fact that the remainder of her visit would be consumed by it.

"Why don't we start with a room-by-room walk-through? We can get an idea of what will go to the flea market, what would sell better online, and what should just be donated." Roxy was already holding a clipboard and pen, ready to take notes on what they decided, so it seemed like her question was more of an instruction.

Since Nic had no better plan for where to begin, she complied.

Some rooms seemed easy. The guest bedroom had a beautiful set of furniture that Roxy was certain she could sell online. And the clothes in the wardrobe were an obvious "donate." But there were other rooms that required a lot of scribbled notes on the clipboard. In the dining room, the regal, dark-wood dining set would be another online sale, but the dishes and various ceramic pieces that filled the china cabinet all needed sorting through and even some items Googled before a determination of flea market or online could be made. Luckily, Roxy seemed to take it all in stride.

"How did my great-aunt collect so much stuff?" Nic mumbled as she opened the drawers in the buffet filled with table linens, napkin rings, and fancy utensils. "There's stuff in the stuff. It never ends."

"She lived here all her life. You've got to figure some of this was her parents' stuff before it was hers." Roxy laughed and peeked over Nic's shoulder before making a note on her clipboard. "Those tablecloths will sell at the flea market for sure."

Nic was suddenly very aware of the heat between them with Roxy standing so close, and when Roxy reached around her to finger the lacy edge of one of the linens and their arms brushed, Nic felt a jolt of excitement that shot straight to her middle. It flustered her. She scooted to her right, breaking the contact between them. Her mind raced to find something to say to fill the silence. "You're good at this—knowing what we can unload where."

"Thanks." Roxy shrugged as she went back to her notes. "I've done it before. Once with my belongings when I moved back here with Mom. And then with some of my mom's once I moved in and she wanted to make more room for me in the house. She said she wanted to sort through it while she could still tell me what was what. Before…" Roxy's lips pulled into a sad line, and she blinked like her brain was forcing a factory reset on her thoughts. "Well, you know."

She didn't have to finish the sentence. Nic could figure out that Mrs. Fitzpatrick would have known what was coming down the track once she received the Alzheimer's diagnosis. Her heart ached for the mother and daughter facing her illness as bravely as they could. The silence between them stretched into the neighborhood of discomfort. "I'm sorry she's going through this. I'm sorry you're going through it too."

"Just the hand we've been dealt." She played with the leather bracelet on her wrist before changing the subject. "Too bad you're going to miss all the fun at the flea market, though."

Nic rolled with it. "Yeah, that's a real damn shame," she said, her tone dripping with sarcasm.

"Don't say it like that. I'm serious—it's a lot of fun, well, as long as the weather holds, but this Saturday's forecast shows nothing but sunshine. I'll call you afterward and let you know how much money we made."

"Oh." The surprise slipped out before Nic could rein it in. She'd never considered they'd be exchanging phone calls or communicating at all after she returned to New York.

Roxy didn't miss it. "Or I can just text you instead of calling. That works too."

Did she look…disappointed? Nic's heart wrenched with regret for putting that expression on Roxy's gorgeous face. "No, you can call. I'd love it if you called. I mean…" Her cheeks burned with embarrassment. She'd overcorrected and said something even worse than her stunned autopilot *oh*. And now Roxy's amused yet sexy smirk was stirring up a warm feeling between Nic's legs. She needed to get out of their conversation, like, now. "Of course you can call me if you want. Or text. Whatever. Hey, I'm going to go check the kitchen for linens too. I'm pretty sure Janie found some in there the other day and we should pack them all up together."

She clocked the bemused expression on Roxy's face, but she didn't let that stop her from scurrying out of the dining room to seek sanctuary in the kitchen. Once there, she did not check for linens, but rather stood with her back against the cold plaster of the wall and counted to twenty-five. She'd meant to stop at ten, only her heart was still beating wildly from the awkward interaction, so she took the extra fifteen to get herself together. Eventually she was going to have to face Roxy again. Hopefully she'd have a little more couth next time around.

What was it about the idea of Roxy calling her once she was back in New York that had caused her to become so flustered? She was an eighties kid—she was fine with talking to people on the phone. Hell, she and Roxy had spent countless hours gabbing away on the phone when they were teens. Often much to their families' annoyance since those were landline days.

Of course, that was before Roxy knew about your crush on her and you blew town without as much as a word to her for thirty years. Nic squeezed her eyes shut, begging those nagging thoughts to subside. *And before you came back to discover Roxy was hotter than ever and had come out as a lesbian to boot.*

She pushed herself off the wall and scrubbed her hands over her face. The "what if" train only stopped at two stations: regret or fantasy, neither of which she had time for. There were linens to pack among other things on her much too long to-do list. Sorting out her weird Roxy feelings was going to have to wait.

It was half past ten, and Nic felt like she hadn't crossed a damn thing off her to-do list. She'd argued with the water department about whether they could get the water bill switched into her name without proof of residency. She didn't exactly win, but at least now she knew what documents she needed to email over to the department to get the process started. Then she had a spirited discussion with a gravelly-voiced woman named Faye at the electric company, trying to do the same thing with them. Faye eventually caved and promised to call back after she checked with her manager, and Nic was counting on her honoring that promise. The clock was ticking, and she still had a lot of house to sort through and pack up.

Roxy had left twenty minutes earlier with a truckload of tchotchkes from the dining room and guest bedrooms she intended to photograph and list online over the course of the next couple of weeks, and Nic was in the parlor carefully wrapping even more knickknacks in tissue paper for the flea market when her phone rang. With a hopeful heart that it was her new friend with an easy solution to a nonresident holding the account to keep the lights on, she stopped wrapping the ceramic cat collection. Shoving the extra tissue in the bib of her overalls, she picked up the call, ready to hear what the electric company manager could do for her.

"Hit me, Faye. What did the boss say?"

"Uh. Nic?"

It wasn't her friend Faye from the electric company.

"Oh, sorry, Peewee." Nic chuckled. "I was expecting someone else."

"Sounds like it. I'll make it quick, then, so I don't hold you up. I've got good news, and I've got bad news.," Peewee said. "I'll give you the good news first. I know what's wrong with your car and I can fix it."

"Great." At least something could be crossed off the to-do list: car fixed. "Let me guess, the bad news is it's going to cost a small fortune."

"Huh." Peewee seemed to be reconsidering. "Let me rephrase. I've got good news and a couple items that are more in the bad news camp."

Nic groaned. This day was something else. "Just spit it out, Peewee."

"See, the thing about fancy cars like your Tesla is sometimes it's hard to get parts for them, and that's what's happening here." Peewee sounded genuinely sorry. "The lower control arm that connects to the shocks on your car is totally jacked from where the car's underbelly hit the edge of the pothole. I'm not going to have the parts I need until Monday."

Monday? Yet another delay in her grand exit. How had this become the visit that never ends? Was Fisher's Creek cursed or something? It certainly shouldn't surprise her if it was. God, this was ridiculous. She needed to get back to New York. She had a book to write and a life to start to put back together. Why didn't anyone understand that?

"Uh, Nic? You still there?"

"Yeah, it's just…this sucks. Is Monday really the soonest you'll have the…control arm, or whatever? Is there anything you can do to get them sooner?"

"I'm sorry, Nic," he said. "It's totally out of my hands. But as soon as I have what I need, I'll get you back on the road. You have my word."

She blew out her breath and then felt bad that she might have hurt Peewee's feelings. It wasn't his fault that she drove a ridiculous car with impossible-to-get parts. "I know, Peewee. I appreciate it. Give me a buzz if you hear anything else. I'll keep my fingers crossed for some kind of Tesla miracle."

"Will do."

At least she had the good manners to hang up the call before she let out her frustrated scream. She dropped onto the plastic-covered sofa and held her head in her hands. That was another three days in Fisher's Creek on top of what she'd already agreed to while taking care of the house. She was only supposed to be there until Friday, and then she would get back to her normal life. Back to writing the chapters that were already overdue to her publisher. She had been counting on having the weekend to write. She knew what Janie would say about it—just be a writer in Fisher's Creek. But would that be as easy as it sounded? Nic's writer life was in New York. That's not who she was here. Here she was just that quiet, scared girl she was in high school. She couldn't exist that way for any length of time. Maybe she'd skirted by like that when she was young, but not anymore.

A knock on the front door pulled her out of her deep thoughts pity party.

Great! The sisters to the rescue. Nic peeled up from the plastic on the sofa and rushed to the door, anxious for the comfort of her sisters—the one good thing about being stuck in town. But when she opened the door, it was someone she didn't recognize at all.

"Hi." The skinny stranger smiled awkwardly as he eyed her up from the other side of the screen door. He pushed his wire frames up the bridge of his nose as he continued, "I hope this isn't a bad time."

Nic couldn't imagine a worse time than that moment when she'd discovered a fancy control arm was basically holding her captive in Fisher's Creek, but good graces prevailed, and she kept that lament to herself. The tall, bald man standing before her had kind eyes behind wire-rimmed glasses that looked upon her with something like sympathy. Well, no wonder. She'd just finished stress-tugging her hair and screaming like a wild beast. She must look a mess. She smoothed her hair with her hands, like that would help anything.

"It's a great time," she began, but his gaze, and subsequent frown, shifted to her chest, prompting her to pull the wad of tissue paper out of her coveralls. "Okay, maybe not *great*, but it's a fine time. I'm sorry." She shook her head. "Can I help you?"

"I actually came over to see if I could help you." When he smiled, the corners of his eyes crinkled. Nic guessed based on that and the salt-and-pepper stubble on his chin that he was a few years older than her. "You're Agatha's niece Nicola, right?"

"You knew Agatha?"

"Sorry, I should've introduced myself at the start. I'm Eric Rogers. I live next door with my husband, Jeremy. We just adored Agatha. I just wanted to stop by and let you know that if there's anything we can do to help you move stuff or get settled in, please don't be afraid to give a yell."

"Whoa, hold on a second," Nic said, needing a minute to catch up. There were a lot of pieces in Eric's statement that she needed to digest. Starting with Aunt Aggie being friends with her gay neighbors. But also, Eric and his husband *adored* Agatha? And when he said *get settled in*, did he think... "I'm not moving in. I mean, I don't live here. Is that what you meant? That I was moving into the house?"

He frowned and shoved his hands in his pockets. "I didn't mean to...I thought that...I saw you with the boxes yesterday and I assumed—" He shrugged, and redness crept up his neck. He probably thought she was a real piece of work. He'd come over to be neighborly, but she was clearly making him uncomfortable. "I'm officially a nosy neighbor, but apparently not *your* nosy neighbor. I'm going to leave now and let you get back to it."

With a wave of his fingers he turned to leave, but something besides guilt about her poor manners toward the guy tugged at Nic's heart. Aunt Aggie left her the house and Nic knew nothing about her outside of her mom's random stories and Bella's sketchy childhood memories. This guy was someone who legit knew Agatha, and Nic felt she at least owed her great-aunt the courtesy of learning a little bit about who she was. It wasn't as if Nic had anywhere to rush off to anyway. She had practically a whole week in front of her now. Stuck in town until the Tesla was ready to carry her away.

"Wait." She stopped him. "I'm sorry. Can we start this conversation over? Would you like to come in for a minute? I have some fresh-brewed iced tea."

"Iced tea sounds great."

As she led the way to the kitchen, Eric seemed to study their surroundings.

"It's all still here," he said, stopping to admire a painting of flowers in a gilded frame.

"What's that?"

"All Agatha's stuff. It's all still here." He looked surprised yet delighted.

"Yeah." Nic sighed as she continued to get their drinks. She wasn't as delighted as he was by the house full of someone else's belongings that she was left to deal with. "Aunt Aggie left me the house and some bonus stuff, I guess."

"Lucky girl. Agatha has a lot of great stuff." Suddenly his bright expression dropped. "Oh, my word. You just lost your great-aunt and I'm talking about her material things with you. I'm so tacky. Jeremy and I truly loved Agatha. She was a wonderful and very interesting woman. Please know that."

He was so disarming with his charm and style. His dark skinny jeans were cuffed once right above his Sperrys and paired with a light-blue button-down. Classic and neat. Nic couldn't help it— she liked him. "You don't have to apologize. It's fine, and honestly, I've been thinking about her stuff a lot the past two days too. It was a bit of a surprise to me—I expected the house to be empty. Anyway, I'm glad she had you guys next door. It sounds like you were good friends to her." She handed him the glass. "And I'm unloading most of this stuff, so if there's anything you want, let me know. I'd be happy to have less to pack up or haul to donate."

Eric nodded and pursed his lips as if he was considering the offer. "In that case, have you packed up her books yet?"

Upstairs, in the bedroom Great-Aunt Agatha had converted into a library, they stood and surveyed the built-in bookshelves that covered two walls, every shelf full of books and more knickknacks. Her great-aunt's treasures.

"Anything in particular you're looking for?" Nic spread her arms, offering her new friend free rein. She was glad to know that at least some of Aggie's things would end up with someone dear to her.

"The *Tales of the City* series." Eric approached a shelf with the nine Armistead Maupin novels on it and ran his fingertips down the line of book spines gently, like he was greeting old friends. "Honestly, I'm not a big reader, but Agatha loaned me the first one and I was hooked. Ended up reading the whole damn series. Twice. If you don't want them, I'd be thrilled to take them off your hands. I promise to give them a good home, and they'll always remind me of the neighbor who first introduced me to that wonderful cast of characters."

Nic was as happy to pass them on as Eric seemed to be to take them. "Have at it."

While Eric collected his bounty, she surveyed the shelves and tried her best to estimate the number of books they contained. They would take forever to pack up. Not to mention the additional tchotchkes in the room. Was Roxy really going to be able to unload all this stuff?

Her thoughts were interrupted when she noticed one of the shelves held about a dozen copies of the same book. *A Dark Thought At Midnight* by Nicola Dickenson. What was Aunt Aggie doing with so many copies of her novel? She must've gasped out loud.

Eric turned, his arms full of books. "Oh, yeah. Your aunt was so proud of you. She gave copies of that book to everyone she knew. Great story, by the way."

"Thanks," Nic said, but her focus was still on that shelf. The fact that Great-Aunt Aggie was proud of her was news. Hell, the fact that she even knew anything about Nic was news. Why did it suddenly feel like Nic was trying to put together a puzzle that she only had half the pieces to?

"Hey, you okay?" Eric appeared at her shoulder, juggling an armful of books and his glass of iced tea. "Did I say something wrong?"

"What?" Nic pulled back into the moment and grabbed some of the books to lighten Eric's load. She could see why her great-aunt invited him around. He was kind and gentlemanly, and that most likely made him a good neighbor. That reminded her of why she asked him inside in the first place—he probably had some insight into who Aunt Aggie really was. "No, I'm fine. I just…Do you know why Agatha left me the house? It was kind of a surprise to me. I mean, we didn't really have much of a relationship. I didn't really know her at all, I guess."

He put a gentle hand on her shoulder and guided her back toward the staircase. "I told you, she was really proud of you. But what can I tell you about her?" His face was thoughtful as they reached the bottom of the stairs. "She loved to read, all types of books, as you probably guessed. She loved watching game shows, in fact, that's pretty much the only thing I ever saw her watch on television. She was a good cook and made a mean roast. Made delicious stews and soups too. She used to make a big batch of ham and beans and then take it out to the Luzerne County Soup Kitchen. She volunteered there a lot, but other than that she seemed to keep to herself. I never really saw her interacting with any of the other neighbors on the street. Guess Jeremy and I were lucky." He paused, and his eyebrows scrunched low. "Is that the kind of stuff you were looking for?"

Nic didn't know what she was looking for, but she was grateful he'd shared something. Avid reader and soup kitchen volunteer was a lot better than *grumpy old lady*. "It is. Thanks." She smiled and traded him the books in her hands for his empty glass. They were back at the door and Eric was about to leave. This could be her only shot to get any of her questions answered. "Just one more thing. What did she do for a living? Before she was a volunteer?"

Eric shook his head. "I don't know. We only moved here about seven years ago. We've always known her as a retired person. She never said much about her younger days. Except that she used to do a lot of traveling with Polly. All over the United States. Europe a few times. Sounded like she enjoyed a good adventure back then."

"With Polly. Right. I heard she lived here with Aunt Aggie for a bit."

Eric's eyes narrowed in confusion, and he looked like he was about to ask a question or possibly say more on the subject, but instead he smiled and lifted his hand in a wave. "I meant what I said before. If you need anything, just let us know. Thanks for the tea."

Nic waved as he walked away. Maybe her family thought Aunt Aggie was just a grumpy old lady, but it sure seemed like she was friendly enough to Eric and Jeremy. And Polly too. An adventurer who loved to travel and cared for others through her volunteer work at the soup kitchen.

Curiouser and curiouser.

CHAPTER SIX

Thursday night, Nic leaned back in the wooden captain's chair and poured herself another beer from the plastic pitcher. She and her sisters occupied a round table in the back corner of a surprisingly busy Zachroll's.

"I can't believe this place." She took a long drink. "It was never hopping like this back in the day. Even when I was in here the other day it was dead as tombs."

"You were here day-drinking on a Sunday." Janie rolled her eyes and reached for the pitcher. "Of course it was dead in here. You should come by on a Saturday night. Roxy brings in a deejay. It's the hottest spot in all of Fisher's Creek."

Well, there was a title that wasn't hard to achieve.

"I guess I can believe that," Nic said between sips. "Middle of nowhere, central Pennsylvania, backward little town. What the hell else is there to do?"

"Okay, Big Apple. You'll be in town this Saturday night. Maybe you should come out and see for yourself." Bella scooted her chair a few inches closer to Nic and gave her a sweet smile. "What are you going to do with your extra time in Fisher's Creek anyway?"

Nic dropped her chin to her chest, defeated. Her sisters had been blatantly excited when she told them she wouldn't be leaving for several more days. She didn't quite share their enthusiasm. "I've been packing boxes for the past day and a half, and based on the amount of crap still in Aunt Aggie's house, I'll still be packing for the rest of my stay."

"You mean your house," Bella pointed out.

"Yeah, yeah." Nic's hand in the air waved off the topic. "*My* house. Thank you for reminding me, Bella. I'll be packing up *my* new house while I'm supposed to be writing a book back in New York. Oh, and attending a flea market over in Ferrisburg Saturday morning with Roxy. I figured since I was here anyway I may as well help out with the unloading of *my* crap too."

"Don't be so negative," Maggie scolded. "It's nice of Roxy to help you out. And it was sweet of Aggie to leave the house and the crap to you in the first place. At least we've confirmed she liked someone in the family."

"I've been wondering about that," Nic said, glad for the shift in the focus of the conversation from her spending more time with Roxy. "Mom always talks about how Aunt Aggie was such a grumpy old bat, but I talked to the guy who lives next door. He described her as kind and interesting. Did you know she volunteered at the Luzerne County Soup Kitchen?"

"Nope," Janie confessed. "But I didn't know anything about Aunt Aggie that Mom didn't tell us."

"Look at you getting into family history. Digging into that family tree." Bella nodded encouragingly. "This could be a new hobby for you. I like it."

"Isn't that the exact same thing you said about Janie Internet stalking Maggie's Perfect Pair matches?" Nic laughed.

"No, I said stalking Maggie's Perfect Pair matches should be Janie's occupation."

"Please, let's don't start up on that topic again," Maggie moaned between sips of beer. "How am I ever going to find a decent date? According to Janie's potential new *occupation*, all that's out there are unsolicited nudes and catfish. That's all I match up with anyway."

Could be worse, Nic thought. *At least she didn't match with Roxy Fitzpatrick.* Nic had avoided dwelling on those weird feelings about Roxy that had stirred up the last time they'd been at the house together. It was like she'd wrapped them up tightly in newsprint and packed them neatly in one of the boxes along with the Depression glass and vintage Fiesta tableware. It had helped a whole lot that between taking care of her mother and working at the bar, Roxy hadn't had time to come by the house and help Nic since Tuesday. Nic had managed to avoid her ex-best friend for most of the night, although she'd delivered the pitcher to their table when the sisters first walked into the place, and she'd greeted Janie with a squeeze and a kiss on a cheek. When had those two become so close? They'd both been cheerleaders back in high school, but they'd only been on the squad together that one year when Roxy was a senior and Janie a freshman. Janie never said anything about the two of them being friends.

"Okay, no more Perfect Pair talk. Got it," Janie said with a shrug. "So, let's turn our attention to the next order of business. Nic, tell us about this book you're supposed to be writing back in New York. You're in a slump, huh?"

Nic took another gulp of beer. The two weeks before she left New York had been an ugly blur of balled-up pages torn out of her notebook, all-night writing sessions, and empty coffee mugs. But none of it resulted in a viable idea to pitch to her publisher at the meeting she had scheduled for next Thursday. She had slid right past feeling nervous about the upcoming encounter and into plain old dread. She couldn't shake the fear that she was a one-hit wonder and she would never be able to write a book like *A Dark Thought At Midnight* again. "It's not a slump. It's so much worse. That meeting hanging over my head feels like impending doom."

"*Impending doom?*" Maggie rolled her eyes. "God, the drama queen cometh."

"I'm not," Nic whined. Her sisters didn't know. None of them was in danger of becoming a one-hit wonder. "They're expecting something brilliant, and I don't even have an idea that's subpar. I've got nothing."

"Come on," Bella said. Her voice was gentle and big sisterly. "You've got to have some kernel of an idea we can talk through and build on. And if you don't, well, can't you just ask for an extension or something?"

"I've already tried that. Twice."

"I know." Janie raised her hand like she was the star pupil at the head of the class. "Call in sick."

"Ha ha." Nic traced a finger through the condensation on her mug and wished Janie's plan could work. "Not an option."

"Seriously." Bella grabbed the pitcher and topped off everyone's beer. "Don't they say write what you know? Why don't you try that?"

Nic inched to the edge of her seat and rested her elbows on the table. Of all the people to point her in the right direction, Bella was the last she'd guess would do it. Bella was smart and pushy enough, but not always the most creative. But this time it was the right kind of push. "Okay, let's go meta and talk this through. A woman goes back to her hometown—a small town—to visit her sisters, and discovers…"

"Hidden treasure!" Janie volunteered, slamming her mug down on the table hard enough to make the beer slosh over the edge of it. "Gold doubloons and jewels in an old chest. This is gonna be great."

"Not hidden treasure. That doesn't make any sense. They're not pirates. Or the Goonies." Nic shook her head. "But I appreciate your enthusiasm. Maybe some other kind of secret."

Luckily, Maggie picked up the thread. "Okay, so this woman comes back to town, and it seems like a really sleepy place, but there's a dark secret. Maybe they pull something out of the creek…no, the lake. Can't make it too much like Fisher's Creek. The location has been changed to protect the innocent, yada yadda yadda."

"Like a dead body?" Bella offered.

"Well, that went from zero to sixty real quick," Janie quipped and flipped the laminated drink menu over and back, studying it.

"No, she's on the right track," Nic argued. "So, she comes back to town where they've just discovered a clue that reopens an old cold case, and the woman—along with the help of her sisters—unravels the town's secrets and solves the mystery. I could throw in a colorful cast of townspeople. That would add some flavor, and of course I'll work the family angle. This…could work."

"Your publisher is probably going to want to know what the town's big secret is, though." Maggie tipped the last of the beer from the pitcher into her mug.

"Eventually, sure," Nic agreed. "I can probably keep it pretty vague in the pitch and still sell it. In the meantime, I'll just nose around in town and try to come up with material to flesh out into a whole story. I've got to make some progress this weekend. I can't afford to lose the time just because I'm stuck here in Fisher's Creek."

"Well, I for one am glad you're going to stick around for a while." Bella smiled kindly at her. "And let me know if you want company nebbing around. Chad's got some school thing Saturday, so my day is open."

"I second the 'glad you're sticking around' part, but good luck with the nosing around thing. There are no secrets in Fisher's Creek. Everybody already knows everyone else's business." Janie's focus remained on the menu as she spoke. "Also, I wish Roxy sold appetizers. I could go for some salty bar snacks."

"Too bad her bar renovation didn't include a kitchen." Maggie sighed. "I could use a nosh as well."

"She could at least buy a microwave. Pop in some pizza rolls or something. That would do the trick." Janie drained the last of her beer and reached for the pitcher. Realizing it was empty, she slumped back in her chair. "Really, Maggie?"

Nic suddenly felt a little lighter. Somehow her sisters had actually made her feel better about being trapped in town for the weekend and even convinced her that maybe the meeting with her publisher wouldn't be a total disaster after all. She stood and grabbed the plastic pitcher to head off any sisterly conflict that might dampen the mood. Keep the good vibe going. "I'll get the next one. And I'll grab a couple of bags of chips too."

"Funyuns too, please," Janie singsonged after her as she headed to the bar.

Nic squeezed between patrons on stools to push up to the bar. She signaled to Roxy, then watched as she worked her way down to her, replacing empty beer bottles and pouring a round of shots on the way. A total boss. Tonight, Roxy's skin-tight blue jeans were paired with a white sleeveless T-shirt that had the Zachroll's logo over her heart. Nic didn't personally know any other forty-eight-year-old women with arms as muscular as Roxy's. Those muscles flexed, showing their sexy curves as the bartender reached, poured, and served. A wave of heat washed over Nic as she absentmindedly drummed her fingers on the empty pitcher, mesmerized by the view. Finally, Roxy appeared directly in front of her, and before she could stop herself, Nic gazed directly into those gorgeous, long-lashed, green eyes.

"Need a refill?" Roxy grabbed the pitcher and stuck it under the tap. "That was light, right?"

Nic nodded. The light beer had been her sisters' selection, not hers. Accustomed to stronger IPAs, she'd been downing the light stuff like water. Perhaps she should get something in her stomach too. "Can I get a few bags of chips too, please?" She squinted at the rack of snacks on the wall behind the bar. "Oh, and Funyuns for Janie."

Roxy grabbed the bags and deposited them on the bar before expertly returning to the beer tap just in time to stop the draught before the pitcher overflowed. A total pro. "This is an improvement."

"A full pitcher? It sure is."

"No." Roxy laughed, and her eyes twinkled like emeralds. "I meant your smile. You seem a lot more relaxed than the last time I saw you. It looks good on you. Did Peewee get your car fixed earlier than expected or something?"

The heat rose up into the tips of her ears, remembering how awkward she'd been when they were boxing up the flea market items at the house on Tuesday. God, now she was blushing in front of Roxy Fitzpatrick. This beer run had just taken an embarrassing turn. "Nothing like that, unfortunately. Just happy to be out of the house and doing something other than cleaning up that mess for a change."

"Well, then, I hate to bring this up, but I wanted to let you know I plan on swinging by tomorrow morning to pick up some more of the items we wanted to list online. I can't stay long, though—too much to do here before the weekend rush. Especially if we're doing the flea market Saturday morning." Roxy paused, her expression hopeful. "We're still on for that, right?"

Something in those pretty green eyes made Nic actually feel excited about driving out to the Ferrisburg Flea Market. "Yep. I'll be ready to flea, bright and early."

"Good. I'll bring the coffee." Roxy smiled. "And since you're going to be in town through the weekend, I was wondering— would you like to come over Sunday night and help me with some of the furniture from your great-aunt's place? I've been working on it in fits and spurts as time allowed the past couple days, but there's still a lot to be done." She shrugged. "It's a good excuse to get out of the house for a bit, anyway. And I have a fridge full of beer in my workshop. Better stuff than this creek water you and your sisters are drinking tonight."

"It's hard to refuse an offer like that," Nic said, clutching the pitcher of second-rate beer. Plus, it seemed only fair that she put a little sweat equity into the pieces Roxy was going to sell on her behalf. "I'm in."

Roxy reached across the bar and covered Nic's hand with hers. Comfortable and still familiar despite all the years gone by since the last time they'd connected physically in any meaningful way. "I'm glad."

The touch sent an alarming shot of feelings from the past rushing through Nic, and even though she wanted to behave better, she instinctively pulled her hand away. Touching Roxy again after all these years—as if nothing ever happened. What the hell was she doing? Working with Roxy on this project was well and good, but foolish was not a look she wanted to wear ever again in front of this woman. She tossed some bills on the bar and gathered the bags of chips. Time for a quick getaway. "Okay, great. Just text me with the time and I'll be there."

Roxy looked confused by the change in the vibe for only a moment before giving her a broad grin. "Maybe I'll even call you." She had the audacity to wink. "Or I could just message you on Perfect Pair."

"A text will be fine," Nic murmured before turning away. Stupid Perfect Pair profile. She should have taken it down after that night at Maggie's. She made a mental note to take care of it in the morning.

CHAPTER SEVEN

Friday afternoon, Nic grabbed at the stitch in her left side and squinted against the bright sun as she walked the trail through Fisher's Creek Park. *Walk* wasn't quite the right word—it was more like a trot to keep up with Janie, who seemed to have become some kind of recreational speed walker to get the maximum bang for her buck in what little free time she had while the kids were still in school. "What are we doing? I thought you said this was supposed to be relaxing."

"This is relaxing." Janie grinned. She didn't seem winded at all. She seemed chipper, like she was gaining strength with every step. "This is how I relax. This is my 'me' time. Now, tell me about the Tesla. What's the deal with that car?"

"Ugh, I know. It's showy and grotesque."

"I saw it at Peewee's this morning when I drove by. It's beautiful and regal."

"I drive it out of spite." Nic would not be swayed by her sister's sunshine thoughts. The car was a symbol of everything extra about Dana. "It's a reminder of past mistakes. My cross to bear."

"It's the only thing you got in the divorce, eh?"

"Pretty much. Can we please slow down?" Nic asked for the tenth time since they'd started on the two-and-a-half-mile trail. This time Janie glanced over her shoulder and seemed to really assess Nic's out-of-breath condition. "I don't know what you've got in those Adidas—some kind of rocket boosters, I assume—but I prefer a leisurely, normal-human-speed stroll through the park."

"Some of us need to make it to the end of the trail with enough time to stop at the market for dinner supplies before the rugrats get off the bus. People get grumpy when their dinner isn't on the table in a timely manner," Janie said, but she slowed down to a more reasonable pace.

"You tell Sean he's lucky—you're still letting him eat meat at least." Nic laughed as she finally caught up. "You could pull a Bella on him and make him go all veggie, all the time."

"Sean's not the grumpy one. The people I was talking about are the kids," Janie said with an overexaggerated wink. *Ba dum dum!* "But seriously, I can't believe Chad's going along with the no-meat thing. Bella's got some kind of hold on him. It's 'cause she's good in bed, I bet."

"Janie!"

"What? It's a Dickenson sister trait—we own that." Janie smirked and knocked her shoulder against Nic's. "Speaking of... how's your Perfect Pair search going?"

"Uh, my Perfect Pair search is going nowhere because I only agreed to make that profile to be supportive of Maggie. I haven't even given it a second thought since the night you posted it." The *yeah right* look Janie was giving her signaled the lie had been detected. One part of the Perfect Pair experience had taken up residence in her mind. There was no denying that. "Oh my God, fine. Roxy mentioned the site last night when we were at the bar. It was so humiliating. She saw my profile."

Janie's hoot echoed in the leafy cover of the trees around them. "That's because you and Roxy make a Perfect Pair!"

Of course Janie would think it was funny, but Nic could still feel her scalp tingling with embarrassed heat the way it did when Roxy had mentioned the dating site at the bar. Her sister didn't get it. Nic had been humiliated in front of Roxy yet again. All because of the stupid dating app.

"God, that is…not funny." Nic shook her head. "When did the two of you become such good friends anyway? I don't recall you and Roxy being bosom buddies."

"I don't recall any rule that said only you could be friends with Roxy Fitzpatrick."

"Seriously, Janie."

"It was about four years ago, and I was dragging two preschoolers through the grocery store, desperate to just get the things I needed to make dinner for the family, and I finally got to the checkout and realized I'd left my whole damn purse at home. Wallet and everything. You remember those days when your whole life is wrapped up in chasing little ones around and catering to their every need, and you're not getting enough sleep because you're up late trying to hold everything in the household together, and you're up early because toddlers have their own schedule and they sure as hell don't care about yours? That was me—total victim of mommy brain fog."

Nic laughed. "Yeah, I know those days. Hard to believe now Asher was ever that young, but I've been in that fog."

"So there I was, all the fixins for fajitas scanned and bagged, and me with no money or phone, and two antsy kids trying to grab every candy bar off the rack, and I was so damn tired I was about to just sit down right there and cry," Janie continued. "When all of the sudden, Roxy shows up at my side, scoops Mia up in her arms, wrangles Mason away from the Mallow Cups, and offers to pay my bill. I didn't even know she was back in town, but she totally saved my bacon."

"She was always a good friend like that."

"Right? After being away all that time, and with everything she was going through with her mom, she was still just sweet as could be and helped me out." Janie nodded. "I met up with her for coffee the next day to pay her back, and we got to talking about how she'd come back to take care of her mother. It seemed like she needed a friend. We made a point to get together for coffee once a week after that. I needed the break from chasing after the kids, and she needed the time out from being a caregiver."

It warmed her heart to think of Roxy helping out her little sister. Just like old times, Roxy was always the friend you could count on when you needed extra algebra tutoring or an extra hand to staff the youth group bake sale. She was faithful. Exactly why it had hurt so bad to lose her. "Huh. I guess she replaced me with another Dickenson sister. Well done, Roxy."

"It wasn't like that at all." Janie looked at her through narrowed eyes and shook her head. "Are you ever going to let go of whatever the hell it was that went down between the two of you in high school? I've never known you to be this damn stubborn about anything else."

She wasn't just stubborn, though, she was…hurt. It had been thirty years, and she was still hurt by what had happened that day with Roxy, and anytime she thought about it she felt like that awkward teen all over again. Like she was right back in high school when they were best friends. Standing at her locker. Embarrassed as fuck. It didn't matter that she and Roxy had been getting along just fine since Nic had come back to town, the wound was still there. It was starting to seem like she might never get over it.

But of course her sisters couldn't understand. She'd never told them what happened that day. Or how she'd felt about Roxy back then.

"Nothing happened between the two of us." Nic tried to brush away the unpleasant memories while ignoring the look of doubt her sister was shooting in her direction. "That was a long time ago, and anyway, that's not the point. As if it's not bad enough my marriage was blown to bits and my career is hanging on by a very thin thread, I'm currently living in my little sister's guesthouse for what has turned out to be an indefinite amount of time while I wait for a car I hate to be repaired. To top it all off, my pathetic complete lack of a life summed up in an online dating profile has been discovered by an old classmate."

"Oh, boo-hoo. First of all, we made you sound pretty damn good in that profile. Definitely not pathetic. You're welcome, by the way. Secondly, we all know Roxy was more than just a classmate to you." She elbowed Nic in the ribs teasingly. Nic sucked in her breath at the contact and held it—had Roxy told Janie what happened back in high school after all? "You two were best friends. You did everything together."

"Whatever. It's still humiliating. I'm so fucking embarrassed I feel that way after all this time."

"Okay, you feel embarrassed, but that's your side of it. No one is saying that's how you should feel." Janie shrugged. "It's all about perspective. There's absolutely nothing wrong with making a fresh start after things blow up the way your marriage did. But not your career. Your career didn't blow up. That's going to be fine. Anyway, a fresh start is healthy. Hell, it's brave."

"Janie, she actually said, 'I could just message you on Perfect Pair!' all snarky." She paused and considered it, remembering the words slipping between Roxy's full, red lips. "Yes, she had a snarky tone. Like she was making fun of me for being gay."

Janie scrunched up her face and squinted at her. "Are you sure she was making fun of you? I mean, she's gay too. Maybe it was her way of letting you know she's on the site too. Maybe she wasn't trying to embarrass you—she was trying to make a connection. You should give her a chance. Get some perspective."

Was Roxy trying to connect with her? Is that what was happening at the bar? Nic was still reeling from the revelation that Roxy was gay. She thought back to the day she got back to town and saw Roxy behind the bar at Zachroll's. The sexy way Roxy's tight jeans hugged her curves when she bent over to stock the bar. She wouldn't totally mind connecting with that body. She shook her head. Those kinds of thoughts and Roxy hadn't seriously mingled in her mind in a damn long time. Maybe that was because high school was a damn long time ago. But still, Janie had made an interesting point. Was it possible Nic had been looking at this Roxy situation all wrong?

Nic glanced over at Janie, who was squinting into the dappled sunlight streaming through the tree branches overhead, her usual calm smile on her face. This was the second time since she'd been back that Janie had hit her with a dose of sisterly advice. Seriously, when did her little sister become so wise? "Perspective, huh?"

CHAPTER EIGHT

"I can't believe how much we unloaded this morning. Who knew people were so into vintage glassware and knickknacks?" Nic was still shaking her head in disbelief. In just a few hours at the flea market they had sold almost everything she had deemed even remotely valuable, and then, to her surprise, people bought some of the remaining stuff.

"I mean, I think I might have mentioned it when we started this venture," Roxy pointed out, but even she looked pretty pleased with the morning's results.

"I can't wait to see how much we made."

"I think you'll be pleasantly surprised." Roxy had insisted they not pull out their cash while they were wheeling and dealing at the market. Instead, the plan was that they would pick up some lunch once they got back into Fisher's Creek, eat at Roxy's, and count the day's earnings then.

"Don't tell my sisters. I'll never hear the end of it from Bella and Janie how I was just going to throw it all out. And if Maggie hears I've come into money, she might charge me back rent for the week I've been camped out at her place."

Roxy's smile faded a fraction. "Aw, she's going to miss you when you leave."

"She was a very good sport about letting me completely take over the guesthouse, and she tolerated me popping into her kitchen at all hours of the day and night."

"Tolerated? Are you kidding me?" Roxy glanced over to meet her gaze. "I bet she loved having you there. She's always been your number one fan. Remember how she used to follow us around when we were kids?"

"Most of the time we let her too." Nic laughed. They had just crossed into Fisher's Creek, and she glanced out the window at the passing town. "Hey, what's the deal with all the bears?"

"The what?"

"The wooden bears that just about everyone in town seems to have in front of their houses. What's that all about?"

Roxy kept her beautiful emerald eyes focused on the road. "They're cute, no?"

"They're kitschy."

"Cute and kitschy." Roxy managed to keep a straight face for a moment before busting out in laughter. "Okay, mostly kitschy. But back in the midaughts, Carl Kramer started carving them and giving them as gifts. I remember he gave my mom one for Christmas one year. Anyway, before we knew it, they were popping up all over town. Like some kind of…"

"Infestation?"

Roxy shot her a sideways glance. "I was going to say fad."

Nic cringed. Mr. Kramer did a nice thing for his neighbors, and she was making fun of it. After she'd had such a nice morning with Roxy too. Definitely cringeworthy. She backpedaled. "I'm sorry. They are kinda cute. I can see how they would grow on you."

"They do," Roxy insisted. "Plus, nobody wanted to hurt Carl's feelings, so they kept the bears there in their yards, standing watch. Like the wooden guardians of Fisher's Creek. Keeping us safe. After a while, they became kind of comforting."

"I guess I can understand that." Roxy seemed unaffected by the wooden bear slight, but not wanting to chance it, Nic changed the subject. "Still only one movie at the theater?"

"They still give each film two solid weeks," Roxy confirmed. "Despite our fine wood carvings, we are not an arts-forward town, but we do what we can."

"Oh my God, remember when we saw *Say Anything* and we thought it was so stupid, but instead of walking out we stayed and made fun of it the whole time?"

Roxy's laugh was a joyful bark, a noise that reminded Nic of middle school sleepovers. She slapped her hand on the steering wheel three times while she caught her breath. "But we had so much fun laughing at that movie, we ended up loving it. We saw it three more times while it was showing at the theater. What was that about?"

"It was a little bit about Lili Taylor, if I'm being totally honest," Nic confessed, and the women shared another laugh as Roxy steered the truck down Main Street.

Nic tipped her face to the sun shining in through the open window and breathed deeply. The earthy smell of fresh-cut grass, the kiss of warm rays on her cheeks—both took her back to childhood days when she would play with her siblings and friends in the town square just across the street from where Roxy was parking the truck. Back then, for a real treat, her parents would take the family to Bo's Diner across the street. Bo's was a real Fisher's Creek institution. It had been around for generations, now owned and run by the original owner's grandson. Nic's mouth began to water the moment she caught a glimpse of the cheerful royal blue and yellow striped awning that adorned the diner's windows. She couldn't wait to taste that delicious bacon and tomato grilled cheese sandwich she'd ordered. Comfort food at its finest. That and a side of Bo's homemade chips would really hit the spot after a morning of hawking tchotchkes at the flea market.

Roxy shifted into park and glanced over her shoulder at the last few boxes in the truck bed. "Will you go in and grab the food?

I want to check what's rattling around back there and make sure everything's secure."

"You got it." Nic hopped out of the truck and headed into Bo's.

Unlike Zachroll's, the diner appeared exactly the same as she'd left it the last time she'd visited. It was clean and the interior paint was fresh, but it still had the same pasty salmon color on the walls, the same chrome and vinyl tables and chairs. Everything about it screamed "blast from the past," and Nic suspected that was part of why it had remained so popular over the years. That and Bo's extensive menu of homestyle comfort foods.

"Hi there," she greeted the young woman at the register. "I'm picking up a to-go order for Nic."

While she waited for the woman to fetch her food, she helped herself to one of the mints by the cash register and surveyed the dining area. The place was buzzing with the weekend lunch rush, but her eyes were immediately drawn to an occupied booth against the back wall. The guy sitting there wore a ball cap pulled down low on his brow, like he didn't want to be seen, but Nic knew him right away. It was Bella's husband, Chad.

Her first instinct was to slide into the booth and say hello, but then he tugged the brim of his cap lower, slouched in his seat, and unfolded the menu in front of his face. Almost as if he was hiding. Why would Chad be hiding in Bo's Diner? Hold up—did Chad have a secret? The other night Bella had said he had some kind of school event to attend. Maybe he was on a lunch break.

Before she had a chance to wonder any further, she heard someone pounding on the front window of the diner. Roxy. And she looked distressed.

Chad would have to wait.

"Grab the food, we gotta go." Roxy's voice was muffled by the glass between them, but her urgency was evident by the way she waved her phone in the air.

Nic paid the check and hustled back out of the diner with the food. "What the hell's going on?"

Roxy already had the truck idling as Nic climbed in. She'd barely waited for her to buckle her seat belt before pulling away from the curb. "I'm going to have to take a rain check on lunch. Sam was supposed to open the bar, but she's sick and overslept and didn't even call until now. We were supposed to open at eleven—almost two hours ago."

Nic doubted that there would be a throng of drinkers knocking down the door to get into the bar at that time of the day, but it was clear Roxy was worried about her business. The mystery of Chad's weird behavior would have to sit on the back burner for now. "I can help you get the boxes out of the truck at your place real quick and you can get over to the bar and open up before your regulars stage a revolt. No sweat."

"Thanks, Nic." Roxy's forced smile did nothing to hide her stress, but it was only a matter of minutes before they were pulling into the gravel driveway that led to the Fitzpatrick house.

"Your mom's roses still look great," Nic remarked. The colorful blooms were always a point of pride for Mrs. Fitzpatrick.

"They're just starting to bloom for the season. I've tried so hard to take care of them since she moved into the nursing home. When they woke up and burst out in color on the bushes this spring, it was kind of like having her home here with me. I need to cut a few blooms and take them over to her. That would probably give her some joy."

"I was so sorry to hear you had to move her to the residence. Was that when you moved back to Fisher's Creek?" Nic asked as they hopped back out of the cab and walked toward the back of the truck to unload it.

"Thanks." Roxy hoisted herself into the bed and slid the boxes toward the tailgate. "I came back right after she was diagnosed with Alzheimer's. About two years before the nursing home became necessary. I moved in, and then I kind of settled in. When I caught word Old Man Zachroll was looking to sell, I jumped on it. Had home health care for Mom while I was working at the bar, then looked after her on my off hours. I was busy and tired as hell. When she moved to the residence, I didn't know what to do with myself. That's when I started fixing up the bar. It became my life. Guess I was meant to be a small-town gal."

Nic bit back the urge to bust out in a Journey song as they moved the boxes. So, small towns were good for some people, just not her. "Well, you've done great with the bar. My sisters and I had a lot of fun the other night."

Roxy glanced at the time on her phone, then gave a sheepish smile. "Speaking of which…"

"You have to open up before the regulars kick up a ruckus," Nic finished for her as she grabbed her bag of takeaway diner food out of the cab of the truck. She'd taken up enough of Roxy's time. She needed to let her take care of her business.

"Can I drop you somewhere on my way?" Roxy locked the door behind them then twirled her key ring around her finger, making an anxious jingle. She was clearly itching to get to the bar despite her offer.

"Go serve your people." Nic winked. "I'll be fine."

Roxy gave a flirty finger wave as she started the truck and pulled out of the driveway.

Did she really just wink at Roxy Fitzpatrick? What the hell was happening?

It was a little after seven o'clock Saturday night when Maggie poked her head in the front door of the guesthouse. "You missed dinner."

"Mmm." Nic was painfully aware of that fact. Her stomach had been rumbling for close to an hour, but she'd vowed she wouldn't leave the couch until she put words on the page. So far, that hadn't happened. She couldn't lose a whole weekend of writing because she was stranded in Fisher's Creek. Her deadline was looming, and she had the feeling "car trouble" wasn't going to be a valid excuse for not having anything to show the publisher.

"Hey." Maggie snapped her fingers before plopping down onto the couch. "I'm serious. You need to take a break and eat something."

"I need to write something."

Maggie rested her chin on Nic's shoulder. "You wrote something. I see almost a full sentence there."

Almost a full sentence was far from the results Nic had hoped for when she'd sat down over two hours earlier. She knew better than to try to rush her creative process, but after wandering around town for a good part of the day, she felt silly having nothing to show for it. "It's not funny, Mags. I have a deadline."

"You have time before you have to turn something in. Don't be so hard on yourself."

"I have to be hard on myself. These people paid me an advance and expect the product they paid for. If I don't meet my deadline, they're going to want their money back."

"Oh, Nic, you spent your whole advance?"

Nic dropped her notebook and pen on the coffee table and slouched back against the plush couch cushions. She'd been avoiding telling her sisters this part of the story because it was just so…pathetic. Her ex, Dana, might have thought letting Nic have the stupid Tesla made the economics between them more equal, but it didn't erase the humiliation Nic felt about the other things she'd lost. "I didn't spend it. Not all of it. Dana's attorney caught wind of it and had it factored into the divorce settlement. Dana fucked the yoga instructor and still ended up with a bigger chunk of my advance than I did. What I had left over went pretty quickly between my own attorney bills and expenses once I moved out of the house. If I have to pay that money back to the publisher, I'm totally screwed."

Maggie slipped her arm through the crook of Nic's elbow. "I didn't know."

"How could you?" She shook her head. "I didn't tell anybody. I was embarrassed. All I could picture was Dana and that yoga instructor having a huge laugh about taking the fruits of being a published author right out of my hands. I didn't want anybody to know."

"Oh, sweetie. It's a divorce. Things get divided up, that's just what happens. I'm sure it's not a joke to anyone. One way or another, you're going to be okay. You're going to meet your deadline and write that book." Maggie squeezed closer and kissed her on the cheek. "But first, you're coming in and getting something to eat.

Just like I tell Collin when he tries to run out the door to school without breakfast—your brain can't work without fuel."

Ten minutes later, Nic was sitting at the counter in Maggie's kitchen while her sister fixed her a plate of eggs and bacon, a quick meal to fuel her brain. While Nic had agreed to come in and eat, she insisted on bringing her laptop along to make another attempt at writing.

"What kind of stack do you want?" Maggie waved her spatula in the air like it was a magic wand.

"The delicious kind."

"There's no other kind in my kitchen. But do you want that short or tall?"

"Um, medium?"

"Fair enough. Grab the syrup and whipped cream from the fridge. Butter too."

Nic did as she was told. By the time she returned to the counter, Maggie was joining her with two full plates.

"No fair," Nic whined and climbed onto her stool. "You get to have an all-pancake dinner."

Maggie laughed. "This is my dessert. I already ate dinner. Oh, crap. I forgot." She hopped off her stool and grabbed her oversized purse from the hook by the back door. "Mom wanted me to give you this."

Nic took the bright red-and-yellow postcard with the Fisher's Creek High School mascot, the Smiling Crawfish, on it. She didn't need to read the text on the back to know she wasn't interested in this particular piece of mail. "Oh, hell no." She tossed the card onto the countertop and went back to her bacon and eggs. "I can't believe you even agreed to deliver that to me. What's wrong with you?"

"What's wrong with me?" There was a teasing sparkle in Maggie's eyes as she took a bite of pancake. Chewing didn't stop the harassment. "You're not looking forward to attending your thirtieth high school reunion in two weeks? What has happened to your Smiling Crawfish pride?"

"It was replaced by gay pride."

Maggie shot her a withering look. "You can have both prides. You contain multitudes."

"I'm not going back to the place that tried to take that pride from me," she said between bites of scrambled egg. Bumping into Roxy and Peewee around town was fine, but a night of mingling on the dance floor with her old classmates held no appeal for her. It was nonnegotiable. A change of topic was in order. "Enough of this high school reunion shit. There's no way I'm driving back from New York for that anyway. Let's talk about something else. How's the man search going on Perfect Pair? Need us to check anyone out for you?"

"I could ask you the very same thing."

"I haven't even logged back in since the night Janie made that profile. In fact, I meant to delete it."

Maggie's fork dropped, clanking against her plate. "Aren't you the least bit curious? Who knows how many women have been sending you the womanly equivalent of a dick pic? What would that be? A puss pic?"

"I think *tit pic* has a nicer ring to it." Nic laughed. Only Maggie could take her from cringing over high school memories to eye-watering laughter over private parts that quickly. She shook her head. "Not that I'm hoping for either."

"Yeah, right." Maggie rolled her eyes and flapped her hand as if summoning the laptop to her. "Pull up the site. Let's see what you've been missing."

Nic groaned but clicked on the browser to pull up the dating site. After tapping in the ridiculous password Janie had selected for her—gimmelove69—she pushed the computer in Maggie's direction. "Have at it, sis. But then I'm deleting it. I mean it."

Nic finished her meal while Maggie scrolled through her potential matches on the app.

"There are some interesting ladies on here, you really should give this a chance." Maggie's eyebrows shot up in surprise. "Oh, this one is nearly a tit pic. Why even bother wearing a dress that sheer? It's not hiding anything. May as well be naked."

"Maybe I *should* give this a chance," Nic joked, reaching for the laptop, but the chirp of her cell phone distracted her.

Just a reminder to bring an extra shirt tomorrow night—could get a little dirty and sweaty!

"Must be a good text to keep you from potential tit pics." Maggie leaned over Nic's shoulder. "Oh, it is! Why is Roxy texting you about getting sweaty tomorrow night? Oh my God, what are you two doing? Is it a date? It's got to be a date!"

"Nebby is not a good look." Nic pulled her phone to her chest and swiveled on her stool to get out of her sister's reach. "And there's no need to work yourself up. It is most certainly not a date."

"But you're doing something. Together," Maggie pointed out. "And she thinks you're going to work up a sweat."

"We're going to work up a sweat because we're refurbishing furniture. In her workshop. Where things are dirty. I'm just going over to help her. That's not a date."

"Do you even know anything about furniture refurbishing?" Maggie's eyebrow quirked up in top sister teasing form.

"No."

"Yet Roxy *needs* your help with the *refurbishing*?"

"Well, she doesn't *need* my help, she just…"

Yeah, Roxy didn't need her help at all. If anything, there was a good chance Nic's presence was only going to slow down the process. But Roxy invited her over anyway. Could Maggie be right? *Was* it a date? Date adjacent?

"She just what, then?" Maggie pressed.

This was ridiculous. The fact was Roxy was doing actual labor to make money for both of them by upcycling the unwanted contents of Nic's great-aunt's house. Asking Nic to put in a little work of her own to achieve results that would benefit them both wasn't unreasonable. It made perfect sense. And it was definitely not a date. "It's just not a date. That's all."

"Okay." Maggie nodded, but it was clear she had her doubts. "Don't get too sweaty on your nondate. That's not a good look either."

CHAPTER NINE

Nic spent the early hours of Sunday morning locked away in the guesthouse, writing descriptions of her favorite spots in Fisher's Creek to use as the small town in her book. It wasn't plot or story, but it was words on the page. And she would take that small victory.

She started by describing the old wooden bridge that crossed the creek on the far side of the town square. She wrote about the tufts of delicate purple wildflowers that bloomed every summer along the path on both ends of its splintery, gray wooden planks, and how she recalled playing Poohsticks there with her siblings on lazy Sunday afternoons after church.

Then she wrote about the gazebo in the square, remembering how the pigeons had strutted around like they owned the place when she sat there the day before. But the memory that had inspired her to include the gazebo in her small-town mystery was a day she had spent there with Roxy when they were teenagers.

The two friends had been bumming around town, just wasting a Saturday, when suddenly a storm blew in. The dark sky opened up and a warm spring rain poured down. The girls had taken shelter in the gazebo, wet clothes clinging to their teenage bodies, the rhythm of the rain pelting the wooden roof, flashes of lightning illuminating the square around them. Nic could still remember how badly she wanted to kiss Roxy that day hiding out from the rain, but she'd refrained from acting on her emotions. She'd been too afraid. Then, less than two weeks later, standing in front of her locker, she'd seen the horror on Roxy's face when she actually did find out how Nic felt about her.

And now all these years later they were, what? Reconnecting?

Whatever it was, it for sure wasn't a date like Maggie kept saying. She was only going to be in town for, like, twenty-four more hours. A date didn't make any sense whatsoever. No. She was going over to Roxy's to help with the furniture because they were working together toward a common goal. Making a little money. That was it. It had nothing to do with the pull she still felt deep down in her soul—the actual heart-clenching tug in her chest that seemed to draw her right back to Roxy. Just like it did all those years ago. She just couldn't resist it. But that didn't mean there was anything happening between them. It was merely her unresolved feelings coming out to play after all this time. Feelings she should probably be pushing back down to wherever the hell they'd escaped from. Or ignoring. But definitely not entertaining.

A car honking out in the drive snapped Nic back to reality. Nine thirty already. Bella, punctual as ever, was outside in her big ol' SUV, ready to go over and finish up at Agatha's house. There were boxes that needed dropping off at the donation site, and one last room to pack up. Nic had taken Bella's suggestion to leave the furniture that was in good shape in place for staging purposes until the house sold. Once they'd pulled the plastic off the sofas and gave the place a good dusting, they'd realized a lot of it was in pretty decent shape and actually added a lot of character to the space. Bella promised when they found a buyer she would handle the arrangements to have Roxy come out and sell the rest of the things Nic didn't want. There was a possibility that by then Nic would have a new home of her own to fill, and Bella could ship some of the items out to New York and save her the grief and cost of having to buy all new stuff. It was old, but free furniture was free furniture, after all.

Bella had a takeaway cup of coffee waiting for her in the car. Always taking care of her younger sisters, even if just to make sure they had their morning cup of joe.

"Thanks for this." Nic took a sip as soon as she slid into the passenger seat. The rich warmth of the drink did the trick, chasing away her morning brain fog. As they backed out of the driveway, she remembered she hadn't gotten closure on the Chad incident from the day before. "I think I saw your husband yesterday at Bo's Diner having lunch. Did he mention it?"

Bella's gaze strayed from the road long enough to give Nic a look that clearly conveyed she thought she'd lost her mind. "At Bo's? No. He was at a seminar over in Frost Lake. Something about environmentally minded school administration. He said it was ridiculous. Chad can be stubbornly analog."

"Oh." If Chad was in Frost Lake for a seminar, there was no way he came back to Fisher's Creek for lunch in the middle of it. She really thought it was Chad she'd seen crouching down behind that diner menu, but Bella seemed certain he was out of town for the day. Before she could give any more thought to it, her sister steered the conversation to the task at hand.

"So, what do you have left to do at the house? Run down the to-do list for me so I'm prepared."

"Mainly we just need to get the last of the stuff I packed up out of there." Nic mentally bullet-pointed the items left to address. Bella would appreciate a concise report, and she wanted to keep a good energy flowing to get through the project as quickly as possible.

The short drive to the house gave them just enough time to come up with a plan of attack. They would load up the SUV with the boxes that were already packed with donations, then while Bella drove them to the Goodwill, Nic would get to work on Aunt Aggie's bedroom.

"This is all stuff to donate?" Bella blinked in disbelief when they stepped into the living room.

The brown cardboard boxes had piled up gradually over the past week, and Nic had become immune to the size of the gathering. It reminded her of when she gained weight that first semester at college. She hadn't noticed the little day-by-day change. But when she'd returned home for Christmas break, her mother declared she'd been a victim of the freshman fifteen the second she'd walked through the front door.

"Believe me, Roxy and I sorted through every last item. We took a whole truckload to the flea market, and we took a few things over to Mom's, but this stuff is all to be donated. Great-Aunt Aggie had a lot of stuff. I'm dreading facing her bedroom. I shouldn't have put it off until last."

"Seriously, why did you wait so long?"

How could she explain it? She'd been asking herself that exact question all morning, and she'd worked up a theory. It still felt weird to speak it out loud. "I think I put it off because it seemed so personal. It's her *bedroom*, you know? Her inner sanctuary. I didn't know this woman at all, and it feels like I'm invading her privacy. I feel like a creepy creeper."

Bella shook her head. "You're not a creepy creeper. You're a family member doing what needs to be done. Better you enter her inner sanctuary than some total stranger."

Nic sighed. "I feel like I am a stranger."

"You're not, though," Bella insisted, giving Nic's shoulder a squeeze. When Nic fixed her with a doubtful glare, she continued, "Aunt Aggie left it all to you. She knew you would have to sort through it. She was okay with that. You have her permission. Plus, if you want to have enough time to go home and shower up before your big date tonight, we're going to be on a real time crunch, so get over it and get to work."

"It's not a da—" Nic caught the teasing gleam in her sister's eye. "Okay. So you've talked to Maggie. You two are very funny."

"What? I was at Zachroll's the other night. I saw how she looked at you. Plus, there was always something special between you two." Bella turned her attention back to the boxes, acting casual like she wasn't still trying to drive her point home. "It kind of makes sense that the two of you would hook up sooner or later."

Hook up? Why did that phrase paired with the thought of Roxy make Nic's chest buzz? Nope, her sisters were not doing this to her.

"For the last time, it's not a date, so you and Maggie can take your little story about whatever it is you're imagining is happening between me and Roxy and shove it." She turned on her heel and marched toward the staircase. There was a bedroom that needed her attention.

"Janie thinks something's happening between the two of you too," Bella called after her.

Nic tried to ignore her sister's teasing and instead focus on what Bella had said about her not being a stranger in the house as she emptied the contents of Aunt Aggie's dresser (mostly throw away) and the small bookshelf under the window (mostly donate, a few keepers), but she still felt like an intruder. The wooden hope chest at the foot of the bed was full of linens—old bedsheets and extra blankets. Nothing fancy, but items the local animal shelter would be able to put to good use.

Apparently, Agatha was a fan of the practical and functional, a quality Nic could relate to. God, the way Dana would get annoyed at her apathy for the latest fashion fad. Nic just never could drum up a passion for the frivolous things her ex-wife obsessed about. To each their own, Nic figured. She never wanted Dana to change and give up the things that delighted her, but Dana didn't share that que será, será attitude. Dana couldn't stand that Nic didn't feel the same way she did about things, be it favorite foods or flashy footwear, and Dana's way was always the best way. Just one of many red flags Nic should've recognized earlier.

It didn't matter anymore. Now Nic was free to like buffalo chicken dip and patterned Chuck Taylors without criticism. Free to be herself, which turned out to be kind of like her great-aunt—practical, independent, wild about books. Maybe it was all handed down through their DNA.

She had started to sort through the storage boxes under the bed when Bella returned from the first donation drop.

"I was really hoping you would be done in here by now," Bella said as she grabbed an empty box and dragged it toward the closet.

"You better get a move on if you want to actually get cleaned up before your big…whatever you're doing tonight."

"You don't think Roxy wants to get up close and personal with sweaty, dusty me?" Nic quipped as she dove back under the bed to pull out a stack of old magazines. Didn't Aggie know that was a fire hazard?

While Nic had been busy with cleaning and packing, her mind had been distracted. She'd managed to push thoughts about her upcoming evening with Roxy aside for a bit, but of course her sister had to bring the subject right back up. She couldn't deny she was looking forward to spending time with Roxy again. Working together. Would Roxy be wearing one of those sleeveless T-shirts like she wore at Zachroll's—the kind that showed off her arm muscles while she worked? A jolt of excitement shot up her spine. *Easy now.* She flipped through the glossy pages of the old journal to redirect her thoughts. "Oh my God, look at these old issues of *Good Housekeeping*. They're from the fifties. Totally vintage. I can't believe they're even still in one piece."

"I doubt they're worth donating. You can toss them in the recycling though," Bella called over her shoulder as she grabbed an armful of clothes hanging in the closet.

Nic was about to flip the pages closed when she noticed a byline on an article on the page in front of her. An essay about the joy and satisfaction that could be found in canning your fresh-from-the-garden vegetables. "Aunt Aggie wrote this! I had no idea she was a writer."

Bella shot her a wry look as she deposited the armload of clothes onto the bed. "In all fairness, we had no idea about anything about her other than she lived in this old house alone and was a grumpy old lady."

Nic considered that as she put the magazines aside to take with her back to Maggie's. *Grumpy old lady* wasn't at all how Eric from next door described Agatha Hill. Why was that the go-to description Nic and her siblings clung to about her? It wasn't as if any of them actually knew her. Despite living in the same town, they'd hardly spent any time with her. She never turned up at holiday celebrations or family dinners. Never invited them to her house either. Nic was starting to think maybe no one in their family really knew Aunt Aggie at all, and for some reason that made Nic want to learn even more about her. She wanted to see if the other magazines from under the bed had articles by her great-aunt. Aggie was a writer. Another thing she and Nic had in common.

Her knees ached from sitting on the floor, and she used the edge of the bed to stand up again. She eyed the mountain of clothes Bella had pulled from the closet and deposited on the bed. Aunt Aggie had a heck of a wardrobe. She grabbed a pink pantsuit and removed the wooden hanger, which she tossed into a cardboard box at her feet. The suit was in impeccable condition, so it went into a separate box marked "donate." Someone at the thrift shop would hit the vintage clothes jackpot.

"I sorted through all the shoes," Bella reported. "She kept them all in the original boxes. Anything worth donating is packed up and ready to go. The rest"—she nodded at a pile by the door—"can get pitched."

"Great." Nic kept at her task of sorting and folding the clothes. She was anxious to get on with her evening. "Go ahead and start loading the car. If we can get out of here in the next forty minutes, we can get it to the Goodwill before they close for the day. Is that everything out of the closet?"

"There's a big plastic tub in here too." Bella's muffled voice came from inside the closet. "Nic, your name's on this."

"What?" Nic dropped a canary-yellow sweater set and turned her attention to the blue Rubbermaid Bella was dragging out. "What's in it?"

Bella popped off the lid marked with its handwritten label. Inside was a scrapbook, loose photos, papers, and open letters still in their envelopes. The ephemera of a life. "She wanted you to find this."

"But why?" Nic picked up one of the photos. An image of well-dressed individuals holding champagne flutes at a party of some sort. Then the next: two young women arms around each other, standing under a dogwood tree in full bloom. "I don't know these people."

Bella squinted at the second image. She flipped it over, but the back was unmarked. "I think that woman there is Aunt Aggie. Anyway, she obviously wanted you to see it." She pointed at the handwritten *Nicola* on the lid of the container. "Aren't you a little bit curious about what else is in here?"

Nic's gaze traveled from the full tote of someone else's memories to Bella's expectant expression. Clearly her sister was excited to dig into the past, but it wasn't her name Aggie put on the tote, it was Nic's. This was something she was supposed to do. Sure, she was curious, but she was more curious to get to her evening with Roxy. According to her watch they were down to thirty minutes to drop off the donations, and they were so damn close to being done cleaning out the house. She couldn't get distracted by digging through old pics and letters. Not then. "Throw it in the back of the SUV. The past is going to have to wait a little longer. I'll take it back to New York with me."

"Wow, this place has had a hell of a makeover since high school." Nic surveyed the space in awe. What was formerly the Fitzpatricks' junk-filled detached garage was now a neat, fully stocked workshop complete with a plush couch and coffee table forming a seating area for breaks. The large-screen television mounted on the wall was placed perfectly to be visible from the work area as well as the resting space. "Did you do all this?"

"You know it." Roxy beamed with pride. "Can I offer you a drink?" She gestured at the fridge against the wall. "Water, soda, beer?"

"Since I'm new at this furniture refurbishing thing and should probably keep my wits about me, I think I'll hold off on beer drinking for now."

Instead, Nic opted for a caffeine-free soft drink. She loved her coffee in the morning, but her consumption had a two p.m. deadline. Any later than that these days and it kept her up at night. It was funny how things like that shifted as you got older. One morning you woke up and discovered you can't handle a night of tequila shots anymore. Or after painting the spare bedroom you realize that old softball injury is now going to haunt you anytime you engage your left shoulder in repetitive motion. Little things whose only purpose is to remind you that you're not a teenager anymore. They didn't hit you all at once, instead they snuck up on you one by one, and you didn't even know the change was happening until it did. Not that Nic would want to be a teenager again. At almost fifty, she felt like she was on the verge of becoming the best version of herself. She'd certainly improved with age, that was sure.

As Roxy led her to the wooden desk they planned to work on, Nic stole a glance at the big screen. "Are you watching *The Goonies?*"

Roxy nodded and laughed. "I thought it would be a fun throwback. I can cue up *Jewel of the Nile* after this. I remember you liked that one too."

She still remembered Nic's favorites from middle school. That was sweet and for some reason made Nic's chest feel warm like it was filled with sunshine even though outside the workshop the sky was streaking purple as evening set in. Of course Roxy remembered. They were her favorites too. They'd shared a million favorites when they were kids. It didn't mean anything. Hanging out together now was totally different from then. This was purely business, and certainly not a date. They were no longer the besties that did each other's nails and watched horror flicks at sleepovers.

"Seriously, I loved *The Goonies* so much when we were kids." Nic fiddled with the center drawer pull on the desk. One thing had changed since their school days about hanging out with Roxy—Nic was nervous. "How many times do you think we saw this the summer it released? I bet a half dozen, easily."

"At least," Roxy agreed with a chuckle. "I was the biggest Mouth fan."

"I recall," Nic said, following Roxy's lead removing the drawers from the desk. "I had the biggest crush on Martha Plimpton."

"What? You never told me that!"

"Yeah, well…" Nic's mind grasped for words as she watched the way Roxy's biceps flexed and rippled as she used a screwdriver to remove the pulls from the drawers. She was mesmerized by the way Roxy's emerald eyes sparkled as she focused on the task. A couple of strands of hair had already fallen loose from her messy bun and danced across her shoulders as she worked. For years she'd wondered what it would be like to run her fingers through Roxy's soft brown hair. "I never told anyone."

"I'm glad you're sharing with me now." She abandoned her screwdriver and locked her gaze on Nic's. "Are you ready to get to it?" She took a step closer—close enough that Nic could smell the sea spray scent of her shampoo.

Was this… Was Roxy actually sending the signal Nic thought she was receiving?

"I, uh…" Nic stammered. "Get to it?"

"Yeah." Roxy's eyes crinkled at the corners as she flashed her bright smile. "Refinishing the desk?"

"Right. The desk," Nic said. She needed to get her sisters' voices out of her head and focus on the job she was there to do. She and Roxy had actual work to do. "Please, teach me your ways."

"I'm going to work on removing the old finish from this desk, but you're going to sand down these side tables that I stripped yesterday."

"I have to sand while you get to strip?" Nic smirked.

"Ha ha." Roxy rolled her eyes. "I'm sparing you from having to work with the chemical stripper. It's some nasty stuff, which is why I've opened all these windows."

"I thought that was just for the ambiance. That Fisher's Creek cricket song is a hell of a soundtrack."

"Are you going to keep going with the jokey jokes, or can we start doing it now?" Roxy stood with her hands on her hips, but her lips quirked up like she found the jokes at least a little amusing. "The longer you screw around, the longer the job is going to take."

And the longer the project took, the longer the two of them would have to spend time together. Nic didn't need Roxy to connect the dots for her for her.

"You trying to get rid of me?" Nic grabbed a piece of sandpaper from the workbench and casually rubbed the top of one of the tables. She didn't know much about furniture refurbishing, but *sanding the side tables* seemed like a simple enough proposition.

"If I am, I'll be crap out of luck based on what you're doing there. It will take you forever to finish if you do it by hand."

Why did everything this woman said to her sound so damn sexual?

Roxy fussed for a moment with an extension cord, draping it from the outlet to the table, where she attached it to a tool she presented to Nic. "Try this electric sander. Your shoulders will thank me later."

Nic took the tool and eyed it dubiously. The jump from using plain old sandpaper to power tools felt major. She was about to say as much, but Roxy was already trying to hand her something else.

"And don't forget protection." She couldn't just say *goggles*, could she? "Safety first."

After donning the protective eyewear, Nic studied the tool. A rotating disk of medium-grit paper—*keep fingers away from that*—a grip that fit perfectly in the palm of her hand, and a switch to turn the unit on and off. Seemed easy enough. She clicked the switch and the tool buzzed in her hand, sending waves of vibration up her arm. She yelped in surprise and clicked it off again.

Immediately Roxy was back at her side.

"Did you get hurt?"

Did she seem that inept?

"No. I just wasn't expecting it to be so…buzzy."

Roxy frowned at her. "You know, screwing around in the workshop can be dangerous. I meant it when I said safety first."

She was disappointed in Nic, and Nic didn't like it. She wanted to prove she could keep up and do her part in this refurbishing deal. "I'm not screwing around. I've just never used one of these before. I was just trying to get my bearings."

Roxy blew out a sigh—*was it relief?*—and her expression softened. "Okay. Let me give you a few pointers." She put on her own safety glasses and positioned herself behind Nic.

Nic desperately tried to force the thought of Roxy bending her over the table and fucking her from behind out of her mind. They were refinishing furniture, for God's sake. Refinishing *Great-Aunt Aggie's* furniture. Show some respect.

But it was hard to think respectful thoughts with Roxy's hips pressed against her ass. Then Roxy put one hand on the table and the other on top of Nic's on the sander. Practically wrapped in an embrace, Nic had to bite her bottom lip to hold in the contented sigh threatening to escape her.

"Turn it on again and follow my lead," Roxy instructed.

This time when the buzzing began, Roxy guided Nic's hand in tight circles on the surface of the table. It certainly wasn't an unpleasant sensation. As they continued to work their way across the piece, the vibrations seemed to take up residence in Nic's chest. And then they migrated south from there. Such a delicious humming paired with the heat of Roxy's body pressed against her. No wonder lesbians loved power tools.

But the spell was broken when Nic's phone came to life with the ringtone she'd set for Peewee.

"Oh my God, my car!" Nic clicked off the sander and fumbled for her phone to answer. "Peewee, what's the good word?"

"Aw, Nic, I wish you didn't sound so happy."

Nic's power-tool high crashed to the ground. "Is this one of your good news, bad news calls?"

"I wish. Unfortunately, this call is just, you know." He cleared his throat. "Bad news."

"Peewee, please just tell me what's going on." Nic ran an impatient hand through her hair. Beside her, Roxy frowned.

"There was a mix-up with the control arm for the Tesla."

"You ordered the wrong thing?"

"No, I ordered the right thing, but they shipped it to the wrong place." Peewee sighed. "The control arm is currently in a truck on its way to Albuquerque."

"Albuquerque?" Nic practically shouted into the phone. She rubbed her temples with her free hand. This could not be happening. "If the control arm is on its way to Albuquerque now, how's it going to be in my car tomorrow for me to drive back to New York?"

"Yeah, I know, Nic." Peewee sounded genuinely sorry. "I feel terrible about this, but once the shipment arrives in New Mexico they'll get it on a transport to come here."

"Well, how long is that going to take?"

The pause on the line basically answered her question. *Not fast enough.* "It will probably be here by the end of the work week."

"Probably? But I have a meeting in New York on Thursday. What am I supposed to do about that?"

"Nic, I promise you, the minute the parts arrive in Fisher's Creek I'll get your car fixed. But in the meantime, maybe move your meeting to a Zoom call to be on the safe side?"

Nic closed her eyes and bit back her groan. This wasn't Peewee's fault. Someone else made the mistake, not him. "Yeah, okay. Thanks, Peewee."

She set her phone down on the partially sanded table and dropped her head into her hands. "Another week in this freaking town."

When Roxy didn't comment, Nic peeked between her fingers. Roxy had removed her safety glasses and was returning the sander to the workbench.

"What are you doing?" Nic glanced at the un-unfinished tables. "We've barely started on the sanding. And what about the beer and *Jewel of the Nile*?"

Roxy shook her head. "I think I'm ready to call it a night." She was coiling the extension cord to put it away. She was ending the work session early. This was all wrong.

"Are you feeling all right?" Nic asked, struggling to make sense of what was happening. Roxy's sudden shift in tone made Nic's stomach twist uncomfortably. "Is something wrong?"

"It's pretty clear you just got some bad news. Your mood has tanked." She squeezed the cord in her fist and gestured at Nic. "And I was never a big Michael Douglas fan anyway."

"My mood's fine. I'm fine," Nic protested. She didn't want this night with Roxy to end. Not now, and not like this. They were finally starting to find their footing as friends—or whatever—again. "Besides, what about Kathleen—"

"Nic, I just don't want to..." Roxy sighed. "Can you just go home now, please?"

Nic bit back further argument as Roxy held the door open for her. There was no use in begging, Roxy was clearly done for the night. Somehow Nic had managed to fuck things up with Roxy all over again.

"It's not even nine o'clock and you're back, so I'm going to guess your date was a dud." Maggie's eyes were sympathetic, which softened her snark. She was sitting in her dimly lit kitchen drinking tea when Nic got back from Roxy's. "You want to talk about it over a cup of tea?"

Nic went directly to the fridge and fished out a beer. She eyed up the carton of leftover Chinese food too but thought better of it. She'd reached the point in life where she had to give more consideration to late-night snacks. Another thing to add to the list with her afternoon caffeine intolerance. "I'd rather have one of these, and there's nothing to talk about."

"Oh no, don't give me that," Maggie said as she pushed a stool out with her foot, inviting Nic to sit. "What happened?"

"Well, it wasn't a date, for one. Far from it." Nic surrendered to her sister's worried glare and slumped onto the seat at the breakfast bar. "One minute we were working on the furniture, getting along just fine, and the next Roxy said she wanted me to leave."

Maggie calmly sipped her tea with an expectant look on her face. When Nic didn't expand on the events of the evening, she finally spoke. "Just like that?"

"Just like that." Nic took a long pull on her beer and reconsidered, playing the scene in her head like a movie. "Well, no. I mean, I guess things went sideways when Peewee called."

"You took a phone call on your date?"

"Maggie, it wasn't a date. Stop saying that. And the call was about my car. I thought he was going to tell me when I could pick it up."

Maggie raised a curious eyebrow. "And you couldn't have gotten that information from a voice mail?"

Nic groaned and picked at the label on the bottle. Taking the call had been a bad choice in the first place. Rude when Roxy was helping her with Aunt Aggie's stuff. She could see that in hindsight. She had been in the middle of doing something meaningful with

Roxy, and she dropped it all to talk to her mechanic. "I've been waiting for that particular call for days. I've been hyperfocused on the car repair. It was like a conditioned response." She shook her head. "Meanwhile, the car isn't even ready. There was some stupid mix-up with the part he ordered, it wasn't Peewee's fault or anything, but it was put on the wrong truck and now it's heading in the opposite direction across the country. Which means I'm stuck in this damn town for, like, another week."

"And that's what you said to Roxy?" Maggie frowned. "Nicola Marie, come on."

"What?"

Maggie sighed and carried her empty mug to the sink. "Nic, you look at this town and you see your past, but this town is Roxy's present, possibly her future. Fisher's Creek is our home, even if you can't get out of here fast enough."

"You think I hurt her feelings? I was just...I just want to get back to my life in New York."

"I know you do." Maggie gave Nic's shoulder a squeeze on her way out of the kitchen. "But no one wants to feel like they're being left behind in the dust."

CHAPTER TEN

First thing Monday morning, Nic took Peewee's advice and called her agent to let her know she needed to change their meeting.

"Hey, Nicola. How was vacation?" Alessa sounded way too chipper for nine a.m. on a Monday. She was probably on her second iced skinny vanilla latte and over-caffeinated.

"It's actually not a…" Why even bother? Nic's agent was always on top of business, but when it came to more personal stuff, she had a tendency to miss a few details. Nic's reason for not yet returning to New York was not the important part of the call. "I'm actually still here in Pennsylvania. That's why I'm calling. I had a little car trouble and I'm kind of stuck here."

"You're still in Pennsylvania?"

"Yes, and I'm not going to be back in New York for our meeting Thursday. Do you think we could move it online?"

"Nic, you know I love you, truly. But real talk, is this the preface to you asking for another extension? Because that's not going to fly with Cindy. She's going to want to see some actual pages eventually, you know?"

"Of course I know." Nic sighed. "I'm not going to cancel."

"Good, because Cindy's been very forgiving, but I know for a fact she's starting to become worried about the project. I mean, you did ask for two extensions already."

"While it's true I asked for two extensions, it was only because I was going through a divorce." Alessa was silent in response. Damn. New Yorkers could be cold. "But anyway, I'm on the other side of it now. I'm fine. I'm focused on the project…this book. And I'm very much looking forward to discussing it with you and Cindy Thursday on a Zoom call."

"Okay, all right. We'll do it by Zoom. I'll set things up with Cindy." Alessa sounded like she was over their conversation and moving on to the next thing on her desk. "So, you're going to vacation a little longer?"

"I'm really not…" Oh, what the hell. "Yeah, I guess so. Listen, I've got to run, but I'll talk to you Thursday."

She clicked off the call, but she had a feeling Alessa had still beat her to it. No matter. She'd done what she needed to do.

Now she just needed to come up with a killer pitch.

* * *

Monday afternoon when her sister got home from work, Nic was in her kitchen again, this time surrounded by ceramic tiles and patterned paper, and up to her elbows in Mod Podge.

"What do we have going on here?" Maggie looked surprised at the state of her craft-supply-covered kitchen but not completely displeased. Her expression brightened when Collin came in through the back door, wearing one of Maggie's old baking aprons. "Oh, you have a helper too."

"They're holding a craft fair and bake sale at school this weekend to raise money for the Drama Club, so we're making coasters out of tiles to sell there." Collin's voice was full of pride.

"I'm stress crafting," Nic admitted as she painted the Mod Podge over a vintage comic-strip-patterned paper, adhering it to a white ceramic tile. "But helping the Fisher's Creek Middle School Drama Club is a happy bonus. God knows I can't bake, so crafting it is."

"Stress crafting?" Maggie raised an eyebrow as she passed Nic to grab a bottle of water from the fridge. "What could possibly have my big sister so stressed out that she'd be cutting out squares of scrapbooking paper and gluing it to bulk tiles?"

"Oh, I don't know." Nic shrugged and added two more papered tiles to the lineup already on the kitchen table. "Maybe the book that won't write itself. Or the ludicrous car that might never be fixed yet I'll owe Peewee a fortune for anyway. Take your pick, really."

"Are you sure it's not the fact that you insulted one of your oldest and dearest friends and you're feeling bad about it?"

"No, I don't think that's it at all." Nic quickly shut the door on that thought. She had to for her own well-being. It didn't have to be about Roxy. It could totally be one of the other things.

The fact remained that Roxy knew damn well Nic was only in town for a brief stay and that stay had only been extended because of the damage to her car. Nic felt bad that she'd hurt Roxy's feelings by saying she wanted to get home, but the reality was, her life was in New York. Roxy hadn't answered any of the texts Nic had sent since they'd parted the night before, but maybe she'd been busy at the bar. Nic could always swing by Zachroll's at some point during the week and apologize, make sure they were on good ground again and had their game plan for the house stuff finalized before she headed out of town.

"Mm-hmm." Maggie toed off her tennis shoes and collapsed into one of the chairs at the kitchen table. Her gaze ran the length of the line of decorated tiles waiting for their felt bottoms to be attached. "This is an awful lot of coasters. I hope the Drama Club is expecting a lot of customers. Or wait, are you two keeping some of these for yourselves? Are you opening a bar?" Her eyes went wide. "Oh my God, I just realized you're stress crafting bar accessories. You *totally* have Roxy on your brain."

"Shut up." Nic sang the words to take the edge off them, but that didn't mean she meant them any less. It was just a random craft. Something she knew how to make that she could gather supplies for quickly and make in time for the Drama Club fundraiser. Nothing more.

"We have a whole batch of them outside with their topcoat drying too." God bless Collin and his teenage enthusiasm. "We made a SpongeBob set and two *Stars Wars* sets. Aunt Nic had all these awesome papers here when I got home from school."

"That's great, sweetie." Maggie smiled at her son before turning her attention back to Nic. "And what exactly are you going to do with this many coaster sets? Surely they aren't all for the craft fair."

"We're getting a jump on our Christmas gifts." Nic smirked back. "And don't go around telling everyone what we're giving out or you won't get a set. That would be a shame because SpongeBob would go great in your living room."

"Ha ha. That's very funny, sis." Maggie pulled her phone out of her pocket and began poking at the screen. "Why don't you two wrap up the crafting and clean up the kitchen. I'll order us some pizza for dinner."

"Hot wings too?" Collin was already gathering up scraps of felt from their work area. Such a sweet kid.

"Sure thing. But after dinner you go straight upstairs and hit the books. Next time, Aunt Nic, no stress crafting until homework is done."

"Ah, homework. I knew we were forgetting something." Nic winked at Collin. "Next time I'll get it right, kiddo."

After their feast, Nic wanted to give Maggie some space and let Collin get back to his homework, but she was feeling too antsy to sit in the guesthouse alone. It was that alluring and much-awaited time in spring where the days were finally long enough to get out and enjoy the evening before the dark of night settled in, a particularly beautiful time of year in Fisher's Creek, so she decided to go for a walk.

Ever since Peewee had mentioned his wife's boutique, Nic had been curious to see it. The soothing effects of her crafting session earlier had her feeling up to the task of socializing with former

Fisher's Creek classmates, so she turned down the road that led into town.

Fisher's Creek was relatively busy for a Monday evening. Bo's Diner still looked full enough of patrons enjoying a meal out, and the grocery market on the corner had people popping in and out, the bell on its front door happily jingling each time someone passed through. That had always been one of Nic and her siblings' favorite part of accompanying their mother to the market when they were little kids. That and the penny candy the store sold. Good behavior on a trip to the market was always rewarded with being allowed to select a few candy dots, root beer barrels, or other treats before checking out.

The second storefront on the block past the corner market was Dazzle, Cathy Palone's boutique. The door didn't jingle when she entered, but the gentle, earthy lavender scent that enveloped her was welcoming enough. The shop was a narrow but deep space filled with inventory on every last bit of real estate in the joint. Some might have considered it chaotic or cluttered, but to Nic it appeared more eclectic and full of wonder. She was immediately drawn to a display of bright colored tie-dyed silk scarves. They were the kind of sophisticated accessory Nic always thought would class up an outfit, but she was never quite sure how to wear them. She was sliding the smooth fabric between her fingers when she heard the friendly voice call out behind her.

"Let me know if I can help you with anything."

Nic turned to smile at her old school chum. "Hi, Cathy. Your place is absolutely beautiful."

"Nicola Dickenson, Peewee told me you were back in town!" Cathy scooted out from behind the counter to pull Nic into a warm embrace. She still had the same willowy build as she did when they were younger. Her electric-blue-framed glasses were striking against her dark skin, and the long-strand beaded necklaces she wore layered over a black tunic top screamed fashionista. Cathy clearly still had the same creative style sense she'd had when they were young. "It's so good to see you."

"You too," Nic said, and she meant it. Cathy had been a dear friend when they were in middle school, and though they ran in different circles in high school, they still shared that connection and remained friendly through graduation. Until Nic had left town and lost touch with everyone she'd left behind. She was still surprised that Cathy had remained in Fisher's Creek all these years when she'd had such big dreams in their youth, but Peewee's family business was there, and staying was probably a sacrifice she'd made for love. Regardless, her boutique was fabulous, so she had that success. "Seriously, your shop is amazing. How long have you been here in this space?"

Cathy released her hold on Nic and threw her arms in the air, pride beaming from her face. "It will be twenty-three years this July. Can you believe it? I just love our sweet little home base here in Fisher's Creek. Excuse me just one minute. Looks like Mrs. Duncan is ready to check out."

Home base seemed like an odd way to describe the boutique, but twenty-three years was certainly impressive. Nic continued to peruse the merchandise while Cathy took care of her customer. A display of stunning beaded necklaces drew her over to the jewelry counter. She admired the intricate patterns and the beautiful handmade glass pendants that adorned several of them. Continuing down the counter, she stopped at a large rack showcasing bangle bracelets decorated with delicate charms and gemstones meant to be worn stacked on your arm. Some were silver and others were gold, but Nic had seen both metals worn together. There had been a brand that was hugely popular back in New York about a year earlier. She scoured her brain, trying to recall the name of the designer behind the trend. Eb-something.

"Eb," she said out loud, hoping that would prime the word and draw it from her lips, but it still didn't come. Then she saw the style magazine article framed on the wall and the name was right there. Eblouissante. Yes, the pricey but high-quality must-have accessory from just a few seasons ago. She scanned the article, and then she saw the picture of Cathy fitted in the block of text because… Cathy Palone was the designer behind Eblouissante? Based on the other half-dozen fashion magazine articles framed and hanging around the boutique, she sure was.

"Oh, those bangles are still my favorite." Cathy returned to Nic's side. "Although, I'm pretty excited for the launch of our new glass on sterling silver drop pendants. I'm such a small-town girl at heart, I still get excited every time I get interviewed for these things. I'm sure you know what that's like with your career as an author."

"Back it up." Nic shook her head. "You're Eblouissante? You've got to be kidding me."

Cathy threw open her arms. "One and the same. Can you believe it? We keep our headquarters right here in Fisher's Creek, but our product is totally worldwide."

"That's so great." Nic clapped her old friend on the back, genuinely happy to learn of her success. She laughed inwardly, remembering how Peewee had told her his wife had a "little boutique" in town. "Your jewelry is gorgeous. My friends back in New York couldn't get enough of those bracelets last year. Totally chic on the scene. I'm so impressed—you totally did what you always dreamed about."

"Well, so did you," Cathy countered. "I remember how you were always writing in your journal. Making up stories, writing lists, documenting it all. And now you're a best-selling author. I guess we're both hometown girls who made good, huh?"

"I guess so." Nic grinned back, but before she could say anything else a loud *pop* from the front of the store made them both jump.

"That stupid lightbulb. I knew it was going to go." Cathy had her hand on her chest as if she was calming her heart. "It's been strobing all day, but I'm too nervous to climb up on the wobbly stepladder."

Nic squinted in the direction of the storefront window, the display now dark without the benefit of the overhead bulb. It would be a simple fix for the two of them. "Lucky I came along, then. Grab a replacement bulb. I'll climb up the ladder if you'll hold it steady."

"You don't have to do that."

"I don't mind. I'm happy to help."

Nic was right—with the two of them working together, the task took less than five minutes. She was climbing back down when she spotted Roxy through the big window out on the sidewalk, staring at them. Or, more accurately, staring at Nic. With a sad look in her eyes that made Nic's stomach twist. "Looks like the class reunion started early," she mumbled and hoped the guilt bubbling up in her belly didn't show on her face as she reached solid ground again.

Cathy was already waving Roxy in as Nic folded up the stepladder.

"Hi, Cathy." Roxy smiled as she poked her head in the front door, but her expression flattened when she turned her gaze to Nic. Somehow, she didn't look quite as happy to see her. "And Nicola. I saw the two of you playing Fix It Felix through the window and thought I'd say hi, but I can't stick around. I'm the closer at the bar tonight."

Nic couldn't help thinking the real reason Roxy didn't want to stick around was more about her and less about rushing to her closing bar shift at seven o'clock.

"Hey, how's your mom doing? I heard she had a little scare a few nights back." Cathy didn't seem at all embarrassed to basically admit the grapevine was abuzz talking about Mrs. Fitzpatrick.

"Just stumbled a little. Bruised her hand and wrist catching herself before she fell." Roxy shook her head, and the wisps of hair that had slipped out of her bun danced around her face. Her expression softened the way it always did when she talked about her mom. "She's okay, thanks."

"Glad to hear it." Cathy smiled. "I'll let you get on to the bar, then. It's about time for me to close up too."

This was it—the chance for Nic to casually say something to Roxy. To let her know she was sorry for the things she said the night before in her workshop. But she didn't want to do it in front of Cathy. The last thing she wanted was to insult another of her old school chums by admitting how keen she'd been to get back on the road out of town. She just needed a minute alone with Roxy to apologize and make sure everything was good between them. If she didn't do it now, who knew if she'd get another opportunity before she left? She owed Roxy more than leaving again without talking to her.

"I should get going as well." Nic found her voice again. "It was great to see you, Cathy. I love the boutique. We'll have to catch up again soon."

"Definitely at the class reunion, right?"

Nic planned to be long gone by then, but she didn't want to be a party pooper. She settled on a noncommittal "Maybe" and followed Roxy back out onto the sidewalk.

They were silent as they walked the two blocks to Roxy's parked truck. There were a lot of things Nic wanted to say, things she wanted to explain. But for someone who made a living writing words and giving characters voices, she was having a damn hard time finding the ones she wanted now.

"So, this is me," Roxy said as she grabbed the door handle of the truck, as if Nic hadn't sat beside her in the passenger seat of it for the entire ride to the Ferrisburg Flea Market only two days before. "Guess I'll see you around."

Nic's heart sank. Disappointment was plainly written on Roxy's face. Had she missed her chance to make things right because she was too concerned about finding the perfect words when all she really needed were honest ones? "No."

"No, I won't see you around?" Roxy's beautiful face scrunched up in confusion. "Are you leaving town again already? I thought your car wouldn't be fixed for a few days yet."

Was it her imagination, or did the level of disappointment on Roxy's face increase? Nic shook her head. "No. I mean, that's not what I want."

"You…*don't* want to see me around?"

Good Lord, could she mess this up any worse? Nic closed her eyes and blew out a long breath, summoning something. Courage? Honesty? The sweet spot where the two intersected on a Venn Diagram of Humanity At Its Best? "I don't want to *just* see you around. I want to see you more. Regularly. While I'm still here in Fisher's Creek." *Ugh. Words. Make words come out of your mouth.* "I want to hang out again like we did last night."

"Really? Are you sure?" The disappointment was gone from Roxy's face and replaced by something that looked like annoyance. Her fists balled on her hips did nothing to soften it. "Because last night you couldn't get out of this…how did you say it…*damn town* fast enough. So, I guess now I'm supposed to be some kind of distraction for you while you bide your time here in this terrible, godforsaken place?"

"No. I mean, yes, I said that about Fisher's Creek, but I was just frustrated about the car. I'm sorry I said it. I didn't mean to hurt you, but I can see I did. I'm truly sorry." Nic shifted her weight, rocking side to side, picking her words again. She was messing this up and she needed to make things right with Roxy—even if Roxy refused to spend any more time with her. "Look, we just connected after not speaking for thirty years. I don't want to go that long without you again. I missed you."

"You missed me? You didn't speak to me at all at graduation. You avoided me like the plague until you left for college, earlier than you were supposed to leave, I might add. I was the one who was left behind in Fisher's Creek. You knew where to find me, but you didn't. No calls, no letters. No contact at all for the past thirty years. So I'm not really here for this *I missed you* version of the story. And I shouldn't be at all surprised that you couldn't wait to leave me behind again." Roxy was opening the truck door. Nic had picked the wrong words and now she was done. "It's fine, Nic. We were kids then, we're both adults now. We're cool. I gotta get to work."

"Wait." It was now or never. "There's more to it than that. There's something I need to talk to you about. Something I should've talked to you about thirty years ago."

Roxy rolled her eyes, clearly exasperated as she hitched her hip onto the driver's seat. Teetering on the edge of hearing Nic out or making a run for it. For a moment, Nic was certain she was going to slam the door and drive away.

"Please," Nic croaked.

Her pitiful pleading must've tempered Roxy's heart. She tipped her head toward the passenger side. "Get in. It's a Monday night and Zachroll's should be pretty dead. You can talk in between me refilling the regulars."

Twenty minutes later, Nic was perched on a stool at one of the tall cocktail tables lining the wall by the bar at Zachroll's. Roxy was right—at seven thirty on a Monday night, the place was quiet. A couple of old-timers sat at the bar nursing drafts and staring wordlessly at the baseball game on the wall-mounted television. A young couple was playing darts in the back corner, but their full pitcher would last them a while. Roxy cracked the caps off two IPAs and carried them over to Nic.

"Okay. Talk," she commanded as she settled onto the stool across from her.

This was it. Thirty years of keeping the hurt bottled up was about to come undone, but the only way to move forward in any way with Roxy was to face the past. And after all the mixed signals on their nondate the night before, Nic definitely wanted to know if there was a way forward for the two of them. But would Roxy want the same? And would it even matter after the way Nic had behaved? Not only by disparaging her hometown and the life Roxy had made there, but also how she'd stayed away for all that time. Speaking the words in her heart would mean facing the humiliation of reliving that day back in school…with Roxy, of all people…but she couldn't leave town again without finding out.

"First of all, you need to know how very sorry I am for what I said last night. It was selfish of me to get so caught up in my own issues. I shouldn't have even taken that phone call. It was rude for me to pick it up while we were in the middle of a project." Nic paused and took a sip of beer. Liquid courage. She'd gotten out the first part. She was doing well. She had to keep rolling. "The truth is, back when we were in school, I had feelings for you that went beyond friendship. It was more like…romantic love."

Roxy chewed her bottom lip. "You're telling me now that you had romantic feelings for me back in school?"

"And I know that back then you weren't into me. I saw the look of horror on your face that day when you heard those fucking gossips say I was in love with you. I couldn't face you after that. I was afraid that I'd ruined our friendship, so I ran. Like a coward." She swallowed hard, pushing on. "But I got back to Fisher's Creek last week and saw you again, and all those feelings started coming back. Then I find out you're dating women now, and we were spending time together. It felt like we were really reconnecting. Hanging out with you was comfortable—just like it used to be all those years ago. But I had to go and say something stupid and act like an ass in front of you. Ruining everything again. There's really no excuse. I'm an idiot."

She got through it. She said all the words, but she still couldn't quite lift her gaze to meet Roxy's. The humiliation and the hurt that she'd felt as a teen that day by her locker came flooding back. She fought the urge to run out of the bar and leave it behind her again. She'd said what she needed to; she'd been honest with Roxy. At least now maybe she could move forward, even if she was moving forward alone.

"Hey, look at me." Roxy's voice was gentle, barely audible over the din of the baseball game on the television and the Led Zeppelin song playing on the jukebox, but held enough command for Nic's curiosity to get the best of her, and she finally looked up. "That day back in school when I saw you standing by your locker and I realized you were in love with me, that wasn't horror you saw on my face. It was surprise and relief because I finally knew you felt the same way I did."

Nic nearly knocked over her beer. She was certain she misunderstood. "What are you saying?"

A look of anguish crossed Roxy's face. Maybe Nic wasn't the only one who'd been holding on to hurt feelings all these years. "I'm saying when we were in high school, I was in love with you too."

Nic took a swig from her bottle, washing down this new information. Not to mention the shock. She'd never considered the possibility that Roxy had felt the same way. She'd just assumed the worst. "Why..." The emotions clogging her throat made it hard to speak. "Why didn't you say anything back then?"

"At first because I was scared too, I guess." Roxy paused to take a drink. Her demeanor had changed since the conversation began outside the boutique. She no longer looked angry. Her eyes carried a lot more sadness than hardness now. It seemed the conversation wasn't easy for either of them, but they were both making an effort to honestly express how they felt. That had to be a good sign. "Then after that day, you became so withdrawn. It was like you didn't want anything to do with me. I figured you just weren't ready, so I gave you your space. It was the early nineties in this small town. It wasn't easy to come out. Believe me, I get it. But then you left without us ever talking about it, and that hurt. A lot." She glanced over her shoulder at the patrons watching the game and their nearly empty beers. "Now here we are, thirty years gone, but both back in Fisher's Creek. Like some kind of second chance."

A second chance. Nic choked down the surge of excitement that bubbled inside of her. Circumstances had lined up. That didn't mean Roxy still felt the same way she did when they were kids. Those days were a long time ago. Roxy had a business to run and a mom to take care of. That was a lot on her plate already. Could she even dare to hope? "So, what do you want to do about it?"

Before Roxy could answer, a gruff voice from the bar barked, "What do we have to do around here to get a refill?"

"Duty calls. I've got to get back to work." Roxy hopped off the stool, her expression torn. She raised her index finger to signal to the guy she'd be right there. "I'm not totally sure what we should do," she confessed. "But I know that you're not planning on staying in Fisher's Creek for long, and my life is here. I had to watch you leave this town once before, and honestly, it didn't feel great. Starting up something between us just to end up watching you leave again might be playing with fire. I just don't know if this is a good idea."

"Barkeep!"

"Cappy, you know my name is Roxy," she called over her shoulder. Turning back to Nic, her eyes were sad. "Sorry, Nic. I've got to get back to it here."

Roxy went back to her business behind the bar and Nic drained the last of her beer in one long pull. It was a lot to process.

How could she have been so wrong about what happened that day? Roxy had loved her too. Had Nic's fear of rejection caused her to miss out on years of being with Roxy? No. *Shouda, coulda, woulda.* There was no use in thinking that way. She didn't regret the experiences she'd had in life—good or bad. If she hadn't left Fisher's Creek and had her life with New York, she wouldn't have Asher. And she probably wouldn't have published her book. The conversation hadn't gone the way she'd hoped, but at least she'd finally had the courage to have it. That would have to be enough for now. Having Roxy back as a friend was better than not having her at all.

She tried her best to put on a smile as she waved to Roxy on her way out of the bar. She was going to have to work out her feelings, and the best way for her to do that didn't involve sitting with the regulars and downing beers. There was a fire in her she hadn't felt in quite a while, and she knew exactly what she needed to quench it.

CHAPTER ELEVEN

Back in the guesthouse after her conversation with Roxy at the bar, Nic immediately pulled out her notebook and wrote. The words flowed miraculously from her pen as she wrote about that day back in high school and her feelings for Roxy. She wrote about the fear that had held her back from pursuing a relationship with her. She also wrote about the hurt and humiliation she'd felt when those girls whispered about her, and how she wasn't totally ready to let go of that pain. The memory still had plenty of bite, but mostly her words were ones of hope.

Her hand was cramped and her wrist was sore by the time she set her pen down more than two hours later. The pages she filled had nothing to do with the small-town mystery novel she was supposed to be working on, but it was more than she'd written since she'd left New York. And it felt amazing.

She stood and stretched, shaking the flow of blood back into her feet. She'd lost herself in her writing. It was the heady sensation that had made her fall in love with her craft in the first place.

Capturing that elusive high again after going so long without it felt totally freeing and was definitely a reason to celebrate.

The cork had just popped out of the bottle of red when she heard the knock on the door. Ten forty-five was a little late on a Monday night for Maggie to make an appearance in the guesthouse. Same with Bella or Janie, for that matter. Unless it was some kind of emergency. She was still holding the bottle of wine when she opened the door. "Roxy? Shouldn't you still be at the bar?"

"Cappy and Frank left and I closed the bar early."

"But what are you doing here?"

Roxy pushed into the guesthouse, stepping Nic backward and closing the door behind her. A couple of loose curls had fallen out of her bun and hung wildly around her face. She was not the same composed woman Nic had left at Zachroll's. Same white tank top, but under it her chest was heaving like she was breathless. She seemed to pin Nic in place with her intense gaze. "I came to play with fire."

Play with fire? Nic dumbly set the wine bottle on the coffee table and let the words sink in. Roxy was there in her space looking hot and bothered and sexy as fuck. Her pulse beat at her slim, long neck and her eyes were wide, pupils dark. A woman on a mission. Nic could take a beat to think it all through or have another conversation with Roxy about what this meant, but there was really only one thing she really wanted to do in that moment.

She pulled Roxy into her arms, their bodies finally crashing together after so many years of waiting, longing, and being kept apart. "I'm so glad you did."

There was only a moment of pause wondering where to begin and struggling against the urge to have all of Roxy at once. The wave of want that had been building for decades could drown them both. She didn't want to get sucked under and flail blindly in the current. She'd waited too long for this. She wanted to savor every sensation.

She began with a few quick kisses along Roxy's collarbone, then one lingering at the place just right of the delicate silver chain she wore on her neck. Paused at that spot, slightly north of Roxy's heart, she could feel its steady beat against her lips. She tasted the saltiness of Roxy's skin, and her head went a little dizzy. The hell with caution and perfect form, she was ready to dive in.

Finally, their lips met in the kiss Nic had waited for forever, and it was warmer and stronger than she'd ever dared imagine. Pure bliss flooded her system. The intimate connection with Roxy felt like heaven on earth. Why had she denied herself this sensation for so long? She slid her hands into Roxy's back pockets, locking her in place. Now that she had Roxy there, she might never let her go.

Fortunately, the feeling seemed mutual. Roxy moaned and deepened the kiss, her hands tangling in Nic's hair. It was a sound straight out of Nic's fantasies. A shock of pleasure jolted through her body. She had the urge to pinch herself to prove she was actually awake. Without breaking their kiss, Roxy moved her hands to the hem of Nic's T-shirt and tugged. "I want this off you," she growled.

Nic responded by grabbing a fistful of Roxy's tank top. "I'll show you mine if you show me yours." She pulled off the top to reveal Roxy's lacy, pale-pink bra. She sucked her bottom lip between her teeth and ran her gaze down Roxy's beautiful body. Every curve so familiar to Nic, yet she'd never been able to touch. Now her fingers ached for their chance to roam over every inch of her.

"Oh, I promise you, I've got plenty I want to show you." Roxy nipped at Nic's jawline before tugging her shirt over her head and tossing it aside. She wasted no time moving to unbutton Nic's jeans.

Nic breathed in Roxy's sea spray shampoo. An intoxicating scent. The whole experience had her floating on cloud nine. She struggled to keep herself grounded in the moment, not wanting to miss a thing. All of the longing, all of the desperate, heart-wrenching feelings she'd kept bottled up and hidden away all that time ago came flooding back. Roxy had been her very first love, and now she was here, half-naked in her arms. Her core fluttered and need pooled between her legs. "And I can't wait to see it."

They continued tearing off each other's clothes as they stumbled toward the bed. Nic shivered with excitement. It was like magic the way Roxy seemed to instinctively know how to touch her—light tickling touches along her shoulders, a heavier pressure as her hands worked their way down her back. Anticipation buzzed between her legs. She lay back against the pillows while Roxy positioned herself on top of her, knees straddling her. Roxy's thong matched the shade of her bra and didn't cover a whole hell of a lot.

"This is very nice." Nic ran a fingertip along the lacy edge. "I'd like to take it off you."

"Mmmm." Roxy ran her tongue along her bottom lip and gazed at her through heavy-lidded eyes. "But I'm on top of you, so I'm calling the shots here."

Nic squirmed and her middle bumped against Roxy's inner thighs. A familiar throbbing started down below. "Bossy. That's very nice too." Her husky voice surprised her.

Roxy reached up and shook her hair out of her bun before pulling it back tighter this time. "We can do this fast, or we could do this slow. What's your pleasure?"

"How about fast then slow?" Nic licked her lips. "And then maybe fast again. I mean, we have all night."

"I like the way you think." Roxy raised a sexy eyebrow at her, and Nic guessed that she could get totally lost in the galaxy of tiny freckles sprinkled across her cheeks.

When their mouths met again, Nic pushed her tongue past Roxy's lips, tasting the cinnamon gum she must have chewed on her way from the bar. Her hands roamed, exploring every inch of Roxy's body. She couldn't get enough.

Roxy seemed to feel the same way. She slid down between Nic's legs and opened her thighs to take her. Roxy's warm breath on her heat set off another flurry of elation in her middle. And then Roxy's mouth was on her, her fingers filling her.

Of all the things Nic thought could happen when she came back to town, falling into bed with her teenage dream had not even been on her bingo card. She'd carried a little bit of Roxy with her in her heart since that day she left—it was a flame that had never fully extinguished, as much as she'd tried to ignore it. But now, after all these years, Roxy Fitzpatrick rolling her tongue relentlessly against the exact spot she needed her…*bingo!*

They rocked together as the wave in her core crested and Nic drew closer and closer to tipping over the edge. She gasped and tangled her fingers in Roxy's hair, messing up that bun all over again as she finally gave in to pleasure. She held on tightly as her orgasm washed over her, and she continued to hold on tightly while she caught her breath and recovered from it. She didn't want to let go. Now that she had Roxy in her arms, she wanted to hold on to her for as long as she could.

CHAPTER TWELVE

Nic woke the next morning warm and content, wrapped in Roxy's arms. She was so comfortable that it took a moment to compute that the clunking noise that woke her from her sweet, sweet slumber was someone knocking on her door.

"Hey, sleepyhead. I made muffins for breakfast," Maggie called from somewhere in the vicinity of the doorway. "They're chocolate chip."

Apparently, her sister had let herself in, and the trifold screen that separated Nic's bedroom from the rest of the guesthouse wasn't going to keep her overnight guest a secret for very long.

Roxy's eyes flew open in alarm as if she'd had the exact same realization. Nic held a finger to her lips, signaling she should stay quiet.

"Gimme a second, Mags," Nic answered her sister. "I'm not dressed."

"I don't care if you're in your PJs," she continued as she appeared from the other side of the screen. Her eyes went wide when she saw Nic wasn't alone in the bed, and she nearly dropped the plate of muffins.

Roxy pulled the sheet up to her chin as if she could still hide, but Nic knew it was too late. She was never going to hear the end of this one.

"Maggie, you know Roxy," Nic deadpanned.

"Oh my God!" Maggie turned around so she wasn't staring at them in bed. "Yes. Hi, naked…I mean, of course, Roxy. Hi. I'm so sorry, you guys, I had no idea…I'm gonna go. Got to, uh, work."

"Okay. That's probably best," Nic agreed with a giggle as her sister scurried back to the other side of the screen again. "Leave the muffins, though. We worked up an appetite in here."

Roxy snorted and covered her mouth with her hand, holding in her laughter until they heard the door shut behind Maggie. "Any chance she's not going to tell your sisters?"

Nic shook her head. "Probably Junior too."

Roxy groaned and pulled the sheet all the way over her face.

"Hey." Nic softened her tone and gently tugged the blanket back down. "My siblings like to tease me, but don't worry, they won't go blabbing around town."

"I'm not hiding because I'm worried about people knowing about us. I'm hiding because I'm embarrassed I put you in this spot. If I hadn't come barging into your home and stayed the night, your sister wouldn't have found us together. You're the one who worries about what people will say." She grinned. "I'm actually quite proud for people to know about us."

Nic propped herself up on her elbow and gazed at the beautiful woman beside her. Her body was sated after their night of passion, and the woman she'd had feelings for since they were teenagers just said she was proud to be with her. Her chest swelled with warmth. "First of all, I'm quite happy that you came *barging* in." She lightly brushed a strand of Roxy's chestnut hair off her face. "Secondly, and maybe most importantly, I don't care about what anyone else thinks. I'm just happy we're here together right now."

"I'm glad to hear that, because I'd like you to be my date for our thirty-year high school reunion."

The damn high school reunion. She knew it was going to bite her in the butt from the minute Maggie handed her that postcard. Nic never thought she'd ever step foot in that school again. She was still surprised she'd even gone near it the other day on her walk through town. But here she was seriously considering returning. All because of Roxy Fitzpatrick—the reason she ran away from Fisher's Creek in the first place. It was kind of mind-blowing.

"You…want me to go to the reunion with you?"

"I do." Roxy nodded. "And I know you're in a big rush to get back to New York and your big, exciting life there. But you're probably stuck here until this Friday anyway. What's one more week?"

"Well, it's seven more days," Nic quipped, stalling for time. She was so ready to get the hell out of town. Not even her sisters had been able to convince her to stay longer. But truthfully, there was no good reason for her to rush back. She'd proved to herself that she could write just as well while living in Maggie's guesthouse as she could in New York. The meeting with her publisher would be over on Thursday, so that pressure would be off, and she could use the extra time to sort through the stuff she took from Aunt Aggie's house and avoid having to haul it back with her. Plus, when it came down to it, this was the chance to finally have the prom date with Roxy she'd always dreamed of. Going back to the school with Roxy on her arm just might bring everything that happened in high school full circle. It could help her heart finally heal. But would Roxy have further expectations for the two of them? Did this mean she wanted to—

"Okay, look." Roxy shifted onto her side to face her. "I can already see the wheels in your head turning, and before they totally spin out because *you have to get back*, I know this thing between us is just while you're here. It's temporary, and we both know that. I'm not trying to hold you here or anything. You're going back to New York because that's where your life is, and that's fine because I've got my own life to live here."

Or, she had absolutely no expectations for the two of them whatsoever.

"So, you're asking me to be your date for the reunion, and that's it? After that we just go back to our separate lives?" Her heart sank a bit, but at least the cards were on the table.

"Yes. Just two friends reconnecting and enjoying their time together while it lasts. Please, Nic?" Roxy was looking at her with those twinkling emerald eyes, and she slipped her hand into hers, intertwining their fingers, and suddenly Nic wondered why she'd even taken the time to think about it. Even if this was only a short-term thing between them, she would do anything this woman wanted.

She tucked a stray strand of hair behind Roxy's ear. She couldn't stop touching her. "Are you going to get me a corsage?"

"I will totally get you a corsage." The slight upward curve of Roxy's lips made Nic's heart skip a beat.

That settled it. Nic was voluntarily staying in Fisher's Creek and enjoying this *whatever* that was going on between them while it lasted.

"Then you have a date."

After Roxy left, Nic spent a few long hours staring at her notebook and Googling articles on unsolved small-town mysteries. She lost all sense of time as she tumbled down one rabbit hole after the next. The Internet was an endless source of stories containing bodies found on train tracks, women who vanished seemingly into thin air, even a few about allegedly haunted houses. Captivating tales, to be sure, but nothing that stirred inspiration in her. None of it felt right for her novel. None of it was anything she wanted to write about.

With no words flowing from her pen, and no one else home to keep her company, Nic shifted her attention to a more physical kind of work—cleaning Maggie's kitchen. It started with her tidying up the bowls and pans Maggie had left behind after making the breakfast muffins that morning, but it quickly evolved into a full deep clean of the room. There was nothing like house cleaning for a procrastinating writer. And if she was planning on camping out in the guesthouse for an extra week, she should probably start pulling her weight around the place anyway.

As she worked, she let her thoughts drift back to her night with Roxy. The feel of her soft skin as they lay in each other's arms, their warm bodies still pressed together when she woke. The delicious fulfillment of a teenage dream. Their night together was better than she ever could've imagined back then. So freaking good that she'd actually agreed to stay in Fisher's Creek for an extra week.

First the crap with the car, then the surprise about inheriting the house, it must have tipped her over the edge. She must be in shock or something. How else could she explain voluntarily staying put in that town for seven days longer than necessary? What was happening to her? Going against some of her strongest, lifelong beliefs, all for a woman. And the weird part was…she wasn't even mad about it.

The chance to spend a little more time with Roxy, and possibly a few more nights of heaven like the one they'd just shared, was just too irresistible. She was under a sex spell—that was it! There was no reason to make it a bigger thing than what it actually was: closure on the mess she'd made of their friendship back in high school. Maturity, really. Making something she'd done wrong in the folly of youth right again. Being attracted to a sexy, smart, big-hearted woman was a normal human emotion. The fact that she felt a tiny earthquake in her nether regions every time she even thought about being with Roxy didn't have to mean anything deeper than that. Nic was going back to New York after the reunion—they both knew that. They both knew damn well what they were doing.

Regardless, she was still pondering the way Roxy made her feel and giving the sink a hardcore scrub when her sister got home from work. Since Collin had gone straight to soccer practice instead of coming home after school, Nic had totally lost track of time.

"Well, there's twice today my sister's given me a shock," Maggie teased, dropping her bag on one of the kitchen chairs. "At least this time, you're decent."

"Ha ha." Nic smirked back. "The muffins were very good, by the way. Thank you for bringing us breakfast."

"Sure, the muffins were very good, but how was the muff?"

Nic barked out a laugh and threw the sponge she'd been using on the sink at her sister. It hit her square in the chest before dropping to the floor. "Don't sully a gorgeous moment between me and Roxy with your dirty thoughts."

Maggie's jaw dropped in mock surprise. "My dirty thoughts are no match for your dirty sponge." She picked up the sponge and tossed it back. "You're the one who said the two of you 'worked up an appetite.' Besides, did you really think I wasn't going to ask what happened after I found you and Roxy in bed together? Did she stay the night with you? Are you two a thing now?"

"Whoa. Yes, she stayed the night with me, but one step at a time, please." Downplay. They talked through the past, and they both had feelings for the other, that was evident. It had to be some damn strong feelings on her end for her to agree to what she did. But there was no point in sharing the details of their agreement with her sister, or anyone. What was happening between her and Roxy while she was in Fisher's Creek was strictly between them. Were they a thing? *No!* Well, yes. But only a temporary thing. Still, she couldn't hold back her smile as she thought about Roxy promising to buy her a corsage. Such a silly thing like they used to laugh about when they were kids. Damn, she'd missed that when she left. She could share a little with Maggie. "She *did* convince me to go to the high school reunion with her."

"Oh, you *must* have it bad." Maggie laughed and grabbed them each a beer from the fridge. "The Fisher's Creek High School Reunion? You, Nic? Hold on, I think I still have that postcard Mom sent over somewhere. You'll want it for your scrapbook, I'm sure."

"That's enough out of you on the subject." Nic snatched a bottle out of Maggie's grasp and twisted off the cap. She had to pace herself for the teasing. She still had two more sisters who would want to make a few jokes at her expense, plus Junior would certainly have a snide comment or two to make. Ah, the joys of a big family. "Maybe we should focus this inquisitive energy on creating a small-town mystery for my novel."

"Oh, Nic." Maggie frowned as she propped her feet up on the chair next to hers. "Still nothing? Is this kind of writer's block normal for you? Is it just part of your process? Like, did it happen with the last book?"

"No, no." Nic shook her head. "That's not what this is. I mean, I don't really believe in writer's block." Her sister just didn't get it. How could she? Maggie's world consisted of caring for others. Nurse stuff. This was a writer thing.

"What do you mean you don't believe in writer's block? It exists, or there wouldn't be a name for it." Maggie smirked. "It's the town, right? It must be killing you to have to write about a town like Fisher's Creek. You hate it here so bad that you haven't been able to write. It's given you writer's block."

"Stop being ridiculous. I wrote a ton the other day," Nic argued. "And it's not the town. I've had no problem writing about the town, or the people in the town. That's not the problem."

"Really?" Maggie blinked her surprise. "We're growing on you, huh? Or is it the magic of Roxy Fitzpatrick?"

"Maybe." Nic laughed. She hadn't considered it until then, but being back in town and seeing old friends wasn't the experience she'd expected. She'd thought it was going to be like squeezing into an itchy wool sweater that didn't fit anymore. Instead, it felt kind of…comfortable. More like a well-worn favorite cotton T-shirt. But she couldn't deny there was still something clogging her creativity. "I just can't seem to write a single word of this mystery. Nothing feels right. Not one idea I've considered inspired me to center a whole novel around it."

"What about an evil swarm of bees that arrives in town and they're, like, killer bees? Oh, or *zombie* bees. Everyone loves zombies."

"No. Besides, that's more horror than mystery. Definitely no zombies."

"Teenagers mysteriously disappearing. The popular crowd."

"No."

"An outsider moves into a long-abandoned house and suddenly all the birds in town start dying."

"Eww." Nic shuddered. "No dead animals. And is that supposed to be some kind of crack about me inheriting Aunt Aggie's house?"

"That house wasn't long abandoned, just newly uninhabited. What about a regular haunted house?"

"Ugh. No."

Maggie laughed and threw her hands in the air. "I just gave you several ideas and you don't like any of them. You can't even extrapolate from point A to come up with an idea you want to write about. Sure sounds like writer's block to me."

Nic sighed with surrender. "No. I believe when this happens it's usually a sign that I'm trying to take the story down the wrong path. It's like I'm trying to force something that's not working."

Maggie nodded slowly, like she was mulling that over. "Okay, so write something else. What about the stuff you said you wrote the other night? Can't you use that?"

"It's not exactly small-town *mystery* stuff." Nic shrugged. "It was more like journaling. Stuff about my life."

"Oh, please." Maggie rolled her eyes. "Your life. You're a whole Fisher's Creek mystery yourself. We don't know what you did all those years in New York."

"Believe me, it was nothing that mysterious." She shook her head. They were talking nonsense. She was under contract to produce. "My publisher is expecting a mystery, and that's what I have to deliver. If I don't—"

"You'll have to return your advance, and the advance is long gone. I know." Maggie grimaced and reached across the table to squeeze Nic's hand. "But can I suggest something that's going to sound like a wild idea?"

What did she have to lose at this point? "Hit me."

"I think you should write that story that does want to come out of you. Who cares if it's not what you're *supposed* to be writing? Get it out of your head. Maybe that will clear you up to write the mystery. Or maybe you'll write something even better."

"You think I should write something different? While the clock is ticking on what I actually should be writing? When I'm forty-eight hours away from a meeting where my agent and publisher are expecting me to report the progress I've made on my brilliant mystery novel?" The idea made her stomach twist with stress.

"I'm no writer, it's just my two cents." Maggie shrugged. "Take it or leave it. But it doesn't seem like you're writing much of anything this way. The kitchen looks great, though. Of course, you should probably be doing this at your own house."

Nic scanned the clean kitchen around them. She'd been super productive that afternoon, but not in any way that got words on the page and not in any way that got Aunt Aggie's house more prepared to go on the market. Maggie was right—this was quickly becoming a *desperate times call for desperate measures* situation. Maybe letting her heart story out would be the cure.

CHAPTER THIRTEEN

Wednesday morning, Nic sat with the three piles on the floor in front of her: scrapbook and loose photos, letters and various papers, and diaries. What was the right way to dig into the story of Agatha Hill? She ran her fingertips along the edge of the scrapbook. Pictures and words together seemed like a good starting point.

The book creaked when she opened the cover, as if it was yawning awake after a long slumber. The first page had a larger print of the loose photo Nic saw the day she and Bella had first found the tote. Bella had been right—one was Aunt Aggie. The caption below the pic was Aunt Aggie's scrawl: *Me and Polly, 1957.*

The following pages held pictures of events, places, times gone by, but in every one, it was either Polly or the two of them. The days of their life together. Nic stopped and studied one page that featured pictures of the yard behind the house. A row of tall sunflowers, a patch of vegetables and tomato vines creeping up stakes. Polly grinning from under a straw-brimmed hat, in coveralls and work gloves, holding a spade. The caption read: *My love in her garden.*

My love. Polly was Aggie's love?

No. That couldn't be right. Nic was just seeing what she wanted to see. She flipped the page to the next collage of photos titled *New Year's Eve in the Village, 1962.* Scenes from an extravagant party—amid balloons and party hats, the gathering of people dressed to the nines looked like they were having the time of their lives. Upon closer scrutiny, she noticed that more than one shot contained couples of the same sex. One showed Aggie and Polly holding hands and gazing lovingly into each other's eyes.

The next page was full of pictures in Paris. The page after that was Aggie and Polly off on another adventure together, this one a more tropical location. The caption under a shot of Polly on a beach, sunlight shimmering on the sea behind her, read: *Elbow Beach, Bermuda.* In another shot, Aggie was holding up the camera snapping a shot of their reflection in the mirror, Polly beside her, kissing her cheek. It became more and more clear with every page Nic turned—they were a couple.

Next, she turned to the diaries. The first one Nic picked up seemed to be from Agatha's preteen years. A young Aggie wrote about her life: lists of tasks completed while helping her mother cook and bake in the kitchen; bits of small-town gossip she'd picked up while running errands with her mother in the shops on Main Street; stories of the world outside of Fisher's Creek her father relayed at the dinner table. An entry dated June 12, 1941 was about her sister Ginny marrying Salvatore Malucci—Nic's grandparents. The wedding at the courthouse, a reception for the family and neighbors at the house.

Happy day for the Hill home as Virginia Elizabeth Hill became Mrs. Salvatore Malucci. Mother made Ginny's floor-length lace and satin wedding dress. Ginny was beautiful in the dress—full sleeves with gathered shoulders, a gathered sweetheart neckline hand-edged in beads. Mother let me help with the beading. She says I have a talent for it! After the ceremony at city hall to make everything official, Father invited all the neighbors for cake. Mother baked it herself and insisted it only be one layer to not be needlessly extravagant while the war was still on. Ginny about had a fit when she heard that plan, but Father ordered a china swan from New York City to decorate the top and soothe her sore feelings. The bride's bouquet was cut fresh from the garden at the side of our house, and Mother even made nosegays for both her and I to carry as well. The groom was handsome in a dark suit and brand-spanking new wingtips. All in all, a gorgeous day full of joy and love.

There were more entries chronicling the day-to-day life of a young girl in the forties. Apparently, Agatha continued to pursue her interest in sewing, which grew into a love of fashion. She wrote paragraphs on the latest trends—halter-top sundresses, wide-legged, high-waisted pants, blouses with rounded shoulders. She mentioned both the on- and off-screen wardrobe of Katharine Hepburn on several occasions. She actually seemed to be quite a fan of Hepburn. The diary went on like this until 1950. Then the entries stopped even though Aggie hadn't reached the end of the pages.

There may have been a missing diary, but the next one Nic could find picked up in 1952. It was a leather-bound book with Agatha's monogram embossed on the front cover. Nic read the first entry.

Father, God rest, gave me this journal on my sixteenth birthday, three years ago. It's about time I put it to good use. Today I made a friend in the park. I was sitting under my favorite oak, rereading The Wonderful Wizard Of Oz, *when a young woman ran past chasing after a cat. A cat! When she caught up with the orange tabby, she spoke to him in the sweetest, most melodic voice I'd ever heard. She was scolding him, and yet it sounded like a song. I was captivated by this young woman and felt compelled to introduce myself. She goes by Polly, and she's new here. She lives with her older brother, who came to Fisher's Creek to work construction at the plant they're building on the outskirts of town. We talked for half an hour before the cat (whose name is Happy!) became too squirmy and Polly had to take him home. I was absolutely enchanted and hated to see her go. We're meeting for lunch at the cafeteria in town.*

Nic skimmed the entries for the next couple of weeks, details of Aggie's meetings with Polly—walks in the park, more lunches at the cafeteria—until one in particular caught her eye.

The skies are bluer today, the birdsong more joyous than ever. Walking through the dappled sunlight in the park this afternoon, Polly and I stopped under that big oak where we first met. It was quiet in the park, the whisper of the breeze through the leaves of the trees the only sound. I gazed upon my beautiful walking partner and, enchanted by her radiant smile, I dared take her hand in mine. I stared at our fingers, how they entwined, a delicate touch and yet strong like we might hold on forever. When my gaze dared meet hers again, there was an instant—barely the beat of a breath—where understanding passed between us, and then our lips met in the most beautiful kiss. I kissed Polly Covington under that old oak, and my life is never going to be the same. Also, I cannot wait to kiss her again.

There it was, plain as anything. Agatha was in love with Polly. Aunt Aggie was gay!

Nic totally recognized that sentiment, the way the whole world seemed to make more sense once you learned your truth. Of course, for her it wasn't the love of her life she had kissed, it was a girl from her freshman year humanities class at the homecoming bonfire. But still, the realization was the same.

She opened the scrapbook again and flipped back to that picture of Polly in the garden. She traced her finger along the edge of the photo and studied it a little closer. This time she zeroed in on the fence post behind the woman. Carved into the wood were initials: *AH + PC.*

Suddenly, Nic needed to know more. She wanted to learn everything she could about Aggie. She had to go back to the house and see things again for herself.

When she got to the old Victorian, Nic went directly around back. She'd barely stepped through the kitchen door onto the back patio while working at the house before, but she'd hadn't spent any real time in the yard. She hadn't noticed then the wooden fence marking off the former garden that was wildly at odds with the Victorian style of the house. The space was a combination of various weeds and dry, bald patches of dirt. Sad and neglected.

Nic turned in a slow three sixty, taking in the entire backyard. The greenery was overgrown, and the plank fence was in disrepair, but if she squinted, she could make her surroundings match up with the images in Aggie's scrapbook.

My love in her garden.

She spotted the fence post where Polly had posed in her wide-brimmed hat. Shielding her eyes from the sun, she bent to examine it more closely. About two inches from the top of the post were the initials. She ran her finger over them, rough and worn by many Pennsylvania winters, but still there decades later. Evidence of a love hidden from most of the world. She closed her eyes in silent tribute, sending positive vibes out into the universe on behalf of those two women, Agatha Hill and Polly Covington.

There had been plenty of times in Nic's forty-eight years when being a lesbian hadn't been easy. But back in their time? Being gay wasn't just frowned upon, it was considered a crime or a mental illness. Discrimination was rampant. Nic's heart filled with respect and love for her great-aunt.

And then she was filled with another feeling, something that boiled in the pit of her belly. Something a lot like hot, thick anger. How could her mother have left this detail out when talking about Aunt Aggie? How could her mother have let Nic go on thinking she was alone, an outsider in Fisher's Creek, while the whole time she had a family member in the same club? Even after Aunt Aggie left her the house, her mom had remained silent on the subject. *What the hell?*

"Hey! Are you thinking about cutting back all that growth? Starting the garden again?" Eric's voice pulled Nic out of her cloud of anger. He was standing on his deck, waving at her and looking so friendly, she couldn't help but smile back.

"I don't know about that. I'm not much of a green thumb," she admitted as she crossed the yard to meet him at the property line. She'd never really looked at the neighbors' yard, but it was well-manicured and neatly landscaped. "Looks like you guys have a handle on things over here, though."

"Can't take any of the credit." Eric shook his head sadly. "This is all Jeremy. It's a real passion project for him."

"He's done a great job." She gestured at the colorful flowerbeds edging the house, then up to the blossoming dogwoods at the far side of the yard. "It's a regular paradise back here."

"Thank you. I'll pass those kind words along," Eric said. His gaze moved to the patch of yard behind Nic. "By the time we moved in the garden was gone, but Aggie showed us pictures of what it once was. She was pretty proud of it."

"I just found some of those photos while going through my aunt's belongings." Nic studied Eric—his kind eyes and easy demeanor. Aggie had trusted him, so she could too. "So, you knew about Aggie and Polly. You knew she was gay?"

"Oh, honey, she was gay as the day was long. That's exactly what she would say any time she got rolling telling us stories about her and Polly. Those two must have really torn it up in their heyday." A fond smile graced his chiseled features. "But you know, back then people couldn't exactly be loud and proud. Agatha and Polly found their people, though. A found family."

"I gathered as much from the photos. It seems like she had a very full life."

"I really believe she did."

Nic glanced behind her at where the garden used to be. She could never make it what it was when Aggie and Polly kept it up, not in her remaining time in Fisher's Creek. Possibly not even if she had all the time in the world. But she could clean it up some, maybe increase the home's curb appeal while she was still in town to help it sell. It might be doable if she had some assistance.

"Eric, you know how you offered to help out over here if I needed you?"

"Sure. Whatever you need."

"Do you think Jeremy would make that offer too?"

CHAPTER FOURTEEN

"I love the small-town angle," Cindy said in a condescending tone that suggested she was much too important to actually partake in small-town life. She was probably only half paying attention anyway. Nonetheless, Nic breathed a sigh of relief. The Thursday morning Zoom meeting with her agent and publisher wasn't going poorly, and that basically meant it was going well. Nic had delivered her pitch, and if nothing else, she'd bought herself a little more time. And this go-around—just like she'd promised Alessa—she didn't have to ask for an extension. "I think it's great that you're right there, experiencing small-town life for yourself. Living the art. So organic."

Nic focused on the screen in front of her, forcing herself to keep a straight face and not roll her eyes. Had she been that pretentious in her old life with Dana? When she was ensconced in life in the Big Apple? She forced a smile and responded the way she was expected to. "Absolutely."

Alessa beamed proudly from the screen and nodded in agreement. "I'm very excited about this whole thing. Real talk,

I think you're on the right track, and readers will be begging for the new book."

"That's the hope," Cindy continued. "And to that end, we have a plan to really get readers buzzing about the release. We've booked a series of appearances for you—bookstores mostly, a couple of libraries. You'll meet, you'll greet, you'll read a little bit from your work in progress."

Read from her work in progress? Nic still didn't know how she was going to manage to turn in the first three chapters by the month-end deadline Cindy had set for her. They wanted her to take the process public?

"I don't know," she said cautiously. She knew in her head she was supposed to agree with whatever terms Cindy presented, but her gut was screaming otherwise. "It's still very much *in progress.*"

"That's what we're going for." Cindy's enthusiasm did not waver. "Our very own small-town gal lifting the veil to give readers a peek at her upcoming release. They'll be invested in the process. They'll be hungry for the final product. Ultimately, they'll buy the book."

Now she was being sold as a *small-town gal?* Oh, hell no. This meeting was spiraling fast. She tried again. "I don't know—"

"It's going to be great," Alessa intervened. "Don't worry about it, Nicola."

She was very worried. But Cindy didn't give her the chance to argue any further. "The first appearance is all set for Saturday, June third, at Benson Books."

Fuck! That's next Saturday—the day after the class reunion. Nic's mind raced. There had to be a way out of this. Maybe if she just explained… *What? That you have a date with your dream girl, so you can't do your job?*

Meanwhile, Cindy was marching on, outlining the plan. "Then you'll do another the following day at Mystery Lovers On Church. Both events start at ten a.m. You'll do Saturday and Sunday events for three weeks in a row. Everything will be fine. Get those chapters over to me and pick a passage to read. Alessa will give you location details. I've got another meeting to get to, so I've got to bounce. Thank you both."

The screen went blank. Cindy had ended the meeting without even waiting for the goodbyes, much less an opportunity for dissent.

"No, no, no," Nic mumbled as she poked frantically at her smart phone to dial up Alessa. Her ears were actually burning with anger. This conversation was not over.

"Hello, Nicola. I figured I'd be hearing from you."

"Yeah, you're hearing from me. Did you know about this plan?" The silence on the other end of the connection answered her question, and realization set in like a lump of lead in her belly. "Oh my God. You knew the plan was to promote me as the small-town girl? You're rebranding me? Why? Why would you agree to that without consulting me?"

"I had to give them something, Nicola. Real ta—"

"Don't you fucking *real talk* me right now. I want the truth."

The beat of quiet on the line sent a jolt of fear through Nic's heart. Had Alessa hung up on her? She'd never cussed at her agent like that before, and though technically Alessa worked for her, Nic needed her if she wanted to keep her deal with Mountain Pass Press.

"Here's the truth," Alessa finally said. "We are at the *jump through hoops* part of getting this book published. If you want to keep the project afloat—if you want to publish your book with Mountain Pass and avoid having to return your advance—then it's nonnegotiable at this point. They say 'Jump,' you say 'How high?' They say 'Small-town gal,' you say 'Yee haw!'"

"Yee haw?" Despite how angry Nic was, she couldn't hold back a bitter laugh. It was like something had shorted out in her brain. Although she came from a small town, she had always considered herself to have more of a sophisticated reputation in the book world. Dana had always pushed her to present herself that way, and it certainly had worked as she navigated the release of her first book. *Small-town gal* somehow seemed like a step backward for her. Everything about this plan went against her sense of logical thought, and yet she felt herself slowly giving in to it out of sheer desperation. What other choice did she really have at this point? "Alessa, where the hell do you think I'm from?"

"I don't know, Nicola. Somewhere in the south."

"Pennsylvania. Remember? Where I am presently…on vacation. I'm a three-and-a-half-hour drive from New York City. That's it." Nic took a deep breath to pull herself together. She remembered Roxy describing herself as a small-town gal at heart when she'd talked about returning to Fisher's Creek to take care of her mom. It certainly didn't make her think any less of Roxy. It was just a part of who she was. There was nothing wrong with being from a small town. Small towns were the heart of the country, really. If playing the part at a few events was what it took to keep her career going and avoid paying back that advance, then she could do it. It wasn't forever. But there was still one other bump in the plan. "Okay, the thing is, I have a commitment here in Pennsylvania on the Friday night before that event, so is there any way you could talk to Cindy and maybe get this first reading pushed back a week at least?"

"Nicola, I need you to hear me," Alessa said. Her voice was taking on a stern edge. She was out of patience. "I don't know what about 'nonnegotiable' you don't understand, but we are not in any position to make demands. Go to your event in Pennsylvania on Friday night, then hightail it back to the city. You just said yourself it's only a three-and-a-half-hour drive. Make it happen."

It was totally doable. She'd just get up early, down a lot of coffee to chase away any post-reunion fog, and make the drive to New York. If she left early enough, she would have enough time to freshen up and change her clothes at Maryann's and still get to the bookstore on time for the ten o'clock reading.

She was going to have to suck it up and make it work. Because there was no way she was giving up her prom date with Roxy.

Nic spent the majority of the day going back through the big plastic tote of Agatha's memories, inspecting photographs and comparing them to journal entries to piece together the whole story. Trying to learn as much as she could about her great-aunt. She was obsessed. The more she uncovered about Aunt Aggie's life, the more she wished she'd gotten to know her when she had the chance. And that notion stirred up that same anger in the pit of her belly all over again. Anger that her mother had hidden this truth from her for all those years. It wasn't right.

It took the entire time she spent dolling herself up for the evening out for her to shake off those hurt feelings. She could be mad later—she wasn't about to let anything spoil her evening with Roxy. She spun around and gave herself one last look in the full-length mirror. The silky, deep-green keyhole peasant blouse Maggie loaned her was a perfect match with her favorite dark jeans. Her hair was clipped back off her face, and a simple, solitaire diamond on a thin silver chain sparkled at her throat. Pleased that she'd created a stunner of an outfit for their first real date, she clicked off the lights and slipped out the front door of the guesthouse to wait for Roxy. She heard the pickup coming down the lane before she saw it. Her heart fluttered with excitement, and she bit back what she suspected would read as a goofy grin. She practically skipped down the driveway to meet her date.

"You look incredible." Roxy hopped out of the cab and greeted her with a kiss on the cheek.

"You clean up okay too." Nic cringed. She was an author and that was the best she could come up with? "I mean, you look incredible too."

Roxy opened the door and waited for her to climb in before running back around to the driver's side. "I hope you are ready for the best cheeseburger of your life. This burger is going to rock your world." She glanced over. "Wait. Oh my God, do you still like cheeseburgers? You haven't gone vegetarian, have you?"

"No." Nic's laugh came easily thanks to a case of the nerves. *Easy, there, Nic. Calm down.* She'd been best friends with Roxy when they were in high school. They'd seen each other naked the other day. There was no reason to be nervous around her now. "I still love a good burger, so you better not be playing with my emotions. 'Rock my world' is a high bar for ground beef."

Ferrisburg was hardly a booming metropolis, but it boasted a metroplex, a bowling alley, two strip malls, and, of course, a flea market. Practically Pleasure Island compared to Fisher's Creek. The twenty-five-minute drive out of town to Ferrisburg passed quickly as they chatted about their days. Nic admitted she'd continued her procrastination streak over the past few days by deep-cleaning the guesthouse, then moving on to tackle Collin's bedroom. She left out the part about going through Aunt Aggie's tote, though. She was having too much trouble processing her emotions about it. She wasn't ready to share her discovery with the world. Luckily, Roxy steered the conversation to some of the upcoming promotions she planned for the bar, including bumping karaoke night up from a once-a-quarter happening to a weekly thing. The one scheduled for the following week sounded like a must-do for the Dickenson sisters. Nic made a mental note to get it on their calendars.

The sign outside of Ruba's Bar And Grill claimed it was home of the best burger in the tristate area, and Nic couldn't stop her mind from sliding to the thought of how that distinction was made. Was there some kind of burger cook-off Ruba had actually won? Had Ruba themself gone from town to town across the three states tasting every burger along the way until they were satisfied that they did, in fact, serve up the superior sandwich? Hell, all it had taken to convince Nic was Roxy's word, but by the time the hostess led them to their table, the mouthwatering smells in the restaurant had her stomach rumbling so insistently that she would've settled for the second- or even the third-ranking burger in the land.

They ordered a cheeseburger each, and fries and onion rings to share. The perfect bar foods to go with the frosty mugs of beer they were already sipping. Once the server left the table, Roxy settled back in her chair and gave Nic a full once-over, as if memorizing her look from head to toe. Her gaze seemed more analyzing than hungry, but certainly not disinterested.

Nervous laughter bubbled up in Nic again. *Seriously, what is that about?* "You look like you have something to say. Care to share?"

"No. I mean, yes. I'm just wondering about something you said on the drive out here, but I don't want to overstep any boundaries."

Good. They had boundaries. That was good to know. Sure, they had slept together in a fit of passion, but that didn't mean they went from zero to sixty, zooming up the relationship scale. This was technically a first date, after all. This was still a getting-to-know-each-other-again time. And, most notably, this was temporary.

"You're not overstepping." Nic shook her head. "You can ask me anything. I'm an open book." God, had she become the most stereotypical author type ever? At least in the tristate area.

Roxy looked doubtful, like she already knew getting an honest answer out of Nic would be like herding cats. "You said you were procrastinating when you were supposed to be writing—"

"And you're wondering if I'll come give Zachroll's a deep clean next time?"

Roxy's arched eyebrow said *Told ya* without her having to speak the words. "No. I was wondering what was holding you back from writing this book."

Nic gazed into those emerald eyes that seemed to be laser focused with concern. Acutely aware of the reinforced first date redo boundaries, she chewed her bottom lip, considering how much she should share. "Maggie thinks I've got writer's block."

"Do you though?"

"I don't believe in it." Nic couldn't help cracking a smile at Roxy's puzzled look. *Here we go again.* "Never mind. The point is, I know I'm *able* to write, I'm just not really into the mystery that I'm supposed to be writing."

"What is the mystery?" Roxy leaned back in her chair and took a long drink of her beer. Like she had all the time in the world to hear about Nic's book.

It was a nice change from what Nic was used to. Dana had never wanted to hear about the brainstorming part of her writing. She was much more into the part where the work was done and the success was evident—both in terms of money and prestige. Roxy's willingness to talk through the process was like a breath of fresh air, but unfortunately it still didn't magically solve Nic's story woes.

"That's part of the problem," Nic confessed, boundaries slipping away. "The mystery itself is a mystery to me."

Roxy screwed up her face as if thinking extra hard. "A dead body shows up."

"No."

"*Four* dead bodies."

"No."

"Blow something up."

Nic stared across the table, a hard blink the silent *no* this time.

"What?" Roxy shrugged. "Isn't that what they tell writers to do when a story seems stagnant? Blow something up?"

"You're not wrong." Nic sighed in surrender. Somehow an explosion didn't seem like a solution to her real problem with the story. "The thing is, I'm not sure this is the book I want to write."

"What book do you want to write?"

Ah. There were the boundaries. Nic felt them slide safely back into place.

Between the conversation with her sister and her assessment of Aunt Aggie's scrapbooks and diaries, she had a fairly solid idea of the story she wanted to write taking form in her mind. But was she ready to share that with Roxy? Not quite yet. Hell, she hadn't even told Roxy about what she'd uncovered in the box her great-aunt had left her. "It's more of a…well, it's a…it's not a mystery."

Roxy reached across the table and grasped her hand. "It's okay. You don't have to tell me what it's about for me to know that it's the book you should be writing. Follow your heart. You can't go wrong writing that."

Nic's head went a little dizzy. She was touched that Roxy respected her time frame on sharing. And she was relieved she didn't have to say it out loud yet. "You think I should write the book of my heart?"

"I really do."

"What if it doesn't sell? What if my publisher doesn't even want it?"

"Then you'll write something else after that."

Nic wanted to jump across the table, take Roxy in her arms, and show her just how full her heart felt in that moment, but instead she settled for a shared smile as their food was delivered to the table.

She was two heavenly bites into what most certainly was the most delicious cheeseburger of her life, just like the sign outside promised, when their meal was interrupted by a thirty-something busty blonde wearing too much eye shadow and a really low-cut V-neck shirt.

"Roxy Fitzpatrick? What brings you to Ferrisburg?" The woman spread her arms. Roxy appeared to take the hint and rose to greet her with a hug. "You look great. It's so nice to see you."

"Same." Roxy smiled politely when they finally stepped apart. She clapped her hand on the younger woman's shoulder and held eye contact a beat longer before she gestured at Nic. "Shannon Sheppard, this is Nicola Dickenson."

Nic waved her fingertips, but Shannon didn't even seem to notice. She didn't seem to be able to tear her gaze off Roxy. Nic nibbled on a fry while Roxy wrapped up her conversation with Boobsy McGee. When Roxy finally took her seat again, Nic raised a questioning eyebrow and hoped she would fill in the blanks. Not that it was any of her business, but she couldn't help feeling curious about the interloper.

"What?" Roxy asked before taking a big bite of the burger.

"Nothing. It's just that I'm wondering about the woman who eyed you up like *you* were the best burger in the tristate area."

"Shannon? I know her from the local business owner's association. She's…"

"Enthusiastic?" Nic supplied.

Roxy laughed. "That's a good word for it." Her brow furrowed, but her eyes twinkled with teasing. "Are you a little bit jealous?"

"Jealous?" Nic repeated and dragged a french fry through the puddle of ketchup on her plate. Was that what that weird tug at her gut was when she watched Roxy hug that over-friendly, bouncing blonde? *Oh.* "Okay. Maybe just a little."

Roxy nodded, finishing the last bite of her sandwich. After wiping her mouth with a napkin, she fixed Nic with a tender stare. "I assure you, there's no reason to be. She's a business acquaintance, that's all." She sucked her bottom lip between her teeth, taking a beat. Looking extra sexy. "You have all of my attention tonight.

And once you're done eating, I'm going to take you into the back room."

"Now *you* have all of *my* attention."

Roxy's laugh was throaty and sexy this time and sent a shiver down Nic's spine. "To play pinball. They've got some awesome vintage machines back there. I want to show them to you."

"You've got a passion for pinball. I didn't know that about you."

"I do. Do you play?"

"I don't, but I could."

Roxy quickly settled their bill at the bar, grabbed a couple of fresh beers, and led Nic to the back room. In addition to the four vintage pinball machines, the small wood-paneled room also had *Pac-Man*, *Dig Dug*, and a foosball table. Very 1980s. Nic loved it.

"Wow." She gasped. "Do you bring all your dates back here?"

Roxy pulled her close and whispered in her ear, "Again, only you."

A wave of heat washed over Nic and settled between her legs. The warmth of Roxy's body against hers was a superb sensation and sent images of where this night could lead flying through Nic's mind. She drew back and smiled. "Then let's play."

They selected a pinball machine called *Alien Attack*, and Roxy produced a handful of quarters from the front pocket of her jeans to get started. Nic stepped into position as player one and placed her hands on the buttons on either side of the game.

"You're going to help me with this, right?" No sooner were the words out of her mouth than Roxy was pressed up hard against her, arms wrapped around to guide her hands on the flipper buttons.

"Don't worry." Her breath tickled Nic's neck. "I got you. Now, just keep your eye on the ball." She let go of Nic's hand long enough to pull the plunger and release the silver ball.

Bells and buzzers sounded while the ball bounced from bumper to bumper on its way down the playfield. Nic was poised for action, fingers on the buttons, trying to focus on the ball despite the way Roxy's chest pressed against her back, making her own nipples harden. When the moment came, they batted the ball with the flippers, sending it whizzing back to the top of the board again. Their hips swayed and bumped as they worked the controls, and the ball made several successful trips up and down the playfield before it managed to finally slip past them. The digital display blinked as their score tallied, and when the number appeared, Nic raised her arms in victory and twisted to face Roxy.

"Not too bad for a newbie, huh?" Nic saw the joy she felt mirrored on Roxy's face. Excitement surged through her as she threw her arms around Roxy and pulled her into a deep kiss.

Heat flooded her body, and she spun Roxy back against the machine. She toyed with the idea of boosting her onto it and parking herself between her legs, but she suspected Ruba wouldn't take kindly to them abusing the game like that.

"That kiss wasn't too bad either." Roxy grinned when they paused to breathe.

"Then maybe we should do it again," Nic murmured as she leaned in again, but before their lips met, an image reflected in the glass of the scoreboard caught her eye.

She wouldn't have let it distract her, except she recognized that green cap pulled low. It was the same one her brother-in-law Chad wore the day she spotted him hiding behind the menu in Bo's Diner. "Oh my God." She turned, but he was already out of her sight line.

"What is it?" Roxy grabbed for her hand, but Nic slipped out of her grasp.

"I'll be right back." She rushed out of the back room and spotted him by the exit. It was definitely Chad, but what the hell was he doing in Ferrisburg? A server carrying a large tray of food cut off her path. She called out his name, but he didn't stop, and he didn't look back. He didn't acknowledge her at all, in fact, Instead, he seemed to move faster as he pushed through the door and out into the dark parking lot.

Why would Chad be in a burger shack in Ferrisburg? Didn't Bella say he was at some meeting at the Lodge? Why would he lie about that and then duck out of town? Unless…

"Nic, are you okay?" Roxy grabbed her arm before she could run into the parking lot. "You look like you've seen a ghost."

"No ghost." She frowned. This was starting to seem much worse than a boogeyman. "But I think my sister's husband is cheating on her."

CHAPTER FIFTEEN

The day after her cheeseburger date with Roxy, the words were finally flowing again, and although she wasn't exactly sure where the story was taking her, Nic was relieved. Relieved that the magic wasn't gone, that her career could still have some breath left in it, and that she was right and Maggie was wrong—there was no such thing as writer's block. Of course, it wasn't lost on her that the times she seemed to be most inspired to put words on paper were after spending time with Roxy. Maybe she'd finally found the muse she needed. Whatever it was, she'd take it. She was making progress.

She'd just set her pen and notebook down for the evening, ready for a break, when there was a rapping on the guesthouse door.

"Y'all decent in there?" Maggie called out from the other side.

Nic yanked the door open and frowned at her sister. "You know damn well I'm the only one in here." She stepped aside and let Maggie in. "Besides, it's Friday night. Roxy is busy working at the bar."

"I damn well know nothing of the sort. For all I know, you're having another naked sleepover in here," Maggie teased. "Anyway, did you turn your ringer off or something? I've been texting you for the past thirteen minutes straight. Janie's at the house, and we need to get our game plan together before Bella arrives."

Nic slipped on her flip-flops and grabbed her phone out of the drawer in the end table. "I had to stow the temptation. Sorry. I'm ready, though. How are we going to tell Bella?"

"Yeah, damned if I know."

They marched across the backyard toward the big house in silence. In Maggie's kitchen, Janie was already making margaritas and greeted them with her typical bright, energetic smile despite the unhappy reason for the gathering.

"Booze already flowing?" Nic planted a kiss on her baby sister's head. "Shouldn't we at least wait until Bella gets here?"

"This sucks and tequila makes everything better." Janie shrugged. "Besides, I can make a second batch when she gets here. I have a feeling this is a two-drink conversation anyway."

"Good point," Nic agreed as she pulled four margarita glasses from a cabinet. "Speaking of the two-drink conversation, what are we going to say to Bella?"

"I'm not so sure we should go jumping to conclusions." Maggie paused while the whir of the blender filled the kitchen. When Janie started to pour the drinks, she continued, "You never actually saw Chad with a woman, did you?"

"Or a man," Janie interjected. Her eyes went wide with forced innocence under her sisters' stares. "What? We don't know *everything* about Chad. Open your minds, people. I expect better from you." She gave Nic a pointed look.

Nic chose to ignore it. "No, I didn't actually see Chad with a…" She glanced over at Janie. "*Person*. But he has been lying to Bella, and he has been sneaking around. So, I think it's safe to say *something* is going on here. Something Chad doesn't want anyone to know about."

"Chad doesn't want anyone to know about what?"

All three of them turned to see Bella standing by the back door.

"What's going on?" Bella dropped her purse on a chair and accepted the margarita glass Janie held out to her.

Maggie grabbed Bella by the shoulders, steered her to one of the stools at the breakfast bar, and forced her to sit. "There's something we need to talk to you about, but we don't want you to freak out."

"Freak out?" Bella's voice came out in a strangled burst. Storms brewed in her eyes as she took a long swig of her drink as if fortifying herself for what was coming next. "The three of you are ganging up on me, but I'm not supposed to freak out?"

"We're not ganging up on you." Nic squeezed Bella's shoulder before climbing onto the stool next to her. It was important she knew they were there to support her. That was one thing they'd all agreed on when they decided to have this chat with Bella. "We have a concern, and we want to discuss it with you."

"How concerned are we talking?" Bella frowned. "Am I going to need more than one of these?"

"You might." Janie carried the pitcher over, ready to serve.

"Honey, you know we love you so much," Maggie began, easing into the conversation.

"Oh, this is bad." Bella drained her glass. Janie refilled it the second she set it down.

"Shh." Nic covered Bella's hand with her own, trying to soften the blow that was coming. "Just remember, we're here for you."

"Someone just spit it out, please," Bella begged.

Nic chewed her bottom lip. Thinking through how to be truthful without jumping to conclusions. Just the facts, ma'am. "I saw Chad last night in Ferrisburg. When you said he was going to be at the Lodge. Did you know he wasn't at the Lodge?"

Bella's face clouded with confusion, like she was trying to make sense of Nic's words. She clearly didn't know. "Chad lied to me?"

"There was another time too. I saw him at Bo's Diner one afternoon when I thought you said he was supposed to be somewhere else." How long ago was that? Definitely before she'd gotten together with Roxy. The day they went to the flea market—that was it. "It was a Saturday. You said he had some sort of school thing, I think."

"Yeah, I remember that, but why would Chad lie to me?"

Maggie cast an uneasy glance in Nic's direction before gently responding, "Honey, do you think it's possible that Chad is having an affair?"

Bella sat up straighter on her stool, hackles raised, and her expression hardened. "Absolutely not." Her blond curls swayed as she shook her head. "Chad would never do that to me."

"But, Bella, he for sure lied to you," Janie argued. "Nic saw him in Ferrisburg when he told you he'd be at the Lodge."

Bella deflated at that and took a long drag of her margarita. "I guess that's true. But an affair? Chad wouldn't. Never."

"Well, you deserve the truth about it." Nic wasn't feeling the same *tread lightly* vibe Maggie was about the situation. She was too familiar with knowing something was off in your relationship but not quite having a handle on what that thing was. She'd been there too many times with Dana. In some ways, the limbo of not knowing was even more excruciating than facing the bad news itself. She didn't want any of that for Bella. "What are you going to do?"

"I just can't go home tonight and accuse my husband of cheating on me because you saw him at a restaurant in Ferrisburg and maybe at Bo's Diner too. That's a big stretch, and as pissed off as I might be about a white lie he told, if I march in there and accuse him of something that ends up being a big mix-up, I'm going to come out of it looking like a total asshole."

"Sounds like we only have one choice, then." Janie raised her glass, a hint of a smile tugging at the corners of her mouth. "We've got to bring back the Dic-tectives."

Nic groaned. "No, don't start that again."

Maggie raised her glass as well, the glee plain on her face. "To the Dic-tectives!"

"Please stop saying that."

"Hush up, all of you," Bella said. Her eyes were squeezed shut and she rubbed her temples. It was possible she didn't find the prospect of her sisters snooping around and spying on her husband especially entertaining.

"Bella's right," Nic spoke up. "This isn't a joke. This is her marriage. Her business, not ours."

"Screw that." Janie paused midpour and slammed the tequila bottle back down on the countertop. "You all know how this works—you mess with one Dickenson sister, you mess with us all. All our spouses knew that when they signed on."

"That's true." Nic sighed her surrender. "You'll never catch Dana in Pennsylvania again for that very reason."

"We'd better not." Bella snapped back to life. "That woman is right to stay far, far away from us."

"There's my big sis." Janie raised her glass again.

"See? That's how we do it," Maggie agreed. "So, what's our plan?"

There was no sense in resisting. Once her sisters set their minds on something, that was that. What the hell—they would do it for her too. "Well, I can't say it's a pattern for sure, but he's missed the last two Sunday suppers. Sunday nights could be a standing date."

"In fairness, you missed the last one too." Typical Bella, jumping to Chad's defense even as they were planning to catch him in his deceit.

"Good point, but Nic didn't lie about her whereabouts." Janie dismissed Bella's comment and picked up the thread. "Let's plan on tailing him this Sunday if he gives you another excuse to miss Sunday supper. We'll check out where he goes, and then confront him when we catch him in his web of lies."

"We're all going to bail on dinner?" Maggie grimaced. "Mom will have a fit."

"We'll have a little look-see at what Chad is up to and circle back to Mom and Dad's before the food is on the table." Nic shrugged. "Besides, they'll be having so much fun entertaining the grandkids, they probably won't even miss us."

"Well, they'll probably catch on that we're not there when we dump our kids on the doorstep," Bella said, getting up to make another batch of margaritas.

"They'll get over it." Janie shoved her empty glass across the counter toward Bella. "How much fun is a sister stakeout going to be?"

"The Dic-tectives are back!" Maggie cheered.

Nic blew out an exasperated sigh. She couldn't even produce a fictional mystery for her novel, and here she was playing amateur sleuth in real life. The truth truly was stranger than fiction. It was just so damn easy to get caught up in anything once her sisters got rolling on an idea. She was swept up before she even knew what she was agreeing to. Surrendering to the power of the Dickenson sisters, she held out her glass for a refill. "Fine. But this is our last mission and then we're retiring for good."

Thanks to that third batch of margaritas with her sisters, Nic was feeling more than a little fuzzy Saturday morning as she walked through town, big-frame sunglasses covering her face to help her cope with the brightness of the day. She might have ignored Peewee's voice mail until later except he sounded so damn excited in his message that he had a surprise for her at the shop. Brighter than the Fisher's Creek ten a.m. sun. The mechanical buzz that sounded when she pushed through the heavy door to the office next to the garage split through her skull, but it did the trick and pulled Peewee in from the workshop.

"Hey, you're here!" He greeted her with his wide smile. "I have the best news for you."

"That's what you said on your voice mail." She tried to smile through the splitting pain in her head. It wasn't Peewee's fault she'd drank her weight in tequila the night before. "Hit me with it, Peewee."

"Your car is done."

"My car." Nic frowned. It was the wrong reaction. Peewee was looking at her like she'd sprouted a second head.

"The Tesla." He scratched his head and squinted at her. "It's all fixed. You can take it today. You can finally get out of Fisher's Creek."

He was right. She had no excuse for staying in Fisher's Creek now that the Tesla was functioning again. She was free to go wherever the hell she wanted. But the truth was, since she had agreed to stay and be Roxy's date at the reunion, she had pretty much stopped thinking about the Tesla. It suddenly struck her that as desperate as she'd been just a week earlier for the car to be repaired, she just didn't give a damn about it now.

"Nic? Are you okay?" He put a surprisingly gentle, meaty hand on her shoulder. "You can pick up the car later if you're not feeling well."

"No, I'm fine." She smiled to prove it. "I'm just…well, obviously I'm going to stick around for the reunion next weekend, so I'm not going to leave town quite yet."

Peewee's eyes went round as pie plates. Clearly word of the big date had not made it all the way around Fisher's Creek. "You're going to the reunion? Cathy said you girls were talking about it, but I said there was no way you'd step foot back in that school. I mean, when I towed you into town you made it perfectly clear that you weren't sticking around a minute longer than absolutely necessary." He seemed to suddenly have a *read the room* moment. He looked at his feet and cleared his throat before taking a different route with the conversation. "Anyway, I'm happy you'll be there. And I know Cathy will be glad too. All the old gang will be at the reunion. It's gonna be a good time."

Nic wasn't so sure about the old gang, but she was certain that being Roxy's date would make any event a good time. This time when she smiled at him, it was much more genuine. "You know, Peewee, I think you're right about that."

CHAPTER SIXTEEN

Sunday evening found the Dickenson sisters crouched down in the upholstered burgundy seats of the twenty-year-old Oldsmobile Nic borrowed from Peewee for the purpose of tailing Chad on his mysterious weekly outing.

"Tell me again why you're driving this hunk of junk instead of your Tesla?" Janie asked.

"Because the four of us don't fit comfortably in the Tesla and it's just about the least inconspicuous vehicle in the world, much less Fisher's Creek. Chad would've spotted us coming a mile away," Nic answered. Peewee had seemed confused about her request to trade him the Tesla for the Oldsmobile for the night, but not opposed to it. Of course, she didn't go into detail about why she needed the vehicle, just said she needed more space for additional passengers.

"But we would've looked so much cooler cruising around in the Tesla," Janie whined.

"Where did he say he was going this time?" Nic changed the subject with a stage whisper over her shoulder—as if they were in any danger of being overheard while hiding in their ride.

"The Lodge to help with post-bingo cleanup," Bella sighed from the back of the car.

"That is not this." Nic felt no joy in confirming Chad flat-out lied to his wife.

With a "humph," Maggie slouched down a little further in the front passenger's seat. She didn't seem to be enjoying the outing either.

"Pull over there," Janie instructed from the back seat as Nic followed Chad's truck into the parking lot of J.T.'s Steakhouse. "Just park by that dumpster and let's see if he goes in."

"Why wouldn't he go in?" Bella leaned forward to stick her head between the two front seats. "He drove all the way out here to Ferrisburg to this restaurant, and you think he's just going to sit there in his car?"

"Shh!" Nic scolded and clicked off the ignition. "There he is."

A hush fell over the sisters as they watched Chad cross the lot and push through the glass front doors of the steakhouse.

"He was alone," Maggie pointed out. "So, there's that."

"That doesn't prove anything," Nic argued. "He could be meeting his date inside. We've got to go in after him and find out."

"Maybe he's going to come right back out." Bella shrugged, but when they all gave her a doubtful look, she seemed to rethink it. "Okay, maybe we should just wait a minute and see if anyone shows up to meet him."

Janie rolled her eyes. "How the hell will we know if someone is here to meet him if we can't see him?"

Maggie twisted in her seat. "Janie, you really are good at this sleuthing stuff. Very logical."

"It's a gift."

"Hush, you two. Look." Nic pointed through the windshield at a red Mini Cooper parking two spots away from Chad's truck.

The tall redhead in tight black jeans and red patent leather fuck-me heels emerged from the car, checked her bright-red lipstick in the driver's side mirror, then sauntered toward the entrance of the restaurant.

"That woman is really working a theme," Janie snarked. "Red-hot mama."

"That's gotta be her. That's our woman." Nic clapped her hands to call her sisters to action. If they were going to solve a mystery, they may as well get to it. "Let's go. This is not a drill. Move it, move it, move it!"

The women tumbled out of the Oldsmobile and scurried across the parking lot. Janie was the last one to make it inside. "There she is—by the bar."

Nic's stomach dipped nervously as she glanced in the direction her sister was pointing. Solving the mystery would be satisfying, but if the redhead was the missing link, it wouldn't be good news for Bella. To her relief, their suspect was being greeted by a group of women already seated at a tall cocktail table. She was obviously there to meet up with them—not Chad.

"Wrong again, sister." Maggie clapped her on the back, but for once Nic didn't mind being wrong.

"So where's Chad?" Janie frowned. "He definitely came in here."

"There he is," Bella said, her gaze fixed on a table in the back of the dining room.

Nic followed her stare to a booth where Chad, sans green cap this time, was seated with his back to them. He appeared to be alone, but was he waiting for someone? Or had his dining companion merely stepped away from the table for a moment?

"He's really here." Bella's voice had taken on a faraway quality, like she was having some kind of out of body experience. "He lied to me and skipped out on Sunday supper to come here. For what?"

Maggie slipped an arm around Bella's waist, bolstering her. "We're here anyway, so do you want to find out the answer to that question?"

Bella seemed to snap back to reality, and her eyes got that steely look that made her a shark in the courtroom. "Let's do this."

Her sister marched toward Chad's booth, and the others filed after her. Nic tripped over her own feet trying to keep up. Smooth as a summer breeze, Bella swept into the bench across from him and Janie and Maggie next to her. As the last one to arrive at the table, Nic got stuck sitting next to Chad.

"Bella!" The color drained from Chad's face. "And *all* of your sisters. What are you doing here?"

Janie slapped her palms on the table. "That's what we should be asking you. So tell us, Chad. What are *you* doing here?"

Bella shot her a warning look. "Chad, what is going on? You told me you were going to the Lodge, but here you are in a restaurant in Ferrisburg. What the hell is that about?"

Chad opened and shut his mouth a few times in succession like a fish out of water gasping for air. No sound came out. No answers. Only a red tomato face full of shame.

Nic's heart sank. Poor Bella. They'd caught Chad in his lie and now they'd all have to face it. Maybe they should give the couple some privacy.

"Damn it, Chad." Apparently Janie couldn't hold back any longer. "How could you do this to Bella?"

"I know. I'm sorry. I was only going to do it once, but then it was *so good*, I did it a second time. And now here we are." He covered his anguished face with his hands.

"A *second* time?" Bella's voice was about two octaves higher than normal. "You bas—"

"Here you go, hon. Ribeye medium rare." The waitress delivered a huge slab of meat to the table and eyed up the sisters with surprise. "I thought you said no one else was joining you. Do you gals want menus?"

"A steak?" Bella's eyes nearly popped out of her head. "You're cheating on me with beef?"

"I'm gonna give y'all a minute." The waitress retreated, looking more than a little confused, and for a beat the table was shrouded in stunned silence.

Until Bella threw her head back and howled with laughter, and her sisters joined in. Only Chad was left looking bewildered and a little bewitched by the force of nature that was the Dickenson sisters.

"He just wanted a steak!" Maggie's hands were shaking in the air hallelujah style, and the sisters cracked up all over again. "The Dic-tectives were on an actual *steak*-out!"

"Wait." Chad shook his head. "Are y'all mad at me or not?"

"Oh, I'm mad," Bella said pointedly, eyeing up the ribeye before reaching across the table and taking her husband's hand. "But, baby, I love you so much."

"All right, sisters." Janie snapped her fingers, rounding them up. "That's our cue."

"Yep," Maggie agreed as the three of them shuffled out of the booth. "Why don't you two have a nice dinner together, and we'll get back to Mom and Dad's for Sunday supper."

"Good night, sisters." Bella dismissed them.

Nic linked her arms through Maggie's and Janie's and directed them toward the door. "Another—and most importantly, final—mystery solved by the Dic-tectives."

Nic enjoyed Sunday supper with the family a little more than usual on the heels of the successful stakeout. She even managed to put her sore feelings about her mom not telling her about Agatha and Polly on the back burner for the evening. But once they finished washing the dishes at her parents' house, she was itching to tell Roxy about the adventure with her sisters. The texts she sent Roxy during dessert had gone unanswered, but that wasn't unusual if things were busy at the bar. A trip out to Zachroll's seemed in order. She could sit and have an after-dinner drink, filling Roxy in on what happened with Chad while she took care of her business. She turned in her tea towel, kissed her mom on the cheek, and headed out to Zachroll's.

"Hey, Ryan," she called cheerfully as she entered the bar. The crowd sure didn't look big enough to require both Roxy and Ryan behind the bar. Cappy and Frank, Roxy's faithful regulars, were in their usual seats and there was a smattering of other patrons occupying cocktail tables, but nothing out of hand. "Is Roxy in the office?"

"Didn't she call you?" Ryan stopped wiping down the bar to rub his stubbled chin. "Her mother had an emergency. They think it was a stroke. Roxy went to the hospital to be with her."

"Mrs. Fitzpatrick had a stroke?" Nic's stomach clenched. "Is she going to be okay? I mean, what happened?"

Ryan's brow furrowed as he shrugged. "That's all she said before she tore out of here. I'm sorry. I don't have any more information."

"It's okay. Thanks, Ry," Nic called over her shoulder as she rushed out of the bar.

It suddenly made sense why Roxy hadn't responded to her texts. Nic had been making cracks about spying on Chad while Roxy was dealing with an actual family emergency. She continued berating herself the entire drive to the hospital, and by the time she made it to the emergency room she was feeling like a royal jerk. But when she saw Roxy slumped in one of the molded plastic chairs in the waiting room, all her inward thoughts dropped away. The only thing on her mind was comforting Roxy.

"Roxy." Nic breathed out her name as she slid into the hard, cold chair beside her. "Ryan told me you were here—that your mom had a stroke. Did you see your mom? Is everything…"

She held up a hand to hush her. "The doctors confirmed it wasn't a stroke. It was just a TIA—a mini-stroke." Roxy's gaze flicked to Nic once more and she added, a bit quieter, "I guess that's better than a full-out stroke? Gave me a hell of a scare in the moment, but she's going to be okay. She's stable now, and I was going to go home and get cleaned up. I just needed a minute."

Nic pulled her into her arms. Roxy melted against her. "Oh, Roxy, I'm so glad she's okay."

"Me too," Roxy whispered.

"You must be beat. Why don't you let me drive you home? We can come back for your truck tomorrow."

Roxy sat back up and looked her up cond down. "Wait a minute. How did you even get here? Did Peewee finally fix your car? Oh my God, do I finally get to ride in the infamous Tesla?"

Nic couldn't help but laugh at Roxy's delight. "Yes, but no."

Roxy narrowed her tired eyes. "Keep saying words."

"Peewee fixed the Tesla, but we'll be riding in an Olds." She shook her head at Roxy's confused look. "I have a lot to catch you up on. C'mon, I'll tell you on the way home."

CHAPTER SEVENTEEN

They'd been working on Aunt Aggie's garden all morning, and Nic was so proud of the progress they'd made. She'd taken Eric and his husband up on their offer to help and capitalized on Jeremy's yard work expertise. The guys had been happy to pitch in and restore the garden to something closer to Aggie's original vision for it.

Nic and Roxy started the project on Monday afternoon by pulling out the smaller weeds and generally cleaning up the yard. But Tuesday morning they really got serious, digging up the bigger weeds and clearing the patch of land behind the house with Eric and Jeremy's help. Jeremy had insisted they do the job without chemicals, and since he was the expert of the group, the others complied.

The process had been a long, grueling one, and the late morning sun had them all drenched with sweat. Proof of hours of hard work. Finally, their morning of toil drew to a close. Eric hosed down the garden area, then Jeremy rototilled it while the others prepared some refreshments. By the time they brought the tray of fruit and cheese and a pitcher of lemonade out onto the patio, he was finishing up.

"Come put on a fresh shirt and cool off with a drink," Eric called to his husband as he filled cups with lemonade.

Jeremy made a few more passes with the machine before powering down and joining them on the patio. He used the hose to soak his head and hands before accepting the change of shirt and glass of lemonade.

"Please tell me that all the manual labor means you're thinking about moving in," he said between sips. "We would love to have another family member in the neighborhood again."

"Again?" Roxy frowned. "I know my bar is on the edge of town, but I only live a few streets away from here."

"Oh, you know what he means," Eric said before popping a cube of cheese in his mouth. He hardly finished chewing before he continued, "Just here on this stretch. Ever since—"

"Okay," Nic interrupted, giving Eric what she hoped was the warning look from hell. It had been almost a week since she'd learned the truth about Aggie and Polly's relationship, but she'd kept that information to herself. Of course, Eric and Jeremy knew, but she hadn't said anything to her sisters, and definitely not to Roxy.

When she originally saw the scrapbook and realized Aggie and Polly had been in love, her first instinct had been to talk about it. Hell, it was more like a full-on gut reaction to scream "It's not just me! Aunt Aggie was a lesbian too!" Only, something about that seemed very…outing. Obviously Aggie had felt comfortable being her authentic self around Eric and Jeremy, but when it came to her own family, it didn't seem to be quite the same. Based on some of the journal entries Nic had read about Aggie's relationship with her sister—and how Virginia had treated her once she knew about Polly—Nic understood.

Still, Nic couldn't stop thinking about how it would've felt to have someone in her family who lived in the very same town and understood what she was going through. What might that have changed for Nic growing up? But she hadn't had the chance to know Aunt Agatha, and it was all because of the way their family had treated her. And she'd thought her great-aunt hadn't known her either, which was why it had been such a surprise to discover all those copies of *A Dark Thought At Midnight* on her shelves and to hear Eric say how proud she was of her. The whole thing had left Nic with a stronger need to process it all than to talk about it. And when she finally was ready to talk about it with Roxy, she wanted it to be a more private discussion than this one.

She attempted to steer the conversation back to the house. "I'm only trying to give the place a little more curb appeal. Bella tells me little touches can go a long way when it comes to selling real estate in this town."

"Too bad. It would be fun to have you around." Jeremy refilled his glass. "And imagine what we could do with this yard if we had more time."

"Maybe you can help whoever buys the place," Roxy suggested as she reached across the table for a handful of grapes. "You're not going to change Nic's mind. She's got to get back to the glamorous literary life of New York. She's got a book tour to kick off."

"That sounds fancy!" Jeremy gushed.

"A book tour would be fancy." Nic laughed at the impressed looks on the guys' faces. "That's not exactly what this is. It's more like a punishment than a…you know what? I don't really want to talk about it." She'd put up a good fight against herself trying to push anxious thoughts about the upcoming bookstore event into a far-off, dusty corner of her brain all week. It was bad enough she was struggling to write the book—now she had to write material to present at readings too. It was a real balancing act to keep the cloud of dread she felt regarding the bookstore obligation from overshadowing the excitement of her high school reunion date with Roxy. One step at a time, and the reunion came first. "I'd much rather be present for the remainder of my visit here in Fisher's Creek."

"Well, slap my ass and call me Sally!" Roxy's eyebrows shot up and a teasing smile flickered across her lips. "It sounds like you might actually be enjoying your stay in town."

Nic's first instinct was to walk it back and deny it, but something about the happy twinkle in Roxy's eye stopped her.

"I'm just excited about a big night coming up at the end of the week." She could tease right back.

"Aw, our special date on Friday." Roxy elbowed Eric. "I'm even getting her a corsage."

"Oh, yeah, that." Nic shrugged, feigning indifference. "I was talking about karaoke night."

"Mm-hmm." Roxy narrowed her eyes. She wasn't falling for it, but apparently she knew how to play along. "Karaoke night is going to be a damn good time. You two should come out for it." She nodded at the guys.

"We should," Eric said, grabbing a few more cubes of cheese. "It will be the perfect way to relax after we plant the garden on Thursday. By then we'll probably all need a drink."

"Or two," Jeremy agreed. "We did some good work today, team. But this job isn't over. We're only halfway there. I can promise you, though, when we're done it's going to be a thing of beauty."

Nic squinted as she surveyed the back of the yard. She could almost picture it restored to its former glory: patches of brightly colored and hardy vegetables, and tall, cheerful sunflowers. The garden would be beautiful, only she wouldn't be here to see it when it all finally bloomed. No doubt Eric would send her pics, but that wouldn't be the same. Her heart sank as reality set in— someone else would get to enjoy Aunt Aggie's garden. Not her.

"Hey, you okay?" Roxy squeezed her shoulder, cutting into her thoughts.

"Yeah, I'm just..." Nic shook her head. She was being ridiculous. "Sorry, I zoned out for a minute there. Too much sun, I guess."

Roxy bit her bottom lip and looked her over, head to toe. "I know exactly what you need. Let's hit the showers and get out of these sweaty clothes."

"And that's our cue to get the hell out of here," Eric quipped, plucking a few grapes from the tray for the road.

"Bye-bye, you two," Jeremy singsonged over his shoulder on his way back toward his own yard. "Let's do it again Thursday once you've had a chance to...recharge. Ugh, lesbians."

"I heard that," Nic called after him. She was one hundred percent sure he meant her to.

"Come on." Roxy grinned and grabbed Nic's arm to steer her into the house.

Forty-five minutes later, Nic and Roxy were clean and fresh and sitting at the Dairy Freeze enjoying a couple of chocolate-dipped cones.

"When you said you knew what I needed, I assumed you meant sex," Nic said between licks of chocolate.

"You don't look completely displeased with this scenario," Roxy mused before wiggling her eyebrows. "Though the day is still young."

"So, after ice cream is the sex?"

"Nope. After ice cream you let me take that bad boy for a drive." She pointed at the Tesla.

"Mmm." Nic licked some chocolate off her lower lip. "We'll see about that. But since we have a quiet moment just the two of us, there was something I wanted to talk to you about."

"You know, it's cruel of you to shut down the sexy banter like that right after licking your lips. A girl could get a real case of blue clit."

"We'll pick it right back up in a minute." She didn't want to shut it down, but she'd sat alone with her thoughts for long enough. She needed to talk it through with someone she knew would understand and who she knew she could trust. "You know how Jeremy made that comment about having another *family member* in the neighborhood?"

"Of course," Roxy said before flicking her tongue across the top of her swirl cone. So effortlessly sexy. "He totally disregarded me as a member of the queer community. Very hurtful."

"It wasn't about you. It was…about my great-aunt."

"Agatha? What are you talking about?"

Nic took a deep breath then launched into the explanation of how Aunt Aggie had left her scrapbooks and diaries for her to find, and how that revealed the truth about her relationship with Polly. In between licks of ice cream, she relayed the story of

Agatha Hill's life including the joys of her travels and adventures with Polly, as well as the heartbreak of her sister shutting her out after learning she was a lesbian.

Roxy worked on her cone and listened quietly until Nic had finished speaking, then she nodded thoughtfully as if putting all the pieces carefully in place before commenting. "I can't say I'm completely surprised. She was shut up in that big house by herself all those years, there had to be some kind of secret there." She paused and seemed to consider that for a moment. "I'm sorry to hear it was heartbreak. You never knew about any of this until the other day?"

"Not a clue," Nic admitted. "My grandmother hardly ever talked about her sister, and when she did it was only to say how Agatha didn't want anything to do with the family. Meanwhile, it was the family who didn't want anything to do with her. It's just so…I don't know. Unfair."

"The way her sister treated her was totally unfair," Roxy agreed.

"Well, yeah." Nic struggled with wanting to say more but feeling stupid about actually saying it out loud. Still, she couldn't deny the emotions that had been eating away at her all week. She glanced up briefly through her lashes to see Roxy studying her with knitted brows. She could be honest with Roxy. She needed to be. Holding it in like she'd been doing was going to push her right over the edge. "I meant…unfair to me."

Roxy's eyes went wide with surprise, but then understanding washed over her face. "You're hurt because no one told you."

Tears stung the corners of Nic's eyes. Roxy understood. "I'm hurt because I missed out on having my lesbian great-aunt to guide me. Do you know what that could've meant for me? Maybe I would've had an easier time coming out. Maybe things could've been different for you and me back then. Maybe I wouldn't have run off to New York the first chance I got."

"Nicola." Roxy's voice was as gentle as the hand she put on Nic's knee. "Don't do that. Don't discount all the beautiful things you've experienced in this life. Sure, some things might have been easier. But if you hadn't left for New York, you might not have followed your dream and written your book, or you might not have had your beautiful son. No shoulda, coulda, woulda. Not when so much good has happened for you too."

"No, I know. I said the exact same thing—shoulda, coulda, woulda and all." Nic squeezed her eyes shut, struggling to get her emotions in check. They both still used the phrase from their school days. Roxy really got her. "I wouldn't trade so many of the experiences I've had, but when I think back on how absolutely devastated I was, how totally alone I felt at the end of senior year…" She shook her head, trying to shake away that old sadness. It would swallow her whole if she let it. "I'm so fucking mad at my mother. How could she keep that from me? If there was one, simple thing you could do that would honestly make your child's life easier, why the fuck wouldn't you do it? Fuck!" She threw the last bit of her ice cream cone at the garbage can as her anger overtook her, but instead of dropping into the bin, the cone skipped off the rim and plopped pathetically onto the pavement. "Fuck," she repeated for good measure as she pushed off the wooden bench and swiped at the tears on her lashes.

Suddenly Roxy was by her side, wrapping her in her arms and holding her steady. "It's okay, Nic. It's okay to be angry."

Nic held on to those words as tightly as she was holding on to Roxy. *It's okay to be angry.* All week she'd carried around this burning ball of emotion in her gut, and only when she finally spoke it aloud, when she named the feeling and Roxy confirmed its validity, was she finally able to loosen its grasp on her.

It was loosened, but not totally relieved. She knew what she needed to do if she wanted to truly move on from her anger. She was going to have to stand up to her mother for once.

Nic said, "I need to tell her how I feel."

At the same time, Roxy said, "You need to tell her how you feel."

"Okay," Nic said, finally stepping back and breaking their hug. "So, I guess that's the plan. God, sorry about that outburst. I'm a mess."

Roxy laughed and used a handful of crumpled napkins to pick up the discarded cone and toss it properly into the trash can.

"You're fine. Or, at least you'll be fine once you work this out instead of trying to hold it all in." She planted a sweet kiss on Nic's forehead. "I think I know exactly what will make us both feel better." She took off running for the Tesla.

"That car is a sensitive machine." Nic chased after her. "It's not a toy."

Roxy reached the car and pressed her face to the driver's side window. "The dashboard looks like a cockpit. I can't wait to get my hands on it." She turned and gave Nic a wink. "Then I'll let you get your hands on me."

The magic words. "That sounds like a deal."

CHAPTER EIGHTEEN

Nic really thought she would wake up and be past the urge to confront her mother about keeping the truth about Aunt Aggie from her, but there she was on Wednesday morning, fired up as ever, knocking on the front door of her parents' house and feeling like smoke could be streaming out of her ears.

Her mother, when she opened the door, was frowning right back at her. "Nicola, why are you knocking? This is where you grew up. It's your house too."

"Come on, Ma. I haven't lived under this roof in almost thirty years. And apparently I own my own house in this town anyway." Why was she rolling right into the first argument with her mother that presented itself? She had a perfectly good subject to be angry about. She didn't have to take the low-hanging fruit. She took a deep breath and followed her mom into the kitchen where she seemed to be midbake. "Speaking of my new house—"

"Are you hungry? There's no kitchen in Maggie's guesthouse. You must be hungry. Have you been eating at all since you've been back?" She bustled over to the fridge and rummaged through its contents. "I think there's some leftover frittata in here. Oh! I could make you an omelet if you want."

"Ma, I don't need to eat. I'm not hungry." She was a little hungry, and as she considered the delicious things that might be in that fridge, her stomach gave a traitorous rumble. But she wouldn't be able to talk if she was stuffing her face with her mother's leftover lasagna or ziti in meat sauce. Could she?

"I'm sorry I don't have any avocado to make that fancy toast you young people love to eat these days." She threw her hands in the air and returned to her flour-covered countertop.

Nic barked a laugh. "I'm the young people? Ma, I'm forty-eight years old. Avocado toast is a millennials thing." She shook her head. She was getting off track. "Mom, I came over here because I've been going through Aunt Aggie's things, and I wanted to ask you some questions."

"It's about time." Her mother dumped a football-sized mound of dough onto the counter and began working it. "I've waited for years to share my bread-baking skills with you, and now here you are, present for the process, and on top of that you have questions prepared? Ask away. I'm making ciabatta today."

"What?" Nic took a beat to wrap her mind around what her mom was saying. Teaching her about bread baking? The woman was a steamroller. "Ma, I'm not here to learn about bread. My questions are about Aunt Agatha."

Her mother wiped the flour from her hands on her apron and shuffled over to the cabinet that held various glass bowls, apparently on the search for an item she couldn't quite locate. "Oh, I know she left you a banger of a mess over in that house, didn't she? The old lady was an odd duck, but you can't say she didn't have character in spades."

"I'm not talking about the stuff, Ma." Nic scrubbed her hands over her face. Her mother was not making this easy. If she wanted a direct answer, she was going to have to ask a direct question. "Aunt Aggie was a lesbian, and you didn't tell me. Why didn't you ever tell me?"

Her mother went stock-still, the search through the cabinet cut short, before she slowly turned to face her. The sad smile in her eyes revealed that she knew damn well she'd been caught in her lie of omission. Her voice was much softer when she spoke. "It wasn't my story to tell." She collapsed into the chair at the kitchen table across from Nic as if the very mention of the subject had worn her out.

"Maybe it wasn't your story, but I am your daughter." To her horror a lump formed in her throat, making her eyes water, but she had to keep going. "Didn't you think it might have been a comfort to me to know there was someone else in this town—someone else in this *family* who could understand what I felt, what I was going through?"

Her mother looked stricken. "Nicola, we've always supported you."

"God, Ma." Nic swiped her palms at the wetness on her lashes. "That's not what I meant. You were all supportive of me. I'm not denying that. But you couldn't possibly understand everything I was feeling. You were never a gay teenager growing up in some tiny little town, but Aunt Aggie was."

The hum of the fridge underscored the silence that stretched between them, and Nic worried she'd pushed too hard. She'd let too much out of the bag by admitting to her mother she'd had those feelings and fears that none of them could've soothed or softened, and now there was no shoving it back in.

Finally, her mother reached across the table and grabbed her hand. "Sweetie, yes, I knew about Aunt Agatha, but it wasn't my place to tell you girls, or anyone, really. Agatha never came around when I was young, and that didn't change as the years went by. She kept her distance from the family. We lived in the same town and we never actually spoke until my mother's funeral, when she introduced herself. I knew my mother had a sister, but her name was like a curse in our house. They'd had a falling out years and years ago, before I was born. Agatha never mentioned what happened, she never said anything much about my mother. But I still felt a family duty toward her after that to, you know, check in on her. Make sure she was okay over there in that big old house. You remember, I took you kids along with me when I went over there sometimes. And she tolerated me in that capacity."

"Yeah, they had a falling out." Nic nodded and struggled to keep her emotions in check. *Falling out* sounded so benign compared to the version of events Nic had read in Agatha's diary. The hurtful, hateful things Virginia had said about Agatha made Nic's stomach turn with disgust. She couldn't hold it in any longer. "Grandma was a homophobe. She cut Aggie out of her life when she found out she was in love with a woman. She was horrible to her. Really, fu—completely horrible. It's no wonder Aunt Aggie stayed far, far away from the whole lot of us."

"My mother was from another time."

"It was the same time as her sister," Nic spat. She had always loved her grandmother dearly, but she never knew the part of her that turned up in Agatha's diary. She couldn't forget those pained words on the page, the heartbreak of a sister's betrayal. "Would Grandma have said those same things about me that she said about Agatha? It was abhorrent, Mom. And Aunt Aggie was absolutely crushed by it. I don't blame her one bit for how she reacted. For building up walls to keep everybody out. She couldn't trust her own family."

"And that was exactly why it wasn't my place to tell you. She wouldn't have wanted me to. But it's obvious that she wanted you to know now. She just needed to tell you in her own way." Her expression was softer now. Full of a mother's love for her child. A look that Nic remembered receiving in abundance when she was a kid. "I think that's something special, honey. Something you should hold on to."

Nic swiped at the last of the tears on her cheeks and took a slow, cleansing breath. That old, lonely pang in her heart eased a bit as the truth of the matter became clearer to her. Aunt Aggie hadn't been able to say plainly to her that she was a lesbian, because in her time it wasn't a subject that was talked about plainly by anyone. Far from it. Her great-aunt had become accustomed to keeping her secret and protecting herself and Polly out of necessity. Especially when it came to her own family. But Aunt Aggie had cared enough to pack up that box with her very personal history—her most intimate truths—with the express intent that Nic would find it and understand that she wasn't alone.

She wanted me to know. The message had come late, but it had been received. Her mother was right—it was special that Aunt Aggie had passed it along to her. And there was definitely a poetry to her doing it the way she wanted. On her own terms.

Up until two weeks ago Nic had thought Agatha was nothing more than a grumpy old bat—God rest her soul. Now she was finding she respected her great-aunt more and more with each passing day.

CHAPTER NINETEEN

"'Ninety-nine Red Balloons!' We've gotta sing that." Janie poked a finger at the laminated page in the three-ring binder that housed the karaoke selections. "I can't believe he has that song in here."

"How do you even know that song?" Bella grabbed the bulky book from her sister. "You were, like, four when that song came out. Besides, we need a song everyone knows. How about 'Girls Just Want To Have Fun'?"

"Wait, do they have any Duran Duran?" Maggie peeked over Bella's shoulder.

An odd sense of peace washed over Nic as she watched her sisters fight over the karaoke binder. They were forces of nature—a strong wind, a rolling river, sunshine breaking through the clouds on an overcast morning—beautiful and powerful. She'd taken this feeling for granted when she was young and then, somehow while she'd been away, she'd forgotten how absolutely wonderful they were when they were all together. Suddenly, she felt like she'd never get enough of it—even these moments of fighting over the best song of the eighties—and she'd most certainly miss it when she left again.

She waited until they had worked through all the titles in the Bangles' catalog before she calmly grabbed the book, flipped ahead a couple pages, and pointed to the ultimate eighties ladies karaoke selection. She cleared her throat to command her sisters' attention before raising a finger in the air to indicate she had discovered the perfect song for them to sing. "Who's ready to rock out and get their Lita Ford on?"

"'Kiss Me Deadly'!" her sisters all exclaimed at the same time.

Janie slammed the binder closed. "I'll put the request in. Maggie, you freshen our pitcher."

Nic dumped the last of the beer into her mug and handed the pitcher to Maggie to take to the bar. As she sipped the warm drink, her gaze moved from the high-backed booths full of patrons excited to get their karaoke on, to the framed vintage photographs on the wall, to the pride flag hanging behind the bar—a recent addition. Things sure had changed at Zachroll's since the old days. Who would've thought? Progress in Fisher's Creek! She'd been surprised by more than a few things in her old hometown since she'd been back. Cathy had taken the fashion world by storm. Her baby sister had turned out to be wonderfully wise under all her quirky weirdness. And the biggest shocker of all—her great-aunt had carried on with her big gay life right there on an offshoot of Main Street. Maybe there was more to love about the town than she'd first believed.

"Hey, you okay?" Bella's question interrupted her deep Fisher's Creek thoughts. "I guess this is kind of your last hurrah as far as your visit goes. I mean, you've got the big reunion tomorrow night, but this is it for the Dickenson sisters for a while. Hope you won't stay away quite as long next time." Her smile was a little watery.

"I won't." Nic shook her head, fighting the tears that were threatening in the corner of her eyes. This was supposed to be a fun night out, not a sappy tear-jerker. But she'd made a mistake in not coming back to see her family more often—she could see that now. "I'm really sorry about that. I got a little too caught up in my life in New York and kind of lost myself in it."

"You think?" Bella balled up a cocktail napkin and threw it across the table, hitting Nic squarely in the chest, breaking the solemn moment, and giving them both a much-needed laugh.

"So, are things okay with you and Chad after the other night? I mean, we sisters can be a lot, I know. Will he still be speaking to us at the next Sunday supper?"

"Not gonna lie, he had a few choice words that evening regarding the Dic-tectives and their theories."

"Nope." Nic held up a halting hand. "We agreed we're leaving that word in the past."

"Fair." Bella nodded. "But, to ease your mind, Chad has been a lot more forgiving toward the lot of you since we've compromised on the meat issue. We've agreed to having either a beef or pork entrée for dinner once a week. I'll serve it beside a very large salad, and I'll just load up on veggies. It's an improvement from hamburgers every week anyway."

"Compromise, huh? Good for you." Nic placed a hand on her sister's forearm. It was a relief to hear the couple was back on solid ground. "Seriously, Bella, I'm happy for you."

Just like that, the tears were threatening again. Her heart was full with love for her sisters. Luckily a distraction was headed their way.

"How's it going over here?" Roxy sidled up to the table and deposited a pile of bagged snacks on it. "I saw Maggie heading up for another refill and thought you might need something in your stomachs. Just so you know, I snagged all the Funyuns we had left back there."

"Thanks, Roxy." Nic smiled up at her. As busy as she was with the full bar, Roxy still took the time to do something special for her and her sisters. "I can't believe the crowd you've packed in here tonight. This is incredible."

"I would like to say it's my brilliant idea to introduce IPAs on tap that drew them all in, but I think I have to admit it's Deejay Crash. They love him. People come here on karaoke night all the way from Ferrisburg."

"I had no idea karaoke was still this popular." Nic grabbed a bag of Funyuns and dug in.

"Well, you know." Bella shrugged and adopted an over-the-top haughty tone, "Middle of nowhere, central Pennsylvania, backward little town. What the hell else is there to do?"

Nic nearly choked on a crispy onion tube and took a big swig of beer to wash it down. Was there anything worse than someone throwing your own words back at you? "I'm sorry," she managed to sputter and took another drink to clear her throat. "I'm sorry I ever said that. If these few weeks here in Fisher's Creek have taught me anything, it's that I've been very wrong for a very long time. This place has a lot to offer, you just need to open your eyes and give it a chance." Bella wasn't the only one who could throw a sister's words around.

"That sounds like some wise advice," Janie said as she and Maggie returned to the table. She plucked a Funyun right out of the bag in Nic's hand and popped it in her mouth before turning to Roxy. "You look beat. You want to sit down with us for a minute?"

"I'd love to. My back is killing me." Roxy rubbed her lower back to drive her point home. "But it's back to work for me." She turned to leave, but Nic grabbed her wrist.

"Hey." She pulled Roxy close to whisper in her ear, "I'll be waiting to rub your back when you get out of here tonight. I can make it all better."

"I bet you can," she whispered back before planting a quick kiss on Nic's lips. "And I already told Ryan he's closing up. I'm out of here as soon as Crash's set ends at eleven." The playful wink over her shoulder she gave Nic made it clear that while things would be shutting down at Zachroll's, their night would just be getting started.

A shiver of anticipation worked its way up Nic's spine, and she took another big gulp of beer to cool the heat in her cheeks. Roxy had a hell of an effect on her. Of all the things Nic had rediscovered during her visit, this thing with Roxy was the one that she could hardly bear to think about leaving behind. But they'd agreed that whatever was happening between them was only temporary. Nic had a life in New York, Roxy had a life in

Fisher's Creek. There was no use getting sentimental about it now when she was set to leave town in less than forty-eight hours. Still, she couldn't deny the attraction that continued to draw them together again and again.

"Next up," Deejay Crash's voice boomed over the speakers, "we have The Sisters of Fisher's Creek singing, 'Kiss Me Deadly'!"

"We're up." Bella led the group to the little stage by the deejay's equipment, Crash gave them the countdown, and they launched into the song.

By the time they hit the chorus, what had begun as a case of the nerves for Nic when she started singing had blossomed into an adrenaline rush. She bopped along to the beat of the music—as close as she could manage to come to dancing while singing— and looked out at the crowd. It seemed like everyone under sixty from Fisher's Creek and the surrounding area had turned up for karaoke night, and they all appeared to be having a blast. Behind the bar, Roxy was shaking her hips while she served drinks. The patrons lining the bar were even bobbing their heads and tapping their feet along to the music. Well, not Cappy and Frank, but the others seated there. Even Eric and Jeremy had come out for the night, both holding up their glasses of red wine in a salute when they caught Nic's eye. She smiled a little more and belted out the lyrics as they reached the last verse, buoyed by the warm vibe in the bar. She was filled with a real sense of community.

Huh. Community. Right here in Fisher's Creek. Who would've thought?

Bella dropped Maggie and Nic off just shortly after ten thirty. They'd left the bar just before karaoke ended, but Nic's ears were ringing, and she was still abuzz with the effects of alcohol and leftover adrenaline from her time on stage.

She turned on the shower and let the steam fill the little bathroom while she peeled off her T-shirt and jeans. She probably had just enough time to wash the sweat and beer funk off before Roxy showed up. She stepped into the spray and inhaled the warm sandalwood scent. She had to hand it to Maggie—she kept the guesthouse stocked with products that made a simple shower feel like a luxurious getaway. The delicious sensation of the hot water rolling down her back lulled her mind into a relaxing oblivion. It felt damn good.

"Honey, I'm home!" Roxy's voice came from the other room.

And suddenly it all felt even damn better.

"In the shower," she called back. Once she heard Roxy moving around in the bathroom, she continued, "I thought you'd still be awhile."

"I left a little early," Roxy confessed, and Nic could just make out the shape of her silhouette yanking her tank over her head. "I couldn't wait to get here and be with you. I didn't even stop home and clean up, so I hope you don't mind if I join you in there."

Nic swiped her hand across the door, clearing the fog on the glass to get an eyeful of Roxy. She was suddenly naked and obviously not taking no for an answer. Not that Nic had any objections to co-showering anyway. "The more the merrier."

"The more the merrier?" Roxy repeated as she stepped into the shower and slid the door back into place behind her. "How many people are you expecting to come in here with you?"

"Yeah, that wasn't exactly the sentiment I meant to express." Nic laughed, shifting slightly to her left to make room under the spray. The beads of water collecting on Roxy's ample breasts as she shampooed her hair were distracting. "What I meant to say is, everything is better with you."

"Is that right?" A sexy smirk graced Roxy's lips as she dropped her head back to rinse.

Nic wanted to kiss that smirk right off her face. Roxy was a sight standing before her—beautiful, confident, and soaking wet. "Mm-hmm." She stepped closer and their hips bumped. Her pulse quickened, and she licked her lips. If only she was licking the droplets of water on Roxy's lips instead. And suddenly, she was struck with a wave of emotion. This was likely the last time she would find herself in this position with Roxy. Could she really let go of what they had started between them? Could she go back to her life in New York and pretend this never happened? "Should we maybe talk about what's going to happen after the reunion? I mean, I know we agreed this is all temporary, but—"

"Don't." Roxy's head snapped up again, eyes wide and wild. Desperate. "Let's don't talk about it. All I want to think about is right now. This moment."

"But I—"

"If I have to kiss you to shut you up, I will."

"That's supposed to be a threat? Like, that's supposed to make me—"

Roxy pinned Nic to the cool tile, and their mouths crashed together as she made good on her words.

Nic's thoughts swirled, her head trying to keep up with the passion stirring in her core. She understood. Roxy was coming off a long shift at work, and if what she wanted was a night of hot sex, if she wanted to just fuck the day away, Nic could give her that. She wanted to give her everything she needed. She raked her fingertips across the muscles in Roxy's shoulders, digging in just enough to make it clear that she wasn't letting her out of her grasp. At least not that night. "Fair enough," she managed between urgent kisses.

She widened her stance and Roxy pressed between her legs. The water from the shower was like drops of heaven pouring down on them as their hands roamed over each other, exploring and teasing. Excitement zapped through Nic as their bodies moved together under the spray. She could never get enough of this feeling.

Roxy tipped her head back, exposing her sexy throat, and Nic peppered the tender, ivory skin there with kisses. The moans she elicited made something in her core melt. Then Roxy was pressing her against the wall again, this time her fingers slipping down the front of Nic's body to her slick opening.

Nic gasped as Roxy filled her, rocking in a rhythm that threatened to tip her right over the edge to pleasure. "Yes," she hissed. "Don't stop."

Roxy nipped at Nic's earlobe, her breath hot against her neck. She increased the pressure of her palm against Nic's sensitive clit. "I want you to come for me, babe."

The muscles in her legs tightened, began to tremble, threatened to give out, but Nic wasn't backing down. She wanted to be consumed by her desire. She wanted the fucking release. And then she got it. Bursts of color flashed on the inside of Nic's eyelids, and she cried out as her orgasm rocked her body. Roxy held her tight as she recovered, helpful since her knees had gone completely wobbly.

When she had caught her breath again, she pressed the lever down to turn off the shower.

"Does that mean our fun time is over?" Roxy pouted and squeezed the water out of her hair. Her ample breasts bounced along with the motion, and a whole new wave of desire washed through Nic.

She grabbed Roxy's hand and pulled her out of the stall. "Oh, we're just getting started."

They grabbed towels on their way out of the bathroom but barely dried off before they tumbled onto the bed, the kissing and groping picking right up where they'd left off in the shower. Nic topped Roxy, pinning her wrists above her head. It was fast and urgent because the whole time Roxy had been fucking her in the shower, she'd been thinking about applying her mouth to Roxy's heat. Tasting her and using her tongue to tease and please her. Making Roxy scream with ecstasy. She pushed on toward that goal, kissing her way down to Roxy's breasts, sucking one nipple between her lips before flicking her tongue over it and moving to the other to give it the same treatment. Roxy's throaty moan was all the encouragement she needed to trail her kisses south until she was positioned between Roxy's legs. She gave her heat a quick kiss, holding eye contact before she said, "Now you come for me."

She watched Roxy's eyes flutter shut as she buried herself in her, wanting nothing more than to bring this beautiful woman pleasure all night long.

CHAPTER TWENTY

With the Tesla all packed up and ready for Nic to hit the road in the morning, Roxy and Nic took the pickup to the reunion Friday night. Once parked, Roxy came around to the passenger side and helped Nic out of the cab, and together they walked into the party.

The high school gym was all done up in red and gold streamers and balloons. A big, flashy disco ball was spinning above it all while a deejay pumped up the early nineties' jams. With a quick scan of the room combined with a recall of the math skills she hadn't used since the last time she stood in that building, Nic estimated at least two-thirds of their class had turned up for the event.

"I can't believe how many people came back for this," Nic said, looping her arm through Roxy's. Solidarity felt imperative to getting through the evening.

"A lot of our class stuck around after graduation, based on what I've seen since I've been back these past few years." Roxy shrugged. "The pull of a career at the power plant is simply too much. They do as their fathers did before them."

"I guess it says something that so many people still have this level of school spirit. Do you think the Fisher's Creek Smiling Crawfish is going to make an appearance and make the night extra special?"

Roxy planted a quick kiss on her cheek. "Relax, Nic. You agreed to the reunion, we're already here. You might as well get into the spirit."

Before Nic could produce a sassy comeback, Cathy rushed over and pulled them both into a hug. "Hey, you two! Isn't this great?"

"It's quite a crowd." Roxy smiled. The disco ball had nothing on her when it came to sparkle. That woman simply had a way of lighting up a room. "Where's Peewee? Already cutting it up on the dance floor?"

Cathy laughed and waved her hand in the air, her bangle bracelets glittering on her arm. "Not likely. Last time I saw him he was by the bar with Tubbs Jeffries and Joey Markle doing shots. Some things never change, I guess."

"Shots at an actual bar is a step up from throwing back stolen gulps from a flask under the bleachers," Nic pointed out. "Could it be that the 1993 Smiling Crawfish are…evolving?"

"Don't get too excited," Roxy countered. "I've seen that gang at Zachroll's after midnight on more than a few wild Saturday nights. Not exactly the picture of class and decorum. But God bless them, they're loyal customers."

The women all shared a laugh as Cathy led them to their table. She quickly introduced them to the guys' wives, and as they settled into their seats, Roxy brought two glasses of wine from the bar.

"So, you're the lesbian author," Kay said. Kay had been two years behind them in high school. Nic had a vague memory of her from back then as a sweet, quiet girl. According to Cathy's introduction, she and Joey got together after he graduated, and they'd been married for twenty-five years. "I've totally heard of you."

"I'm a lesbian and an author, so I guess that is accurate." Nic smiled politely.

"Well, sometimes I think you people have it right," Tracey chimed in. "I love Tubbs and everything, but sharing a bathroom with a man is not my favorite thing. Toilet seat left up, chest hair on the floor, whiskers in the sink—let's face it, it's a nightmare. And you never have to worry about any of that. Maybe I should become a lesbian, you know what I mean?"

"Oh, I know what you mean." Nic winked over the top of her wineglass as she took a long sip. It wasn't the first time she'd heard a straight woman make a comment like that. "Although that's really not the compliment you think it is."

Roxy kicked her under the table—a reminder to suck it up and put on a happy face. Fortunately, the dinner hour went smoothly, and when the guys started telling funny stories about the parties they used to throw in the field out behind Tubbs's grandpa's farm, Nic even started having fun.

Nic grabbed Roxy's hand under the table and gave it a squeeze. She would've never come to the reunion if it wasn't for Roxy being her date, but she had to admit, it was good to remember the fun times. She'd spent so many years focusing on that one bad moment that she'd forgotten there were so many good ones too.

She leaned in to whisper, "Roxy, I'm really glad we—"

"Okay, Smiling Crawfish, the night is just getting started." Andy Miller was the 1993 class president. He was taller than Nic remembered him but still skinny as ever. He was also wearing the same bow tie he used to wear for debate club competitions. He always knew how to rock the geeky-chic vibe, even back in the day before it was cool. "But before we get to the dancing and heavy drinking—yeah, I'm looking at you, Tubbs—we have a few awards to hand out. I present…The Smileys."

"May as well just bring 'em all to this table," Tubbs called out. "All we do is win."

The crowd laughed along, but Andy quickly reined it back in, happily acting as the host with the most as he handed out awards for Couple Married The Longest, Farthest Traveled, Still Looks Like Their Yearbook Pic, and various other corny subjects. Even Tubbs won a Smiley—Best Dad Bod—which he accepted with his usual swagger.

"Okay, almost time to bust a move." Andy kept the show moving along. "Our final Smiley goes to our classmate who has changed the most since our Smiling Crawfish days. You've come a long way, baby! The award for Most Changed goes to...Nicola Dickenson!"

Nic was middrink when she heard her name called. The room around her went silent as she choked it down. *Most Changed.* As in, *you once were straight, but now you're not.* Her stomach sank. In an instant she was transported back to her teenage days. The only thing notable about her to her classmates was—

"Dyke!" Someone at a table behind theirs fake-coughed the word.

There it was. For a minute the gymnasium spun around her, and it wasn't from the two glasses of wine. Nic sucked in a deep breath as her gaze slid to the exit. Was making a run for it an option? In the moment that was the only thing she wanted—to get the hell out of there as quickly as possible.

Roxy's soft touch on her shoulder grounded her. "This is bullshit. We can just leave," she whispered.

She could run like she did thirty years ago, or she could stand up for herself and speak her truth. A glance around the table at Peewee's and Tubbs's shocked faces, Cathy's tear-filled one, and Roxy's outraged expression was all it took to know what she needed to do. She had people who cared about her. People who loved her. What other people thought didn't matter. Their sour feelings were on them—not her. She stood but she didn't run. Despite the whispering voices around her, she held her head high and marched up to the stage to take the award and the mic from Andy.

Nic looked out at the sea of faces below her and almost lost her nerve. But then she spotted Roxy, who was nodding her head with her fist held against her chest, a silent *You got this.* A deep breath to calm her nerves, and she was ready.

"Thank you, Andy. And thanks to all of you for this." She paused and held up the award—gold-painted plastic in the shape of a fancy double-handled cup. Chintzy. But a symbol of something more for her. "I have to admit, my gut reaction when

Andy called my name was to laugh along with the joke. I sure have changed. Back in high school I dated guys and now I'm a lesbian, right? Then my second reaction was to run out of the gym."

A round of nervous laughter from the crowd. Roxy's gaze was fixed on her. Holding her in place. Giving her strength to continue.

Nic swallowed hard. She had to stand up for herself. "That's what the old Nic would've done, but I'm not going to do either of those things tonight. Instead, I'm going to accept this award because I *have* changed a lot. Only, not in the way you think. Back in high school, I was the girl who would run for the door. Hell, I did. I ran right out of town after graduation, too afraid to let everyone know the truth and to face their reaction to it. That's not me anymore. And it's been a long journey to get here, but I'm proud of who I am. I'm not afraid of what people will think, or say behind my back—or under their breath. I've changed a whole hell of a lot. We all have in one way or another. Jeff and Susan have six kids. Cathy designed last year's must-have fashion accessory. Garrett was one of the first generals in the US Space Force. We all have a lot to celebrate, and a lot to be proud of." She caught Roxy's eye, and they shared a special smile before she held up the award and addressed the crowd again. "I know I'm proud. Thanks, everybody."

She left the stage to applause, but before she made it back to her table, Roxy met her in the middle of the gym floor, took her in her arms, and kissed her, right there in front of everybody. Then the applause really ramped up, accented by hoots and whistles from their former classmates.

"The world has changed, Fisher's Creek," Roxy declared loudly enough to make herself heard when they finally broke apart. "Don't get left behind."

Nic couldn't stop the smile that split her face. She didn't know what she'd done to be blessed with a do-over with the beautiful, kind, wonderful woman standing before her, but suddenly she was filled with desire to hold on to the joy with both hands for as long as she could. Maybe it was worth thinking about what was going to happen between them when Nic left town. Or what could happen if they tried.

"Hey, Rox, I think maybe we should talk about—"

"Roxy!" Cathy rushed over, holding out Roxy's phone. "This has been blowing up. I think you better answer it."

Roxy squinted at the number on the screen, and recognition registered on her face. "Excuse me, I'll take this and meet you back at the table."

Nic took the moment while meandering back to her seat to think about what she wanted to say to Roxy. Was she about to ask her to start a relationship with her? When she pulled into town three weeks ago, she didn't think she wanted to be in a relationship with anybody, much less someone who tied her back to Fisher's Creek. Now she couldn't imagine simply saying goodbye to Roxy and moving on. She'd stood up for herself to her old classmates and the other people in town she needed to. She'd made her peace with her hometown. She didn't need to run anymore. By the time she settled in her chair, she was buzzing with anticipation to tell Roxy how she felt.

But the look on Roxy's face as she clicked off the call put a deep chill on Nic's plan.

"Roxy, what's wrong?" She hopped back up from her seat. Were those tears in her eyes?

"It was the nursing home. My mom is, uh…They said she's stopped eating. I guess it's not a good sign." Roxy shook her head. "I'm so sorry, I have to go. I just have to make sure she's okay."

"Of course," Nic agreed. "I'll come with you."

Roxy put her hand on her shoulder. "No, there's no reason for you to do that. It could be a false alarm. Plus, my mom will be furious with me if I bring a guest along when she doesn't have her face on." Her expression softened and a weak smile even graced her worried lips as she said the phrase Nic recalled hearing more than a few times when they were kids and turned up unexpectedly at the Fitzpatrick house with a group. "I'll just check in, make sure everything's fine, then swing back by and pick you up. Our night can pick up from there."

"You're my date. You go, I go."

"Absolutely not." Roxy grabbed her clutch from the table. "You can't leave after the speech you just gave. You can't run out of here now. Stay and celebrate your victory." She paused and gave her a quick kiss on the lips. "You definitely deserve it, and I want you to have it."

As expected, the reunion lost a lot of its luster after Roxy left, but nonetheless Nic stayed, caught up with old classmates, and danced the night away with Peewee and the gang. When the party ended shortly after eleven o'clock with no word or texts from Roxy, Nic began to worry.

"I think I better get a ride out to the home and check on her," Nic said as she clicked off another call routed directly to Roxy's voice mail.

"We can give you a lift." Peewee swayed slightly as he spoke.

"Dude, I watched you throw back whiskey with Tubbs and Joey all night. You're not driving anywhere."

"Agreed." Cathy jingled the ring of keys in her hand as she joined them. "Designated driver, right here. I'm happy to take you wherever you need to go, Nic."

A short ride later, as she walked into Rosewood Manor, the familiar smell in the building took her back to the days that summer before her senior year when Maggie roped her into volunteering at the home with her. She checked in at the front desk and got a room number before heading down the hallway to the long-term-care wing. Her feet ached from wearing high heels all night and her head throbbed from the loud music and box wine, but neither was a match for the tension that was rising between her shoulders from worry about Roxy's lack of communication. She blew out a breath of relief when she finally spotted her through the open door sitting by her mother's bedside.

"Hey," she whispered, crossing the room. "I got worried when I didn't hear from you."

"I'm sorry. I turned my ringer off when I got here, and I just haven't paid any attention to the phone."

"Any improvement?"

Roxy shook her head and her gaze dropped to the floor. She looked beyond worn out. A huge change from the brightness in her eyes a couple hours earlier when they'd kissed on the dance floor after Nic's acceptance speech. She looked like a lost child—scared and alone. "I'm not even sure she knows I'm here. The doctor who was on earlier said that not eating or drinking and the loss of lucidity can be end-stage signs."

Nic's heart sank. She dragged another chair beside her. "Come here." She wrapped an arm around her.

Roxy snuggled against her shoulder and sighed. "This isn't how our night was supposed to go."

"There will be other nights," she said to herself as much as to Roxy.

"You have to go home and get some shut-eye before your book thing tomorrow." Roxy's voice was sleepy. "It's okay. I'll be fine."

"I've got some time before I have to hit the road. Why don't you try to close your eyes for a minute?"

The only thing Nic wanted to do was be there for Roxy. She could take a little nap there in Mrs. Fitzpatrick's room then run back to the guesthouse, shower, and get on the road in plenty of time to make it to the book event in New York City. Right now, she needed to be with Roxy.

CHAPTER TWENTY-ONE

The clang of metal crashing jolted Nic awake. She blinked hard, trying to make sense of her surroundings while hushed voices issued orders just beyond the walls of the room. Mrs. Fitzpatrick's room in the nursing home. They had fallen asleep. She untangled her arm from under Roxy's and grabbed her phone from her bag. Five minutes after six. She was supposed to be in New York by ten.

Crap.

She clicked on the contact she needed to reach while she slipped into the hallway.

"It's early, Nicola. It's real freaking early," Alessa said by way of greeting. "I assume you're calling me from the road."

Nic swallowed hard. Her mouth was dry from sleeping in the stale air of that room, especially after downing spiked Smiling Crawfish Punch and wine all evening. "I'm about to be, I just—"

"Nicola. Do *not* flake on this. You have got to be at the bookstore at ten o'clock to read and smile nice and talk to the readers who all want to hear about this book, or you will be in breach of your contract with Mountain Pass. All you have to do is show up and play nice. It's so freaking easy. Please, Nicola, get in your car and drive here now."

"I'm not flaking. I'm just running a few minutes behind," Nic whispered her protest to keep from disturbing the residents. She did the math in her head again. She could still make this happen. It would all be okay. "I'll be there. I'm just asking you to stall a little. It's fine. I'm on my way."

She clicked off the call, closed her eyes, and took a deep breath.

"Hon, are you okay?" A nurse wearing heavy eyeliner and a hot-pink scrunchie holding back her frosted hair was looking at her with genuine concern. "Do you need something? We've got coffee at the nurses' station, and water. Or I could probably find some juice for you."

She didn't have time for juice or coffee. She barely had time to answer politely. Not if she had any hope of making it to New York on time. "No, thank you. I'm fine," Nic insisted. She had to get back to Roxy and let her know she was leaving, but the nurse put a hand on her shoulder, halting her retreat.

"It's nice to see someone here supporting Roxy for a change," she said with a kind smile. "You're sweet to stay with her all night. She doesn't have anyone to help her out with her mom, no siblings or anything. Has to shoulder this all on her own, poor thing." She shook her head and tutted. "Anyway, let me know if you two need anything."

As the nurse bustled on to her next task, Nic's feet filled with lead, holding her in place. The thought of Roxy sitting in that room alone, afraid of losing her mother, made her stomach twist. Nic was so accustomed to her own big family with a sibling always there by her side when she needed them that she never even thought about how Roxy must feel going through this—taking care of her mother all this time—without any family to help her.

Now she was going to leave Roxy to go to some stupid event in New York that she didn't even want to attend. How could she even consider it? She wanted to make Roxy feel supported and cared for, just like she had done for Nic the night before at the reunion. She wanted to be there for her.

Then it hit her—she could do the event in New York and come back afterward. She could be back in Fisher's Creek by four—five at the latest. She would have to go back again Sunday morning for the second event, but it was doable.

With hurried footsteps she returned to Mrs. Fitzpatrick's room, practically bursting with her revelation. She needed Roxy to know she would be by her side—she had a plan.

She need not have worried. When she got back to the room, Mrs. Fitzpatrick was awake and asking the nurse for breakfast. Roxy was standing by her bedside and greeted Nic with a big smile.

"Look who's up and demanding brown sugar in her oatmeal." Roxy tipped her head in her mother's direction. "She's a tough girl."

"She sure is," Nic agreed.

Roxy faced Nic, her eyes suddenly wide. "What are you still doing here? You should be on the road by now."

"Yeah, about that." Nic bit the inside of her lip. Stalling. This was big, but she was ready. "I was thinking maybe I should stick around. You had a heck of a night last night, and I hate to leave you alone right now. I can stay."

Roxy took a step back and eyed Nic like she'd suddenly sprouted a second head. "Absolutely not. You have to get your ass to your book event before you get yourself into any more trouble with your publisher. She's fine." She gestured at her mom. "I'm fine. I don't need you to stay."

"You don't—" Nic swallowed hard. She felt like she'd been punched in the gut. "You don't need me?"

"No, that's not…" Roxy pinched the bridge of her nose and closed her eyes. When she finally opened them again, she grabbed Nic by the arm and pulled her out into the hallway. "That's not what I meant. C'mon, we both knew this was a temporary thing. You were always going to go back to New York in the end. That was the plan all along. And you have an event to attend in a few hours. People are expecting you."

"They'll get over it."

"Nicola." Roxy exhaled her name and took her hand. "Once you ran away from Fisher's Creek, but you came back and made things right for yourself here. This time you ran from New York—from your divorce and your book troubles—but now you have to go back and make things right for yourself there. It's okay. This is how it's supposed to be."

A heaviness settled in Nic's chest. She didn't want her time with Roxy to end, but everything she'd said was true. They knew this was just a visit. Totally temporary. And she knew in her heart she needed to go back and get her career in order before she could move forward. She had to go. "So, I should get on the road."

"You should get on the road," Roxy repeated with watery eyes. She gave Nic's hand a squeeze before one last quick kiss on the lips. "It's okay."

Nic forced a smile to hide the sour feeling bubbling up inside of her. It hurt, but she would have to accept the truth: A temporary fling was all Roxy had expected from her, and apparently, all she'd ever wanted in the first place. She couldn't expect Roxy's feelings to change just because hers did. She had to respect that. Despite the planning and agreeing, she'd ended up with an aching heart nonetheless. Leaving still hurt in the end, but there was no other choice. Roxy had made her stance clear.

She schooled her face into what she hoped was a kind but resolved expression. "You take care, Roxy."

CHAPTER TWENTY-TWO

"Nicola, let's get these extra copies boxed up and out of here. We don't want people to see you slumped at this table all alone with a sad stack of books and no readers to be found." Nothing like Alessa to turn a moment of satisfaction into a potential public relations blunder.

Nic stood and helped with the books, but she wasn't about to let Alessa throw a wet blanket on her good mood. With the exception of Nic arriving to the previous day's event a full forty-five minutes late after a mad dash from Fisher's Creek, both of the bookstore events that weekend had gone off without a hitch. Both days she'd had a line of at least a hundred folks waiting to have her sign a book or say hello and shake her hand. Meeting her readers—and people who were book lovers in general—gave her a buzz. It was like the endorphin rush people got from running, only with less physical activity required. All she had to do was talk about the stories she dreamed up in her head and recorded in her notebook. A writer's high. Best of all, she had found the more she talked about her plans for the small-town mystery book with readers who were hungry for more of her writing, the more the actual story began to take form in her mind.

When the books were all packed up, Nic and Alessa thanked the store manager for hosting the event. Nic signed a few extra books for their inventory and assured them that if there was a demand for them, she would happily stop by again sometime and scribble her name in more.

"Now, listen." Alessa frowned when it was just the two of them outside on the sidewalk. "You're not taking any more vacations, are you? You're booked Saturday and Sunday for the next two weekends at four different bookstores around the city, and I don't want to have to vamp for you again like I did yesterday. I expect you to be on time."

The image of Alessa telling corny jokes and warming up the crowd flashed in Nic's mind, and she bit back a chuckle. Somehow, she doubted that was what had actually occurred. "Don't worry, Alessa, I'm back in New York for good."

"Wonderful," she said, eyeing Nic from head to toe. "Real talk, you looked a little sad just then, but you should feel good—these book talks with the readers the past two days have been very successful. You should celebrate or something." She gave a quick wave, turned on her heel, and walked away.

Sad? Nic wasn't sad. She had a great story idea for the mystery book, and the bookstore events had been a lot more fun than she'd been expecting. She *should* celebrate. And she should get her ideas down on paper before they slipped away. Luckily, since the bookstore was Time Square adjacent, she only had to walk a few blocks before finding a sports bar where she could accomplish both.

Sitting at a cocktail table in Bombed Yankees with a frosty tumbler of the only IPA they had on draft, Nic began to outline the tale of murder in a small town, the all-too-convenient trial of the drifter who stands accused, and the town's dark secret from the past that surfaces along with the investigation. The discussions she'd had that weekend helped her lay out the plot, and with the town descriptions she'd penned during her time in Fisher's Creek, she would have no trouble fleshing it out into a full novel. She could already picture several key scenes as if they were movie clips playing in her mind.

She finished putting her notes on the page just as she finished her second beer, and not a minute too soon. While she'd been absorbed in her mystery, baseball fans had been trickling into the bar to watch their beloved team play, and when Nic looked up to signal the server for her check, the bar was decidedly jam-packed. Very different from the last time she sat in a bar writing. Even on karaoke night, Zachroll's didn't get a crowd like this. The first pitch hadn't even been thrown and the fans were already edging toward rowdy. It was time to pack up and clear out. The check the server handed her was another glaring difference between a bar in New York and Fisher's Creek. What she was paying for two beers would have bought her two pitchers at Zachroll's. Maybe a few bags of Funyuns too.

Janie and her Funyuns. Nic should grab some on her way back to Brooklyn in honor of her sisters. It might have been the bookstore events that finally shook the story out of her, but it was definitely the three of them who kept her afloat while it was still swirling around in her brain. Her sisters never gave up on her. They were all probably gathering at her parents' house for Sunday supper right at that moment. Her heart warmed at the thought of everyone gathered around the big dining room table, and for the first time in possibly forever, she wished she was there with them.

Back at the apartment, Nic had barely walked through the door when Maryann came out of her bedroom, dressed to kill in a silky black pantsuit and red patent leather stilettos, buzzing with an air of anticipation.

"You're heading out already?" Nic couldn't hide her disappointment as Maryann crammed items into a tiny clutch purse. Nic had been hoping for a girls' night in—yoga pants and T-shirts, lounging on the couch, maybe some margaritas. Sure, she could still do that without Maryann, but she was really itching to tell someone about how great the event had gone that day, how she'd *finally* figured out the book she'd been struggling with, how damned excited she was about her writing career again. She couldn't do that alone.

"Tim got tickets for a fundraiser at the Botanical Gardens. Cocktail hour starts at six. I'm running late." Her lips pouted for a sorry second before she fiddled with the clasp on the cultch and headed for the door. "And don't wait up—I'll probably stay at Tim's tonight."

No surprise there.

"Okay. Well, I hope you have a great time at the—"

"Bye!" Maryann called over her shoulder as she pulled the door closed behind her.

Nic blew out a long breath and slumped onto the couch. It wasn't really Maryann she wanted to tell about her little victories that weekend anyway. She pulled her phone out of her bag and scrolled through her contacts, searching for one name in particular. But tempting herself with the prospect of reaching out to Roxy wasn't going to help matters.

The few texts she had sent to Roxy since she'd returned to New York had been met with one-word replies or emojis, and the one call she'd made had gone straight to voice mail. Nic had to face facts—they had made an agreement. Their reconnecting was over and they were going back to their separate lives. *The way it was meant to be.* Roxy didn't want her to call. She had her own life in Fisher's Creek.

Alone in New York City was Nic's life now.

CHAPTER TWENTY-THREE

By the time a second weekend of successful author meet and greets came and went, Nic had settled back into her life in New York. Not only had she managed to get the first eight chapters of her still untitled mystery novel down on paper, she'd also sold the Tesla. With the plentiful public transportation city living afforded, she didn't need the obnoxious thing. Parking it in Brooklyn had been a nightmare, and she hardly ever drove anywhere anyway. Plus, selling it eliminated the temptation to simply hop in and road trip back to Fisher's Creek. She needed to keep her momentum up and focus on her life in New York, not look backward to what might have been.

After the third and final weekend of bookstore events, Nic had worked up the courage to pitch the book of her heart—the one she'd started writing while staying in Maggie's guesthouse—to Alessa.

That was how she ended up sitting in Alessa's art deco styled office with the floor-to-ceiling windows overlooking Manhattan that Tuesday morning. Nic sat in front of Alessa's glass-and-chrome desk, wearing a business suit she hadn't buttoned herself into in years, and anxiously sipped her overpriced coffee-cart coffee while Alessa's gaze stayed trained on her laptop. She was presumably staring at the pitch email Nic had sent just the day before.

"Mountain Pass won't publish this," she said as she closed the laptop and leaned back in her white leather chair. "But I've got to tell you, Nic, I love this story. Of course, I'll need to read the full manuscript before I make any promises, but the town you've created has such charm, the main character's growth over the arc is heartwarming, and the plot is solid. It's a winner all around."

Nic's chest fluttered with excitement. She'd had a gut feeling that Alessa would like it, but she'd needed to hear it out loud from her. Confirmation from an industry professional that this story Nic loved so much wasn't just a vanity piece—that it held appeal to others as well. The relief flooded out of her in a rush of words. "It was the story of my heart. I just knew I had to get it on the page and tell it. I don't know what it is about Fisher's Creek, but my stay there just—"

"Nicola." Alessa's tone was sterner this time. "Don't get ahead of yourself. Real talk. I love this story and I can sell this book, but I'm going to need a minute. And I can't make you any guarantees on the kind of advance I'll get you while switching genres, especially if word gets out about how long it took you to get your second contracted book over to Mountain Pass Press."

"The draft is nearly done now," Nic protested. "A few more weeks and I'll have it to the editor. I promise."

Alessa gave a stiff nod, then seemed to make up her mind. "Okay. Then it's settled. As soon as you turn in the book you owe to Mountain Pass, we'll get to work selling this project. There's just one more thing—you're going to need to use a pen name on this one. If we try to sell it under Nicola Dickenson, people are going to expect a suspenseful mystery. And that's going to result in some very disappointed readers."

"A pen name?" It was such a personal book. A book about appreciating your roots and being true to yourself, and yet she would be writing it under a name that wasn't actually hers? A big part of why she wrote the story in the first place was because she was inspired by her great-aunt Agatha Hill living her truth despite the homophobia and discrimination she faced every single day. Could she still honor the lessons she'd learned from Aunt Aggie if she released the book under a name other than her own? Maybe, if… "What do you think about Nic Hill?"

Nic returned to the apartment with some celebratory Italian food she'd picked up for lunch on her way back to Brooklyn. She poured herself a glass of iced tea and plated the chicken parm and pasta. Even by looks it was no match for her mom's version of the dish, but this reasonable facsimile would have to do until the next time Nic made it to Sunday supper.

As she ate, she found herself longing to share the good news about her meeting with Alessa, so she clicked her phone on speaker and dialed up Janie.

"Tired Mom's Taxi Service," a harried-sounding Janie answered on the third ring.

"One of those days, huh?" Nic laughed. Although her little sister might be having a stressful afternoon, Nic was ready to burst from not yet sharing word of her success with anyone else on the planet.

"Just picked the kiddos up from swimming, made a quick stop home to change into dry clothes, and now I'm off to drop one at Scouts and the other at dance. While they partake in those activities, I'll run to the market and try to come up with something that will serve as a quick dinner we can all shove in our faces before we need to be at the field tonight for the T-ball game. So, yeah, it's one of those. What's up?"

This wasn't going to be a long chat. Janie sounded so frazzled, she'd probably only hear half of what Nic was saying. But still, her sisters would all be excited to know the book was moving forward, and since Bella and Maggie were still at work, Janie was the one who would get the news first. She could be trusted to send it down the pipeline.

"I met with my agent this morning, and she's going to try to sell the book I wrote while I was staying in Fisher's Creek. The nonmystery one."

"That's great," Janie managed before apparently detecting some behavior in the back seat that required her attention. "Would you two knock it off back there?"

"So, I just wanted to let you know. And I was just calling because I wanted to…" *What?* Talk to someone who loved her? That sounded pretty pathetic. Nic was a grown-ass woman. She could handle being on her own.

"What's that? The kids are fighting over a package of gummy bears and I couldn't hear."

Nic's gaze shifted from her sad, take-out Italian meal for one to the empty living room. It wasn't fair for her to expect her sister to fill the void of her loneliness. Janie had her hands full with her own family. Nic would just have to be satisfied with celebrating alone for now.

"Nothing. I was just saying everything's going fine here in the Big Apple."

"Good, good." Janie was clearly distracted. "Maybe we can talk more this weekend. We're pulling up to Scouts now and I've got to…Oh, crap. Sorry Nic, gotta run. Love you."

Before Nic could respond, Janie hung up.

Nic sighed and trailed a slice of garlic bread through the tomato sauce on her plate. Her sisters all had lives back in Fisher's Creek just like Roxy did. She couldn't expect them to drop everything anytime she got the urge to chitchat. She knew that. And still, the empty apartment left her with a loneliness that gnawed at her heart. Maybe she needed to make some friends. All her old ones had kind of dropped off back when she was with Dana. Mainly because she'd neglected all other personal relationships to focus all her attention on Dana. Maryann had been the only friendship that had survived. And now she had a significant other of her own to fully focus on. It certainly wouldn't be fair of Nic to fault her for that.

Nic hadn't been surprised when she came back to an empty apartment that afternoon—Maryann was working, and after that she would have dinner with Tim and spend the night with him, per usual. It seemed more and more the couple was spending time at his place, probably to avoid having Nic play third wheel on their dates. Perhaps it was time for Nic to find a place of her own.

Maybe she should get a dog to keep her company. That would be nice. Of course, if she had a dog, she'd want to have a yard for him to run around in, and a place like that was hard to come by in this area. Especially if you didn't have unlimited funds to put toward it. The New York City boroughs weren't like Fisher's Creek in that regard. Or in any regard, really.

Nic couldn't help the bitter laugh that escaped her lips as she deposited her dirty dishes in the sink. She technically owned the exact kind of place back in Fisher's Creek that she was dreaming of living in—the one she'd asked her sister Bella to oversee the sale of. *Isn't that ironic?*

She pushed the Alanis Morrisette lyrics out of her mind and leaned against the kitchen counter, afraid that if she didn't, her knees would give out under her. Suddenly, her heart pounded with a fresh wave of excitement and realization—she already had exactly what she wanted. It had just taken her a damn long time to figure that out.

With no regard for the office hours of anyone back in Fisher's Creek, she dialed her phone again.

"Hey, Bella. Can we talk about Aunt Aggie's...I mean, *my* house?"

CHAPTER TWENTY-FOUR

Nic had slept well after making up her mind about moving back to Fisher's Creek, but the next morning she woke with a start. She had a lot to do to make this reality. Figuring out transportation back, for one, since she sold the damn Tesla. Maybe she would rent a car, or maybe her dad would drive up in his pickup and help her. Of course, she was going to have to have a conversation with her mom—Marie Dickenson was going to love that *I told you so* moment. And she should probably reach out to Roxy and let her know she wouldn't be selling off the furniture from the house since she'd probably need it until she bought new.

Roxy. Would this move mean a fresh start for the two of them? The thought was almost too overwhelming for Nic to consider. Getting her career back on track and realizing how she wanted to move forward in life seemed like such a complete victory. Another chance with Roxy would be the icing on the celebratory cake. But would Roxy even want that now? Their arrangement when Nic was visiting in town had been contingent on just that—Nic was only visiting. Their relationship had included a built-in expiration date, and that seemed to be exactly how Roxy had wanted it. There might not be a future for the two of them together, and that was something Nic would just have to accept. They could just be friends. Or people who used to be friends in school but were now just people who lived in the same town and said a polite hello when they crossed paths at Bo's Diner or Cathy's boutique. It might sting at first, but eventually Nic's heart would heal on the Roxy front. She pulled the sheets up to her chin to shield herself from the Ghost of Heartbreaks Future.

Stop it. She was getting way ahead of herself. Maybe she and Roxy would end up as just friends, but she had been handed a new beginning in so many other ways. She couldn't deny herself excitement over that. And that meant putting one foot in front of the other and making her plan happen.

One hot shower and a couple of hours later, she was doing just that—taking steps to move to her house. *Her house!* She was in the middle of updating her address in the millions of places that required it when her phone chirped with an incoming text message.

Please say you're in the apartment.

It was a weird text to receive from Roxy out of the blue, so Nic responded simply:

I'm in the apartment.

Look out at the street.

In her haste to reach the street-side of the apartment, Nic tripped over the edge of the area rug in the living room, launching her forward and ending with her face pressed right up against the front window. Her breath caught when she spotted the old, beat-up red pickup blocking one side of the street down below, its owner leaning against the door waving her hands over her head.

"Roxy, what are you doing here?" she shouted through the pane, but it was doubtful she could be heard above the din of the city.

An impatient driver in a shiny Toyota hybrid beeped their horn angrily before giving up and circumventing the truck. Roxy ignored them and continued waving at Nic, now gesturing to her to come outside.

Of course. Get your ass down there!

Nic held up one finger, signaling she wouldn't be long, but she didn't waste a second. She rushed down the building's musty stairway as fast as her hopeful heart and flip-flops would carry her and pushed through the front door out into the humid July air. It hadn't been a mirage—Roxy was actually standing right there at the bottom of the steps on the sidewalk.

"Roxy, what are you doing in New York?" She didn't wait for an answer. She ran into Roxy's open arms and the touch she'd missed so much over the past month. Clung to her. Inhaled the familiar sea spray scent of Roxy's shampoo. Remembered every thrill of being together.

Roxy pulled back just enough to look into Nic's eyes, a solemn, earnest gaze that indicated she was laying all her cards on the table. "I'm here to tell you I love you, and I know we have a lot to figure out, but we can do it. We can do long distance for a while and, oh!" She dropped her hold on Nic and turned to the truck, grabbing something out of the passenger side that was big enough to fill her arms, yet smaller than the traditional Fisher's Creek front yard version—a bear carved out of a log. "And I brought you this to remind you of Fisher's Creek while you're here in New York. I know you don't have a front yard to put it in, so I had this smaller one made special for you. It will fit in your room, or on a balcony or something."

Another angry honk blasted as a driver maneuvered around the truck. Nic shook her head, taking in Roxy's rambling. She couldn't suppress a smile as she imagined Roxy making the three-plus-hour drive from Pennsylvania with a wood bear buckled into the passenger seat beside her. All that way. To tell Nic she loved her. And bring her a wooden bear. Nic's belly fluttered.

"I love you too," Nic blurted out as she took the bear from Roxy's arms and set it on the sidewalk, freeing them so she could take Roxy's hands in hers. "We'll figure it all out, but we won't have to do long distance for very long."

Roxy's face scrunched up, cute and questioning, as if trying to work out the meaning behind Nic's words.

"I called Bella last night and told her to pull the house off the market. I'm moving back to Fisher's Creek. When I saw you out here, I figured she told you."

"No." Roxy shook her head, but her expression was full of relief. "I hadn't heard. I only knew I had to come here and tell you in person how I feel."

"You came after me this time."

"I did."

Nic's limbs tingled with excitement, and she silently prayed this wasn't a dream that she'd wake from any minute. "Why this time?"

"Because this time I knew there was a chance you wanted me to. I saw you change in that time you were back. You came in a little rough, but I watched you ease into Fisher's Creek life."

"What are you talking about?" She laughed. "I don't remember doing anything especially notable. Other than inheriting a house, I mean. But that wasn't anything I did really."

"Sometimes it's the little things, Nic. Like how you helped people right and left while you were home. I saw you do it. You helped Cathy change that light bulb in her store. When Collin needed help fundraising for the Drama Club, you stepped up. And, in your own weird way, you and your sisters helped Bella when you thought her marriage was in peril."

"I'm not so sure Chad would say we were all that helpful." Nic chuckled, but she was starting to see Roxy's point.

"You all meant well, that's the important thing."

Nic thought back to that evening at Cathy's boutique. She would've never guessed in that moment that merely hours later the history of how her high school friendship with Roxy had crashed and burned would be completely turned upside down simply by listening to the other side of the story. From looking at things from a different...*perspective.* Then Roxy put words into action at the class reunion when she stood up and kissed her right in front of everyone, making it clear there was a place for Nic in Fisher's Creek if she wanted there to be. But then the night went sideways, and Roxy had to rush off. Nic had never even told her how much that meant to her. She squeezed Roxy's hand. "It occurs to me I owe you a thank-you for standing up for me at the reunion. It was really brave of you to basically come out in front of everyone. You're a business owner, and public opinion is a thing. Are you worried being out in a town like Fisher's Creek will impact that?"

Roxy kept her gaze locked on Nic as she shook her head. "I didn't think about that, and I don't regret what I did one bit. The only thing that mattered to me was being there for you. I was so proud of the things you said when you accepted that award in front of our old classmates. You stood your ground and stood up for yourself. Besides, I highly doubt it will stop anyone from coming into the local watering hole for cheap draft beer, but if it does, screw them. It's their loss, not mine." A gentle smile graced her lips. "Our little town isn't some kind of perfect utopia. I know that. There are always going to be a few jerks like those cowards who shouted insults from the back of the gymnasium at the reunion, but mostly Fisher's Creek is good people."

Tears prickled at the back of Nic's eyes. She never thought her detour to Fisher's Creek would have that kind of impact on her. She'd returned reluctantly after all these years of thinking Fisher's Creek needed to change its attitude, but it turned out she needed an attitude adjustment as well. She swallowed back the tears and smiled. "Of course it's good people. And I've been lucky enough to fall in love with the very best of them. Roxy Fitzpatrick, I have loved you since we were in school. I was just too afraid to say it back then. So, I guess you're right—I've definitely changed."

"One thing about you hasn't changed." Roxy placed her warm hand tenderly on Nic's cheek. "You're the one I've loved right back this whole damn time. That's why I couldn't wait one more minute to come up here and tell you. And I had this bear to give you." Her eyes were red-rimmed now too. Happy tears, Nic assumed. "Damn. I was going to totally surprise you and just knock on your apartment door with this carved symbol of my love, but I couldn't find a parking space anywhere. It was going to be so romantic."

Nic swallowed hard to keep the tears at bay. It wasn't a dream. It was the best possible scenario she could hope for—Roxy felt the same way she did, and they had an honest-to-God shot at making things between them work. "Roxy, I promise you, it was."

There was a steady drumming in Nic's chest as Roxy pulled her back into her strong arms and their lips crashed together in a kiss that was sweet and powerful in equal measure, and so very overdue. A promise of the wonderful things to come as they opened their hearts to moving forward in life together.

CHAPTER TWENTY-FIVE

Three Weeks Later

"Now this is how you charcuterie!" Nic artfully arranged rustic crumbles of parmigiano as a finishing touch next to the crock of olives and gherkins. "I love this honey beer mustard. Have you tried it?"

Roxy peeked over her shoulder and reached around to dip a slice of pepperoni in the sauce. "Damn, that is good."

"Okay, hands off the board," Nic scolded. "Save some for the party."

Soon enough they would have a house full of family and friends celebrating Nic's official move into her house, and she had to admit, she was feeling pretty excited about this fresh start in Fisher's Creek.

"Who would've thought folded meat would be so popular?" Asher bounded into the kitchen and pinched some prosciutto from the board. He had gotten into town the night before to spend a little time with his mom and help get her settled into her new home, and he hadn't stopped eating since he arrived. Nic began to wonder if he had even eaten a single square meal since he'd been staying at the beach. Lucky for him, Nana Marie would happily send him back with a packed cooler and plenty of sweets to share with his roommates.

"Asher! Did you not hear me say hands off the charcuterie?" She swatted playfully at her son.

"It's super popular," Roxy said, grabbing some limes from the fridge to slice up for margaritas. "I'm considering making it an offering on our new snack menu, but Ryan can't pronounce it. He keeps calling it a 'shark and lava' board."

"That would make me want to order it even more." Asher shrugged. "So, who's this guy Aunt Maggie is bringing? Will her nephew approve?"

"Jonathan," Nic and Roxy singsonged in unison. It was hard not to use that tone when talking about the man who had Maggie floating around like she was filled with helium—like a big smiley face mylar balloon.

"He's the package delivery guy for her office," Nic explained. "They flirted and joked for months when he'd bring in packages, and then they ended up matching on Perfect Pair. They really got to talking then, and eventually he asked her out."

"A regular fairy tale for the digital age," Roxy added. "Seriously, he's really great and Maggie's very happy, so go easy on him, okay?"

"We'll see." Asher winked as he snagged a chunk of cheese off the tray and hopped out of reach before his mother could smack his hand. "Okay. I'll be back. I'm going over to Eric and Jeremy's to get the party tub for the drinks. Should I stock it too?"

"Might as well. People will start arriving any minute," Nic said, pulling a family-size bag of tortilla chips out of the pantry. As Asher dashed out the back door, she turned to Roxy. "By the way, I think the new snack menu at Zachroll's is a great idea."

"You're not the only one who can embrace the new."

"I can't wait to embrace some new paint on these walls." Nic frowned at the obnoxious flowers on the wallpaper.

"But I'm glad you didn't wait to put up your collage of pictures."

Nic glanced up at the cluster of framed photos she'd arranged on the wall by the kitchen table like her mother and her sisters had in their homes. She smiled when her gaze reached the picture in the middle of them all—the shot of Aunt Aggie and Polly in front of their garden, the one she'd found in the scrapbook. "Yeah, I couldn't resist. I guess the Dickenson genes got the best of me. Embracing the new. Well, I guess the photo collage idea is actually old, but you know what I mean."

Roxy put an arm around her and gave her a comforting squeeze. "Speaking of old, what about the Tesla? Have you missed it since you sold it?"

"Nope. I'm perfectly content with the last bit of that time in my life gone," Nic confessed. "I have my trusty bike. Plus, if I really need to, I can always have Junior cart me around in the squad car."

"Oh, he'll love that." Roxy rolled her eyes before scooting over to the counter to slice the pan of brownies Nic's mom had sent over earlier in the afternoon. "You're always welcome to my truck if you need it."

"I may take you up on that." Nic nodded. "But you know, one of the great things about Fisher's Creek is you can cover a good bit of it on foot."

Roxy set the knife down and put a hand to her chest as if stilling her heart. "Nicola Dickenson, are you telling me there are actually *great* things about Fisher's Creek now?"

"I guess I am. But that one's not the *best*."

"What is?"

"This." Nic joined Roxy at the counter and planted a gentle kiss on her lips. "I love you, Roxy."

"I love you too." Roxy squeezed Nic tight against her. "And I love that you're back in Fisher's Creek to stay. Let's get ready to celebrate your new, old home and your future here."

"Our future here," Nic corrected and kissed her again, deep and strong with a swell of love that she couldn't deny. It was the way she planned to kiss Roxy for the rest of their lives.

Bella Books
Happy Endings Live Here
P.O. Box 10543
Tallahassee, FL 32302
Phone: (800) 729-4992
BellaBooks.com

More Titles from Bella Books

Jones – Gerri Hill
978-1-64247-598-2 | 260 pages | Mystery
One weekend getaway, six friends, and a deadly secret that will wash away everything they thought they knew.

Merry Weihnachten – E. J. Noyes
978-1-64247-610-1 | 292 pages | Romance
Christmas traditions aren't the only things getting mixed up when these two hearts collide beneath the mistletoe.

Sweet Home Alabarden Park – TJ O'Shea
978-1-64247-570-8 | 362 pages | Romance
She came to restore a royal estate—she never expected to rebuild her heart.

Dr. Margaret Morgan – Christy Hadfield
978-1-64247-628-6 | 286 pages | Romance
Facing the professor on campus everyone hates is terrifying—but falling for her might be even worse.

Overtime – Tracey Richardson
978-1-64247-630-9 | 278 pages | Romance
A charming romance about second chances, found family, and scoring the goal that matters most.

The Big Guilt – Renée J. Lukas
978-1-64247-657-6 | 206 pages | Romance
What if the one who got away became the one you can't have?